LOST LETTER

BY

NEIL MULLIGAN

ISBN:1-4392-2636-9
ISBN-13: 9781439226360

Visit www.booksurge.com to order additional copies.

ACKNOWLEDGEMENTS

To my wife, Sandra, for all her love and support
during the writing of Lost Letter.

Special thanks to Glenn Herdling for his
assistance in the project.

From: PFC JAMES McDougal
106th Battalion 1st Army
ET OO Allied Command

V ··· — MAIL

To: Maggie McDougal
2251 Sedwick AVE
APArtment 4C
Bronx, NY 10468

V-mail service provides a most rapid means of communication. If addressed to a place where photographing service is not available the original letter will be dispatched by the most expeditious means.

INSTRUCTIONS

(1) Write the entire message plainly on the other side within the marginal lines.
(2) PRINT the name and address in the two spaces provided. Addresses of members of the Armed Forces should show full name, complete Military or Naval address, including grade or rank, serial number, unit to which assigned or attached and Army Post Office in care of the appropriate postmaster or appropriate Fleet Post Office.
(3) Fold, seal, and deposit in any post office letter drop or street letter box.
(4) Enclosures must not be placed in this envelope.
(5) V-Mail letters may be sent free of postage by members of the Armed Forces. When sent by others postage must be prepaid at domestic rates (3c ordinary mail, 6c if domestic air mail service is desired when mailed in the U.S.)

1

I HATE MONDAYS

The mixture of snow and rain turned the sidewalk a deeper hue of gray. Snowflakes quickly turned to slush under the constant barrage of footsteps from people hurrying to work. Exhaust fumes rose in the air from the street, as cars, buses, and trucks blanketed the early-morning Manhattan sun with thick exhaust.

Street vendors set up shop, cranking umbrellas, lighting coals, unbundling newspapers. Melting snow that had settled atop the umbrellas dripped off the edges. Fresh brewed coffee, Danish, pretzels, commuters jockeying for position speaking languages from the four corners of the Earth—another morning rush hour had begun.

The flow of footsteps on the sidewalk subsided momentarily to watch a Great Dane do its business. A dog walker and the five other dogs in his charge looked patiently at one another. The dog walker waited for the hound to finish, cleaned up its mess, looked to the crowd, and said, "When you gotta go, you gotta go." The comment elicited a few laughs and grins from the crowd, and the commute was back on track.

Snow began to accumulate as the mixture switched to a full-blown winter storm. The city always looked peaceful in snow. It gave a feeling of rebirth and somehow muffled the noise. Soon three inches of soft snow had blanketed the roads and sidewalks.

A large Jamaican fellow, sporting dreadlocks beneath his knit Rastafarian hat, threw a large box upside-down outside a subway entrance. He placed a board over the box and urged passersby to partake in a quick game of Three-Card Monte. The cards flew from his knit gloves, which had been cut so that his fingertips protruded. She moved to the outside of the sidewalk to avoid the unsuspecting victims of the street vendor. Staring at her watch, her blood pressure rose as she realized she was more than ten minutes late at mid-way point of her commute.

Mary kept a swift pace to her stride. The snow made no difference to her, and she used her umbrella like a horsewhip to keep others at bay. She liked to get to the office by seven o'clock, but now she would be late. She picked up the pace, her sneakers squeaking.

At fifteen minutes past her self-imposed arrival time, the doorman wished her good morning. Mary closed her umbrella, shook off the wet snow, and placed it neatly into its sleeve. She sat on the lobby bench, removed her soaked sneakers, and replaced them with heels for work. Mary had worn a black pantsuit with gray pinstripes. She liked how it made her look professional while still complimenting her figure.

Mary glanced through the clouded window at the name of the accounting firm on the marquee. The gold script logo of Murphy, O'Connor, and Dooley was trimmed with new-fallen snow. She took a deep breath and grabbed her umbrella, leather portfolio, and shoe bag. Another doorman nodded and held the elevator door for her. He instinctively pushed "12" for her. Mary returned the nod and entered.

The door closed, but Mary distinctly heard one doorman tell the other, "Gotta be nice to Mary McDougal. She's gonna be somebody in the MOD Squad."

Murphy, O'Connor, and Dooley was a prestigious accounting firm. MOD had leased the top three floors of the building for over fifty years. Mary still felt the sense of nobility that others in the accounting community affiliated with its name. As the elevator opened, Mary walked down the hall to her office. "Good morning, Rosarita," she said to the Cuban woman sitting at the reception desk.

Rosarita and Mary were good friends. Rosarita was a Cuban immigrant and a single mother. Her family had escaped Cuba years earlier. Her father was a human rights activist who had been targeted for arrest by the Cuban police. A friend inside the police department had warned Rosarita's family of her father's pending arrest. That night the family spent their life savings on a small boat to the United States to escape persecution.

Rosarita worked at MOD during the day and attended St. John's University at night, studying to be a lawyer. Mary respected her hard work and desire to better herself.

Rosarita followed Mary's dripping raincoat down the hallway before she turned left into the office kitchenette. Mary entered her office, hung the drenched outerwear on a coat tree, placed the umbrella in a stand, and tossed her portfolio on her desk.

She settled herself in her tall leather chair and shuffled through her mail. Rosarita tapped on the open door and walked in unbidden. Mary made no eye contact and continued reading her mail. Rosarita placed a steaming coffee cup on Mary's desktop coffee warmer and a low-fat yogurt with a spoon in front of her. "Can I get you anything else, Mary?" Rosarita asked.

Mary raised her eyes slightly. "No, but thank you." As Rosarita walked out, Mary called out, "Close the door, please."

When the door clicked shut, Mary flipped the mail back into her inbox, picked up her coffee, and took a sip. Rosarita knew exactly the way Mary liked it—piping hot. Otherwise Mary wouldn't stop drinking it.

Mary spun in her chair and looked out her penthouse windows. On the windowsill, two pigeons strutted back and forth. She stared at them as they darted this way and that, as if to avoid the heavy snowflakes. Two loud knocks disrupted her thoughts.

The door to Mary's office opened halfway, and Mr. O'Connor stuck his head in and joked, "You're late. What's this, a half day?"

His abrupt entrance startled Mary. She tried to pull the coffee quickly from her lips so that it wouldn't drip and burn her. Half-annoyed, she shot back a smile. "Sorry," she said. "I slept in." O'Connor returned the smile and closed the door. She knew that he slept only five hours a night and was the first one in the office every morning—promptly at six.

O'Connor was eighty and had never contemplated retirement. He was a multi-millionaire, but still wore suits that were old and worn. He put in twelve-hour days and still handled some of his clients personally. Mary liked him best of the three owners. She had always considered him a father figure, and she tried her best to emulate him. She had never met her own father. He had died before she was born.

O'Connor was also extremely fond of Mary. She had been with the firm six years and had more than proven her worth. She had increased their client list—especially profitable clients. Her nose was to the grindstone and she possessed a "do what it takes" attitude. She reminded O'Connor of himself at her age. She knew that he was planning to recommend Mary for partnership in the firm at the next board meeting. The sacrifices were many. Social life, family, and dating had all taken a back seat as she struggled to get ahead. But it was all going to pay off. MOD was an "all boys club," and Mary was about to pierce its machismo.

With an air of confidence, Mary took some lip gloss out of her purse. The cold air had made her lips feel hard and dry. As she applied the gloss to her lips, Mary reviewed her calendar for the day.

Appointments all afternoon.

It was not going to be an easy Monday.

Mary spent the morning reviewing ledgers and preparing for her afternoon meetings. She was diligent about being organized. She hardly noticed the eight loud chimes that rang out from the grandfather clock in the MOD lobby, signaling that the workday had officially started.

2

THE CALL

The carillons of the oak grandfather clock sounded down the corridor, sending a few workers scurrying to get in the front doors before the last peal of the bell. Old man O'Connor's office was across from reception. Murphy and Dooley had situated their offices in the rear of the top floor. O'Connor liked to stay visible. He thought it was important for clients not to feel out of touch with the firm's upper management.

O'Connor backed his chair from his desk and approached reception. Employees heard the telltale thump of his cane as he idled down the hallway, fixing his gaze on the entrance. O'Connor had a standard lecture for a minute late to the guilty party. But those who knew the drill would wait until 8:15—after the old man had left reception.

Some of the staff insisted that O'Connor kept the grandfather clock running five minutes fast, just so he could practice his "early bird gets the worm" speech. O'Connor's wife had made him remove the clock years earlier. The clock had been in O'Connor's family for generations, but the chimes had scared his children. So O'Connor had it relocated to the MOD reception area in the hope that it would have the same effect on his employees.

Mary was accustomed to the old man's morning ritual and paid little attention to it. She spent the first four hours of her day huddled over her desk reading ledgers. She always liked to be fully prepped for any client question or comment. She clasped her hands over her head and stretched the stiffness from her back as the old grandfather clock chimed once for the half-hour, eleven-thirty. Best be on to lunch to beat the crowd, she thought.

Mary rarely brought her own lunch. She grabbed her raincoat and descended to the lobby in the elevator. She asked no one to join her. She needed to use the time to review additional files and didn't feel like engaging in office gossip or politics. This was one of Mary's biggest challenges. The old-boy network was infamous for its liquid lunches. Befriending the right people could be beneficial to one's career, but the wrong ones could be equally detrimental. Mary felt she should be judged by her work, not by whom she associated with. She tried to steer clear of the gossip and politics and had become adept at playing the common ground.

Stepping into Conroy's Grill for a quick soup and salad, Mary sat with her back to the door to avoid anyone who might want to join her. She ate slowly, savoring the beef and barley soup that eased the chill from her bones. She took almost an hour and a half to finish. Mary threw twenty-five dollars on the table for the twelve -dollar tabs. She had served tables in college and knew that she had probably cost her waitress an extra customer by taking so long to eat.

On her way back to the office, dodging puddles of slush and ice, Mary mentally reviewed the account she was going to advise at her one-thirty meeting. Five Borough Coffee was her largest client. Anyone who had visited New York had to have run into one of their locations. The coffee shop, a local chain, competed with Starbucks but offered a local atmosphere. It served coffee, Danish, and other breakfast items at sixty-two locations throughout the five boroughs. Each shop also sold historical memorabilia from the tri-state area. It was a family-owned business that had started with one location and had franchised rapidly.

Mary had been Five Borough's accountant from day one. She felt comfortable with the owners, Charlie and Elaine Perkins. They were in their fifties and had entrusted Mary with most of their financial decisions. The Perkinses, ever punctual, arrived at 1:25. Rosarita buzzed Mary, who met the couple in the reception area and escorted them back to her office. They passed two MOD employees at the water cooler. The conversation hushed as she ushered the couple past them into her office. Obviously they had been discussing Mary. Rumors of her partnership? Were they jealous? Pleased? Annoyed?

Charlie and Elaine exchanged quick pleasantries with Mary as she closed the door behind them. Charlie asked, "How have you been, Mary?"

Elaine chimed in before Mary could answer, "That suit looks great on you."

Mary looked at each of them before answering. "I've been great. How have you two been? And I got the suit at Saks. What a deal."

"That's another story and why we wanted to meet with you," Chuck blurted out.

Mary's head turned askew. Elaine added, "We're tired, Mary."

The Perkinses worked extremely long hours. The five a.m. to ten p.m. hours had taken their toll. Mary nodded in an understanding manner.

Charlie spoke up. "We feel as though we've paid our dues. I think it's time to let someone else take care of the day-to-day operations and we're gonna start living life."

His wife gave a deep sigh. There was obviously a little hesitation and trepidation in their decision. She opened up and said, "We're going to hire professional management to take over our responsibilities and we'd like you to help us safeguard our business."

Mary had been listening the entire time. She responded, "I'm excited for the both of you and I'm flattered that you trust me to assist you in this decision. You two have worked so hard and I see that we'll have to implement some safeguards during this transition, but it's nothing we can't handle together."

The couple looked pleased at her response and reassurances. The decision had been painful for them, workaholics that they were. They had been hands-on from the first day until this moment. They still visited each store location biweekly to ensure the integrity of their business model.

Mary asked, "You'll both be able to let others make decisions and run the daily operations, right?" She was referring to their anal obsessive, hands-on management style.

Charlie joked, "We've heard the 'control freak' term before, but we're in recovery."

The three shared a laugh before Elaine added, "Hell, we were ADD before doctors even knew what it was."

The meeting had started at one-thirty and Mary had only blocked out an hour for their "review the books" meeting. She had not planned on the Perkinses' bombshell. They had asked Mary to plan their future and help them with their personal lives. She quickly realized it would take days of planning on her part. In addition, she would have to bring in the "big guns," the financial planners, to assist. Her CPA degree would not be enough.

Mary turned to the couple. "Congratulations on your decision. You two will be so happy and will enjoy the fruits of your labor." The Perkinses squeezed each other's hands, acknowledging Mary. "I am going to have to consult with some associates and the planners. I suggest we make an appointment for late next week to review what we put together for you."

The couple looked a little perplexed at Mary's suggestion. In their excitement, they had overlooked that it would take some time to put a plan together. It was an extremely emotional moment for them, lost in the enormity of their decision.

Mary asked, "Is Wednesday at nine a.m. alright? I'll block out the entire day."

The owners at first were taken aback, but quickly agreed. "That'll be fine," Elaine said, cutting Charlie off. They proceeded to review the books as the clock chimed three times.

Mary began to speak faster and rushed the meeting along. Twenty minutes later she finished the review. She apologized, "I'm sorry, I have a three-thirty. Let's plan on Wednesday then."

They nodded in agreement and each gave Mary a hug when she escorted them to the front door. As they walked out the clock chimed once for half past the hour. Mary shook her head. She did not like to play it so close.

Mary's following appointment was with Matt Klein, who owned six pharmacies in the Bronx with his son. Mary's affiliation with Klein was far different from the tight relationship that she shared with the Perkinses. She never liked to say that she disliked anyone, especially a client, but Matt Klein was a pompous ass. Unlike the Perkinses—unlike herself—in all the meetings she had ever had with Klein, he had never been on time.

By 3:45, the self-proclaimed "pharmacy king Rx Rex," as he liked to call himself, finally arrived. His tardiness always forced her to compress her counsel into brief snippets. Yet somehow her meetings with him always seemed to last an eternity.

Rosarita buzzed Mary on the intercom. Mary answered, "Yes."

Rosarita snarled into the receiver, "Your three-thirty has arrived. You know, the Pharmacy Prick."

Mary laughed and said she'd be right out. It was 3:45, on time by his standards. "Hi, Matt," she said as she walked into the lobby. His back was to her as he spun 180 degrees to acknowledge her. He looked her up and down, as though performing an inspection. "Hey there, darlin,' how's it shakin'?" He wiped his nose across his sleeve before extending his hand.

Mary's skin crawled. He was disgusting. She often thought that if he hadn't inherited his father's business, he might be running a roadside fruit stand. Her stomach turned as she returned his handshake, having wondered where it might have been.

"Shall we get things started, Toots?" he blurted out. Rosarita rolled her eyes at Mary as they headed to her office

Mary pressed the intercom button on her phone. "Rosarita, please hold all my calls."

Klein was a stickler about reviewing the books. A half-hour into the meeting and Mary's mind started drifting. "When's this going to end?" she asked herself. She likened their meetings to having a cavity filled— painful but necessary. The man would review the same page over and over.

Klein mumbled to himself, "This looks good." Moments later, "What the hell's this?" Looking up momentarily at Mary, "You people gotta do better."

Mary knew not to engage him. Not answering would expedite the meeting. Finally she could not take the aroma of his cheap cologne and his rants anymore. "Matt, would you like something to drink?" Mary needed a break, a distraction, anything to break up the monotony.

"No," he quipped.

She took a deep breath, annoyed by his curt response. It was four-thirty. Watching Klein ramble on was like watching a glacier melt. Through the frosted window on her door, Mary saw Rosarita pacing uneasily. Mary cocked her head. This wasn't like Rosarita.

Finally the Hispanic woman knocked gently and opened her door. "I need to speak with you," she said timidly.

"We're almost done here," Mary replied. "Can it wait?"

Rosarita said, "I need to speak with you now." There was a sense of urgency in her voice. Klein sniffed, but nodded that it was okay.

Rosarita took Mary by the wrist and led her into the kitchenette. "Mary, there's a problem with your mother." Mary looked at her blankly. "Your mother is at Presbyterian Hospital in the Bronx. She's in the emergency room. That's all I know."

Rosarita handed Mary a pink slip from a message pad on which she had scribbled the hospital address and phone number. She touched Mary's shoulder. "If there's anything I can do, Mary," she began. She then slowly withdrew her hand.

Mary took three deep breaths to compose herself. She walked back into her office, grabbed her raincoat, sneakers, and umbrella. "Matt, I have a family emergency I have to attend to. Have Rosarita reschedule our meeting."

Klein shook his head. "My old man died last year. The big C." That was Klein's way of being consoling, she thought. Mary rushed out of the office and hit the down button on the elevator.

Outside, the snow had stopped falling, but the temperature had dropped, turning much of the soft fallen snow into crusty ice. Mary asked the doorman to hail her a cab and was surprised to get one relatively fast for rush hour. She gave the cab driver the hospital's address and frantically called the emergency room on her cell to check her mother's condition. She had not spoken to her mother for a week. Usually they spoke every other day, but Mary had been busy with clients every day after work the previous week.

Different scenarios raced through her mind. Was it a fall, heart attack, pneumonia? She felt anxious not knowing. She was all about numbers. Numbers don't lie. Uncertainty, however, was something she could never deal with.

The hospital switchboard put her on hold. The waiting was interminable—worse than the eternity she had just spent with Klein. Finally, a nurse with a Filipino accent got on the phone and told Mary that her mother had fallen. She was stable, and they were running some tests. Her mind raced: **Stable.** That could mean anything.

Rush hour was harder than usual because of the ice and snow, but Mary wished the cabby would drive faster. He did not make small talk as many cab drivers did. Mary leaned forward and ran her fingertips over the driver's beaded seat cover. "How much longer do you think?" she asked.

"Fifteen minutes, Miss," the driver replied in a Middle Eastern accent.

Fifty-five minutes to go eight miles. Mary called Mrs. Hanley, her mother's neighbor, thinking she would know what happened. The phone rang and rang. No answer. "Don't these people have an answering machine?" she mumbled. She redialed, thinking maybe they were eating dinner.

"Hello?" came the voice of Mrs. Hanley on the other end.

"Mrs. Hanley?" Mary cried out. "It's Mary McDougal! My mother—she's in the hospital. Can you tell me . . . ?"

Her voice trailed off as Mrs. Hanley explained that the paramedics had left with Mary's mother on a stretcher at about three p.m. Mrs. Hanley's voice cracked as she struggled not to cry on the phone. She and Mary's mother had been friends for years. Mary was desperate for answers, but politely stayed on the line as Mrs. Hanson assured her that she would look after her mother's apartment and cat. Mary had forgotten all about Mr. Wiggles.

The taxi pulled up to the emergency room. Mary tossed some bills at the cab driver, threw open the door, and raced across the wet sidewalk, paying no attention to the crunch of salt pellets beneath her sneakers. She practically slid to the patient information stand. "My name is Mary McDougal," she breathed. "I'm here to see my mother."

For the first time in her life, Mary wondered if she was too late.

3

THE HOSPITAL

Every seat in the waiting room was occupied. Mary grew increasingly anxious standing in line at the hospital information desk. When she finally reached the front of the line, a demure nurse typed her mother's name into the computer. The nurse tried to tell Mary about her mother's condition, but Mary could not understand her thick accent, which Mary guessed was Russian.

Growing more agitated, Mary decided that she would wait to speak to the doctor. The nurse handed her a card with her mother's room number printed on it. Mary followed the nurse's directions as closely as possible. After a few wrong turns, she was about to ask directions from someone who looked like they spoke English when she came across the room almost by accident.

Mary stepped into room E218. Her mother lay in the bed as a nurse cleaned dried blood from a wound on her head. Mary took a deep breath and held it. Her mother had not seen her yet. Her head was turned toward the window so the nurse could tend to her wound.

"We called your doctors to notify them," the nurse said to her patient. "Dr. Donahue and Dr. Dockendorff." Who was Dr. Dockendorff, Mary thought. The nurse finished tending to the wound and said, "I'll be back to check on you. We need to run some more tests."

Mary's mother turned to address the nurse and saw Mary standing behind her. Mary stretched her lips in an attempt to give her a reassuring smile. Her mother looked almost ashamed of her predicament. She held her arms out to her daughter and they embraced.

"Are you okay? What happened?" Mary had to fight from choking on the words.

Her mother paused as if to consider what had happened. "I don't know. One minute I was vacuuming the living room, next thing I know I'm lying on the ground with blood on my head."

The nurse addressed Mary and nodded. "Mrs. McDougal's wound was too deep for conventional stitches. We had to use staples. The EMT's report states that she fell and hit her head on the coffee table in the living room. They found a shattered vase on the floor, which is probably what alarmed the neighbor to check on her."

Mary tried to comfort her mother. She reached for a button on the side of the bed, glancing inquisitively at the nurse as if to ask permission. The nurse nodded assurance, closed the curtain, and stepped out of the room to continue her rounds. Mary elevated her mother's head and got her another blanket. She lifted a glass of water to her mother's dry lips.

Before Mary could speak again, a voice bellowed, "You're looking much better," and the curtain was pulled away again. The emergency room attending physician removed the oxygen mask from his patient's face and checked her head dressing. "That was some bump to your head. We're going to be running some more tests and we've notified doctors Donahue and Dockendorff. They'll be visiting you in the morning."

"Doctor, is there anything you can tell me before then?" Mary pleaded.

The doctor removed the chart from the basket at the end of the bed and glanced through its pages. "Are you her daughter?" he asked.

Mary nodded once, and the doctor interpreted the chart for her. "All her vitals look normal, with the exception of her red cell count. We'll see if we can get those up during her hospital stay." He placed his hand reassuringly on Mrs. McDougal's lower leg. "We'll be moving you out of the ER to another room. Do you have any questions?"

Mary's mother shook her head no. "Thank you, doctor," she said in a raspy whisper.

The hospital was more crowded than on a typical Monday. The weather had caused a number of accidents, and some of the homeless had sought reprieve from the frigid cold in the large waiting room. The security guards let them gather in a corner as long as they did not beg or bother the waiting patients and their families.

Mary's mother fell asleep, so Mary waded through the crowd to get something to eat in the cafeteria. She had not seen her mother in six weeks. She could not believe how tired and old she looked. Even at eighty-five, Mary always thought that her mother looked vital for her age. She had always been relatively healthy. Maybe one cold a year, tops. They spoke often, but Mary's career got in the way of personal visits. Her mother did her own cooking and cleaning, and she walked to the church and the grocery store daily. Mary tried to reassess the situation. She tried to tell herself that it was just the medical surroundings, the image of her mother in bed, no makeup, oxygen, and other machines hooked up to her that gave her a pallid appearance.

Mary returned to the ER and her mother was awake. Attendants and orderlies were already in the process of transferring her. "We're going to be moving you to the fourth floor, Mrs. McDougal," said one of the orderlies, mispronouncing her name. They pulled wires off her and inserted an IV into her arm that was attached to a mobile unit.

Two orderlies assisted her mother out of the bed so that she was sitting up, her legs dangling over the bed. She looked like a limp rag doll. Mary picked up the chart: 113 pounds. She knew that her mother usually weighed 130 pounds. Never a scarecrow—just healthy.

As the orderlies lifted her mother into a wheelchair, Mary examined her more closely. Her hair was thin and dull. She knew there may have been dried blood in her mother's hair, but something about the way it sat lifelessly on her head just wasn't right. Too much gray—too thin.

Mrs. McDougal always took great care in her appearance. Heels, dresses, never slacks, and her makeup was always perfect. Mary's apprehension grew.

The orderlies wheeled her mother out of the ER and down the hall to the elevators. The hospital was old and needed remodeling. The hallways were dark and narrow. They ascended to the fourth floor and entered room 431. Mary was convinced that her mother would be sharing a room in light of all the emergencies the winter storm had created. But as they wheeled her into the room, Mary spotted only a single bed. At least luck was on her side in that matter. Most of the rooms had two beds.

The orderlies assisted Mary's mother into bed. The nurse reconnected the IV to the metal tree beside the bed and attached a pulse monitor to her chest and to her frail, bruised wrists. "There you go," said the nurse, gently patting her arm. "Hope you have a good night."

"Yeah, a great night," Mrs. McDougal said sarcastically. She looked at Mary. "Can you believe she said that? Have a good night. In *this* godforsaken place."

In a consoling voice, "You're alright now, Mom."

"I'm alright. Speak for yourself," she replied huffily.

The painkillers must be wearing off, Mary thought. Her mother's personality was returning to its old sardonic self. Her wired hand reached for the television remote, and she turned on the ten o'clock news. She barely acknowledged Mary's presence. When she did, she avoided eye contact, as though to avoid the onslaught of questions that her distressed daughter would be asking.

Mary felt isolated. It deeply saddened her that her own mother did not want to confide in her. So instead she reached out and held her mother's hand and asked the question as delicately as possible, "What's wrong, mom?"

Her mother cleared her throat and slowly turned her head to look at Mary. With a deep sigh, she looked at Mary point-blank and said, "I'm sick, Mary."

Mary grasped her hand tighter and dragged her chair closer. "Mom, what do you mean, sick?"

Mrs. McDougal grimaced and spoke from the side of her tight-lipped mouth. "I have cancer. Dr. Dockendorff is an oncologist. He diagnosed me last month."

Mary's eyes welled up. "We'll get through this, Mom." she said. They both gazed at each other, each woman trying to be strong for the other and struggling to keep her composure. Mary leaned over the rail of the bed, and they wrapped their arms around one another.

One or two minutes later, Mary's mother took a deep breath and let go. She continued to hold Mary's hand in hers. "I know," she said, rubbing her daughter's hand. "The 'C' word. The one no one wants to hear." Mary tried to keep her composure as her mom continued. "The diagnosis isn't good. I've already been through an aggressive radiation regimen over the past month."

Mary stifled a gasp. A month? And she was only learning about it now? She felt nauseous, but did not want to upset her mother more than she already was. "At first, Dr. Dockendorff was more optimistic. But he didn't like the last set of test results. I was supposed to start chemotherapy next week."

"Mom?" Mary interrupted. "What type of cancer?" she stammered.

"Pancreatic," was the quick but sullen response.

4

I WANT TO GO HOME

The man recognized Mary and looked genuinely glad to see her. He took her hand between both of his in a warm greeting. He then turned his attention to Mary's mother.

Dr. Donahue was in the twilight of his career. He was in his early seventies and continued to practice medicine just for his love of it. But he had not taken on any new patients in years. His white coat seemed too big for his frame and the back of his pant legs were frayed from where he continuously stepped on them. He had donned a bowtie and black-rimmed glasses. Gray eyebrows seemed to grow from the top of his glasses. Gray strands also grew from his nostrils and ears.

The old doctor put his hand under her chin and said, "I bet it's been thirty years or more since I saw you last, Mary."

Mary laughed. "I bet longer."

"You still got those beautiful baby blues, I see," as he touched her cheek with his trembling hand.

Mrs. McDougal grew agitated that he was not examining her and exclaimed, "I'm the patient, you know. Are you going to examine me or what?"

Donahue whispered to Mary, "I better look at your mother now. I see her fall hasn't affected her rosy disposition." Mary turned away so that her mother would not see her chuckle.

Donahue examined Maggie McDougal's head and looked at the chart. He checked her blood pressure, pulse, and then felt around her neck. "You had quite a fall. How do you feel?" he asked, pushing his glasses up his nose.

Maggie rasped, "I'm fine, doctor. I just want to go home."

Donahue nodded and said, "Let's see what Dockendorff says. We'll try to get you home as soon as possible." Mary and her mother seemed surprised by his response. The doctor grabbed Maggie's bony foot over the blanket and said, "Hang in there." Mary and her mother both looked eager and excited about the prospect of leaving the hospital.

The doctor ushered Mary out the door. "I don't see any reason we can't discharge your mother sometime this afternoon. She's a very sick lady, though. You realize that don't you, Mary?"

She replied, "No, I don't know. I mean she only told me yesterday."

Momentarily surprised, he said, "I guess that really doesn't shock me, Mary. You know had headstrong your mother can be." Walking off, he said, "We'll see what we can do to expedite some tests results and get you out of here."

At two-thirty in the afternoon, Dr. Dockendorff entered room 431. He was a very tall man, six feet five inches tall, slim, and tan. Dressed in a blue fitted suit, red tie, and black dress shoes, he had a much more professional air than Dr. Donahue. Maggie gently patted her daughter's arm and whispered, "He'd be a good catch for you."

Mary shook her head and shushed her. Her mother wouldn't even know what she liked in a man and it annoyed her to no end when she tried to set her up.

The doctor reviewed the charts. "We'll have to draw some more blood and get a CAT scan for later today. But I see no reason to keep you overnight again." As he left the room, he reminded Maggie of her appointment on Thursday.

He closed the door behind him and the two women waited again. The hospital waiting game was brutal. Wait for the attendant, wait for the nurse, wait for the technician, and wait for the doctor. It's all they did the rest of the day.

At seven o'clock in the evening, the waiting game was over. Blood had been drawn and CAT scans had been completed. Maggie's discharge was actually easier than Mary had expected. Medicare was picking up the bill, and that's all it took. The hospital staff reviewed Maggie's medicines and their dosage, instructed her on how to keep her wound clean, and they were off. The attendant wheeled Maggie to the exit. Mary hailed a cab and they left for the Bronx.

Mrs. McDougal lived in Riverdale, New York, on the Henry Hudson Parkway in the Bronx. It was a nice apartment, more than big enough for her. The taxi pulled alongside the curb. Mary settled the fare and walked her mother to the front door. She pressed a button to announce their presence to a large doorman, who was busy watching the Knicks. He looked irritated that he had to buzz them in and then get off his chair to open the inner door. Maggie thanked him anyway.

They proceeded to the elevator and pushed "11." Mary stood behind her mother, inspecting her head wound but trying not to be obvious. When the elevator reached the eleventh floor, Mary and Maggie shuffled down and across the hall. They entered the apartment and took their shoes off. Both of them were tired but hungry. Neither had wanted to test the dinner menu at the hospital.

Maggie opened the refrigerator. She had cooked a ham two days ago and most of the prized pig was still on a dish, wrapped in foil. Maggie removed it from the refrigerator, smiled at Mary, and began slicing it for ham sandwiches.

They sat at the kitchen table and enjoyed their simple, tasty meal. Halfway through, there was a knock on the door. When Mary opened the door, Mrs. Hanley was standing in the hallway holding a gray tabby. "I saw the light on and wanted to see if everything was okay."

As Mary invited the woman inside, the cat leaped out of her arms and jumped onto Maggie's lap. "Mr. Wiggles!" Maggie shouted with glee. She got up from the table. Thank you, Terry, for watching him. I hope he didn't cause too much trouble."

Terry Hanley teased, "Not nearly as much trouble as you caused!" She started to inquire about Maggie's health when the whistle from the kettle disrupted the conversation. Maggie offered Mrs. Hanley some tea and the three women sat down at the table to enjoy a little impromptu tea party.

"I was sorry to bother you with all of this, Terry," her mother said somberly.

"That's what friends are for, Maggie. Don't be foolish."

As Maggie explained her ordeal at the hospital, Mary noticed that her mother was starting to wince. She could tell that she was in pain. Mary left the table to get her mother's prescriptions. Two pills—one to inhibit the swelling and one for pain. She removed the pills from their containers and handed them to her mother at the table. "Mom, take these," she said, as she rested her hands lightly on her mother's shoulders.

Mrs. Hanley finished her tea and said, "You two must be tired." Terry stood up and walked across the room. "I'll check on you tomorrow. Thanks for the tea." She opened the apartment door and left, waving a finger at Mary. "You take good care of her, now."

Mary poured them both some more tea, and they struggled to start a conversation. Usually they could talk for hours about anything. But right now topics were difficult. Small, meaningless, one-sentence blurbs were all they could express.

"Mr. Wiggles looks good," Mary said.

"Terry . . . Mrs. Hanley . . . is so nice," her mother replied.

These little one-liners continued for an hour as Mary battled the urge not to talk about the "c-word." Finally, she couldn't evade the topic any longer. "When's your appointment with the oncologist?" she asked.

Her mother said, "Ten o'clock, Thursday morning."

Mary looked at her. "I'm going with you."

Maggie didn't meet her daughter's eyes. "You better not miss any more work because of me. You don't want to get your boss mad at you."

Mary walked around the table so that her mother could see her face. "Don't you worry about that," she insisted. "We're in this together." Her mother had always taken care of herself. She had been on her own since she was seventeen. Mary's parents had married when her father was eighteen and Maggie was seventeen. She was a very private person and never wanted to be a burden to anyone.

It was late, so Mary decided to stay at her mother's that night. She set an alarm for four-thirty so that she could make it to her apartment, shower, and arrive at MOD by seven. She had left on Monday and called in for a personal day on Tuesday. She would have to reschedule appointments to make the oncologist appointment on Thursday.

She felt as if she had just lowered her head to her pillow when the alarm sounded. Mary had never been one for the snooze button. A bad Top 40 song was enough to make her get up. She looked in on her mother before leaving and took the subway home. It was so surreal. It felt like a bad cable TV movie. She couldn't keep her mother off her mind.

Mary arrived at the office at seven o'clock, second only to Mr. O'Connor and Rosarita. She sat down at her desk and Rosarita entered with her coffee, yogurt, and a comforting smile. "Is your mother all right?" she asked.

Mary nodded and said, "For now. We have another appointment tomorrow with a specialist."

Rosarita smiled and said, "I'm glad." She dropped some mail off on Mary's desk and left. Five minutes later, Mr. O'Connor walked in and fell into a leather chair behind the mahogany table in her office. He motioned for Mary to join him at the table. Mary stood up, smoothed out her skirt, and sat across from O'Connor. She knew that he would be concerned.

"How's your mother?" he asked. She told him everything she knew about her mother's condition and Mr. O'Connor listened attentively. After she was done, O'Connor took her hand and said, "Anything you need, the firm is behind you. Take care of your mother. After all, this is just arithmetic."

"Thank you, sir" she said, choking back. O'Connor got up from chair and put his hand on Mary's shoulder before leaving her office.

Mary felt comforted by Mr. O'Connor's words and went about her day. She called to check on her mother once in the morning and again in the afternoon. She told her that she would be sleeping at her apartment again that evening so that she could take her to the oncologist. Maggie tried to talk her out of it, but Mary would have none of it.

Mary asked Rosarita to reschedule all of her appointments the next day, and she left the office at six o'clock. She first went to her apartment to pick up an overnight bag. She hopped a taxi to her mother's and arrived before eight. Her mother had made spaghetti and they both enjoyed a late supper. Mary always loved her mother's cooking, even when it was just sauce from a jar. They stayed up to watch the 10 O'clock News, but Mary's eyes began to flutter about six minutes into it. Her mother urged her to go to bed. Tomorrow would be a big day.

5

CONGRESS IS IN SESSION

The sun peeked through the early morning haze, adding a slight golden hue to the white exterior of the Capitol building. Two Marines unfurled a flag while a third pressed a trumpet to his pursed lips. The wind caught the flag as it ascended its perch, welcoming the lawmakers and lobbyists to the noble building below.

The House had been reviewing and debating a ten-year report on the state of the Armed Forces, domestic and international. Meeting after meeting, deal after deal, base closures was a hot button item. No lawmaker wanted a base closed in his or her district. A closure could sink a local economy. The millions of dollars in expenditures a base represented to a community was its lifeblood. The report came out every ten years and the debates would last up to a year. But this was the final stage of the closures. Some would make the cut, others would be mothballed. The last two national bases on the table were Holloman Air Force Base in New Mexico and Fort Monmouth in New Jersey.

As the lawmakers took their seats, some still had smiles from the previous day when their local bases had been spared. Others still bore the frustration and anxiety of knowing that their constituents would hold them responsible for the closure of their local base. Surely anyone up for re-election with a base closure carved in his or her back would be an easy target for a GOP candidate in the next election. The representatives knew their careers would be over, no matter how long their tenure had been. Contributions often were linked to contracts with local businesses, which would likely not be in a friendly mood to donate to their lame duck campaign.

The sergeant at arms convened the session. The gavel came down several times, calling the meeting to order. The deals had already been cut, so this was a mere formality. Local media from New Mexico and New Jersey were outside awaiting the outcome. The lives of thousands of military families as well as civilians that worked on the bases were in jeopardy. The House would make its recommendations to the Senate. From there it was just a signature from the president that pronounced life or death for a military base. The representatives from the affected districts sat forward in their chairs as the speaker reviewed the votes.

Holloman AFB would be closed. In a sly deal, the New Mexico congressman had begrudgingly agreed to the closure as long as it included a five-year phase out plan. He would be able to tell his constituents that there was no alternative, but he had succeeded in allowing them to bring home the bacon for another five years. This deal might be enough to get him re-elected.

The New Jersey congressman leaned forward and heard the axe fall with the gavel. He was looking for a last minute reprieve that did not come. His late night back-room deal had fallen through.

The session had taken most of the morning and the speaker convened for lunch. As the lawmakers left the Capitol building, reporters from the respective local media swarmed the congressmen like hornets. The New Mexico congressman tried to sugar coat the recommendations and argued a glass half-full approach. The New Jersey representative, on the other hand, unsuccessfully tried to blend in with the crowd to avoid the reporters.

But the Jersey reporters were like killer sharks, frenzied to reach their prey. The cameraman looked to the reporter and said, "There he is!" They both lunged at the New Jersey congressman. The congressman knew he could not escape their tenacity, and he surrendered to the interview. He squirmed as a reporter asked pointed questions. "What happened? Didn't you say there was a good chance Fort Monmouth could be saved? What's going to happen to all the local workers? Do you think it will affect the local economy?"

The congressman answered as best he could. He deflected some of the attacks to the Senate, adding that nothing was final yet. Duck and dodge strategy. When the inquisition was over, the reporters looked like they had just finished a big meal. The steps to the House were vacated.

The House would vote for the international closures that afternoon. Foreign reporters replaced U.S. reporters on the steps of the House. German, French, Spanish, and Turkish reporters camped on the Capitol steps. The air smelled of fast food and local cuisine as the foreign press ate its lunch awaiting the lawmakers' return.

The concerns of the international base communities were no different than those of the domestic ones. A closure at some of these foreign bases could be catastrophic to a local overseas economy. Some of these countries depended on their base for a significant part of their GNP. The end of the Cold War had made many of these changes necessary. The reallocating of funding troops and bases was a necessity for the security of the United States and its allies.

Many foreign diplomats of the highest ranks had been lobbying in Washington the prior two weeks to keep the bases open in their countries. The president had seen some of the diplomats, but many were given audiences with members of his cabinet or aides depending on their rank or foreign importance.

The dollars and jobs at stake were astounding. More than two hundred-fifty thousand uniformed personnel worked at international bases. To support these uniformed personnel, forty-five thousand foreign civilians were employed at the bases. Seven hundred foreign bases would be reviewed that afternoon. This number did not include the satellite or "mini-bases" that supported each main base. House members who had a large number of constituents in a country where a base was located would fight tooth and nail on the "Hill" to keep the base open. Any lesser attempt could rile the voters against them in the next election.

When the lawmakers returned from lunch, the foreign press took aim. Some first-year House members were more than willing to provide interviews. This was a good opportunity to get their faces in front of America. With free air time, they could make themselves noticed. The reporters and cameramen tried to get more of the senior congressional speakers to talk. Most ignored them and walked briskly by.

Inside the Capitol, the sergeant at arms reconvened the meeting. Arguments had been heard by all the affected parties, and the final recommendations would go on to the Senate. After the numbers were crunched, world strategic defense considered, and all political savvy put aside, there were twelve bases to be considered for final termination. The House members cast their votes and it came down to six bases. The first was Camp Butler in Japan. To appease the Japanese allies, the base was not terminated, but downsized. Camp Butler had eight satellites and had been "feather bedded" through the years. It was recommended for a 30 percent reduction in staff and budget dollars.

The remaining five bases were not so lucky. They were the Royal Air Force Base in the United Kingdom, Qatar, Romania, Turkey, and Diji Bouti. All would be recommended to the Senate for termination in the next five years. The political wrangling was over.

The gavel came down and the House was excused for the day. Discontented House members were eager to plead their case to the media. They would hope to ride public opinion before the Senate could vote. Some pleaded for voters to flood their senators with calls. Others played the world order on the terror card. Nonetheless, the recommendations went on to the Senate. The Senate would review the motion for forty-five days before passing its recommendations on to the White House.

The president would have thirty days to either veto or sign the measure. Budgets were tight and the recommendations by Congress would save five billion dollars a year. Although the president was keen on a strong military, he would have to make a difficult choice. Sign, and the military and his right-wing affiliates would label him soft on defense. Veto, and he would be viewed as a president that spent taxpayer monies recklessly. He had already been labeled a big spender by the GOP with the increasing deficit spending. The president would consider other options available to him. He would ultimately choose to do neither. By not signing or vetoing the measure within the thirty-day review period, it would default and become law—a political juggernaut. This way, he could ride both sides of public opinion.

On the thirty-first day, the bill became law. The five bases would close, the sixth would be downsized. The president made phone calls to the heads of state of each country affected by the new bill. He would also call the heads of state of the other six of the twelve bases that were saved, claiming he interceded on their behalf.

Politics.

6

WHEN WERE YOU GOING TO TELL ME?

Mary and Maggie each took a deep breath as they stood and entered the examining room. "Here we go," her mother gasped as they both took deep breaths.

"Everything's going to be okay." Mary said in a soft voice. The nurse walked in with Maggie's chart and left the room, closing the door behind her. The McDougals sat in silence awaiting the doctor's arrival. Excruciating minutes ticked by before Dr. Dockendorff gently rapped on the door and entered. Maggie introduced him to Mary, who raised her eyebrow in concern. Had she already forgotten that she had tried to set her up with him earlier in the week?

The handsome doctor asked Maggie how she was feeling. "The test results are back and I want to go over your prognosis." Mary had an uneasy feeling about what was to come.

The McDougals stared at the oncologist. His face and demeanor had changed. He was straight faced and stoic as he examined the chart. Setting it on the counter, he looked to Maggie and said, "Despite the aggressive treatment regimen that we chose to combat the cancer, we have not made any gains in battling the disease. I don't think we should continue this course."

Mary took a deep breath, thinking to herself, *What the hell does that mean?*

Mrs. McDougal nodded in agreement. The doctor continued, "We knew the odds weren't in our favor to begin with, but you were very brave to try the chemo. From here, we'll treat the disease as needed, to give you comfort from any pain you might have. My best estimate is sixty to one hundred-twenty days. Each patient is unique. I'm sorry I don't have better news."

"Thank you, doctor," Maggie said, as if the doctor had just seen her for a common cold.

Dockendorff looked at Mary. "Thank you for being here—for supporting your mother." Mary sat dumbfounded. Somehow she had expected good news or at least a ray of hope.

Maggie snapped her out of her trance. "Are you ready?" she said, as though they had just discussed a recipe or a business deal. Mary got up and hugged her mother, not wanting to let go. Maggie held on to her, trying to think of something to say. After a long pause, she said, "It's just my time, Mary. It's just God's plan. Not our job to question it."

Mary just held on until her mother gently pushed her away. Mary began to cry and her mother grabbed her by her shoulders and in a strong Irish brogue said, "There'll be no crying for the likes of me. Be strong."

They both composed themselves and left the exam room. Proceeding to the checkout window, they signed forms and made an appointment for the following week. Doctor Dockendorff wanted to see her every week. They left the building and walked to the bus stop. They did not talk.

On the bus ride home, Mary was grief stricken knowing that her days together with her mother were numbered. She began thinking of all the good times they had shared in their lives. Her mother was the only family she had ever known. Like a little girl she laid her head down upon her mother's shoulder as tears filled her eyes. Drops rolled down her cheeks and her nose began to run.

When they arrived back at the apartment, Maggie began thinking of all the things she needed to do. "I should make a list so I don't forget anything important. Oh dear, Mary," she said apologetically, "I don't have anything in the fridge for lunch."

Mary couldn't even think of eating. *How could she be hungry? She was just pronounced a death sentence.* Mary looked back at her and said, "I'm not hungry, Mom. Don't worry about me."

"That's ridiculous. You've got to eat something now. I'll make you some soup then."

She sat at the kitchen table while her mother made tea. Mary looked exhausted. The stress of the news had hit her hard, but her mother looked unfazed. "When were you going to tell me?" Mary asked.

Maggie looked out the window, waiting a few seconds before answering. "I'm not really sure when I was going to tell you. I always had the notion that I could get better if I had the radiation and chemotherapy. I'm sorry I wasn't honest with you, but I knew you were busy at work and I didn't want to bother you."

Too busy at work? Mary was going to argue, but she knew that's how her mother was. Maggie McDougal was extremely independent and would not impose herself on anyone, no matter what the circumstances.

Just like her daughter.

7

OFFICE BRAWL

On Friday, the MOD board met to discuss the subject of new partners. But first, the accountants insisted on addressing the firm's budget. The executives sat around a long antique mahogany table. Ice water in pitchers lined the middle of the table. Freshly baked Danishes and fresh fruit sat on silver platters at each end of the table.

There were nine board members, three of whom were the founding fathers of the firm. Each had their own personal agenda or crusade. Murphy was the brains of the outfit. He always had a savvy business sense. It was under his leadership and vision that the firm had sustained exponential growth. His ongoing mantra was that steady growth paid better dividends than rapid, unplanned growth. Together with his two junior partners, they reviewed their plan for new business and returns.

Dooley was the Scrooge of the original partners. His personal agenda was always how to cut costs. He also had hand-picked two protégés, who encouraged him to take the better part of two hours to discuss controlled spending. The three of them could take two pennies, rub them together, and get a nickel.

The last of the threesome included O'Connor and his two junior protégés. They were the heart of the firm. O'Connor was concerned about *people*. His presentation focused on compensation packages, bonuses, vacations, pro bono cases, and new partners. His two protégés filled out the remainder of the nine-member board.

O'Connor's presentation lasted over an hour. He could see Dooley grimace, as if stabbed by a knife, each time he mentioned the new bonus structure or adding a scaled bonus for office staff members. At the end of his presentation, he brought up Mary McDougal.

O'Connor pleaded his case for offering Mary partnership in the firm. "She's been with us now for sixteen years. She's helped MOD retain business, brought in new business, and applied her education and business accreditation to every task that comes across her desk. Some may think that partnership is offered for only younger employees. I say that it is merit based and that Mary McDougal is not only qualified, but long overdue this reward. "

While presenting his case, O'Conner scanned the table, carefully examining each board member's facial expression—but especially their eyes, the mirror to their souls. He stopped to gaze intently into each person's eyes while making his case. O'Connor needed a 60 percent majority to approve a new partner. Normal business decisions took a 51 percent majority. He knew the vote would be close. He could count on his two protégés, but Dooley was a lost cause. He had no soul. And Dooley's protégés were clones of him. He knew he could not count on their support either. He would focus his attention on Murphy's group.

The grandfather clock tolled noon. The board members broke for lunch and O'Connor asked Murphy to join him. O'Connor had to close the deal at lunch. He knew that if he could convince Murphy about Mary's value as a partner, Murphy's junior partners would follow their mentor in voting.

Long gone were the days when the founding fathers of MOD were inseparable. They had started the firm over twenty-five years ago. "Work hard, play harder" was the philosophy back then. They would finish work, close the bars, and sometimes bring the party back to the office.

Times had changed. They each had their personal demons to face. Alcoholism, divorce, and death had all hit them hard in their younger years. Murphy had been sober twenty-three years now. He tried limiting his exposure to alcohol. The desire to drink still sat deep in his conscience. O'Connor's young bride of five years had been a victim of a fatal hit and run. He had waited until in his forties to wed. She had been the love of his life. An emptiness still clung to his heart.

Dooley had been the first of the three to wed. He had married a daughter of the Hennessey empire. She had filed for divorce and her family had the Vatican annul the marriage. The Hennesseys had tried to erase the marriage before the public and Church's eye. Dooley had borne a disdain for women ever since.

Dooley saw Murphy and O'Connor depart together. He knew office politics were at play. He quickly rounded up his junior partners and asked Murphy's junior partners to join them. Sides had been drawn. They would reconvene at one-thirty. The afternoon had been set aside for the junior partners to make thirty-minute presentations.

Murphy and O'Connor, accompanied by O'Connor's two mentorees, Chris Lally and Bobby Stafford, exited the building and walked down to Ryan's Tavern. They took a large round table in the back of the establishment and shed their overcoats. O'Connor whispered into the seated Murphy's ear and motioned for him to follow. "Excuse us," he muttered as Murphy and he took a separate booth. Lally and Stafford remained at the original table and ordered. The old partners joked about lunches of years past—martinis and steaks. Now it was diet sodas and salads. After the two old friends had finished their meals, O'Connor launched into his case for Mary. He got up from his side of the booth and sat next to his old friend, placing a one-page summary of Mary's credentials on the stained placemat before him.

"Murph," he began, "Mary would make an invaluable asset to the firm. You know that." O'Connor knew he would have to concentrate on the benefits for the business, not the intangible assets of Mary's personality. "Look at this column, where I've detailed the monies and accounts she's responsible for. Hell, she's brought in more dollars to the firm than either of your junior partners—or mine, for that matter!"

"I dunno," Murphy started to protest. "She would bring the number of partners to ten. And what about Dooley? We could be setting ourselves up for a real donnybrook within the firm."

"C'mon, Murph—didn't I go to bat for you when you motioned for your protégés' partnerships? And you know that as a partner she would set a great example for employee morale. Some of our clients are looking at us like we're still in the Stone Age. We've even lost some to smaller minority- and women-owned firms. Don't you think it's time for a qualified woman partner?"

Murphy began to get edgy, but O'Connor kept hitting him with one qualified reason after another.

"Alright, alright, you got my vote!" Murphy finally blurted. "You could beat a dead horse. Really."

"Thanks, Murph." O'Connor slapped him on the shoulder and picked up the tab. Murphy threw ten dollars on the table for the tip and said, "I don't want you to think you can buy my vote, at least not for a salad." They both chuckled and returned to the round table with Lally and Stafford. The four discussed the pending vote and the further direction of the firm.

A few blocks away, Dooley was planning his own counterstrike. He had brought his protégés and Murphy's protégés to JR's in Hell's Kitchen. It was a dark place with dim lighting and in dire need of remodeling. Dooley had gone there for years because the drinks were cheap and the food was cheaper. The waitresses always argued about who would serve his table. None of them wanted the job because he was a notoriously poor tipper who demanded a great deal of service. On this day, the bartender chastised the newest waitress and she relented.

The professional gathering dined at a large round table with graffiti carved into it and ancient gum plastered on its underside. Dooley reinforced his position that the firm did not need additional partners. His protégés nodded in agreement. Murphy's protégés ate and listened to Dooley's embittered diatribe.

Dooley's youngest protégé, Jim Cossell, added, "I'm with Mr. Dooley. We don't need ten mouths to feed instead of nine, especially that old bitch! She thinks she's the cat's meow 'cause she gets in so damn early in the mornings. I mean really. If she worked as hard as we do, she could come in at eight a.m. like the rest of us."

His second protégé, Billy Farrell, tagged in, "Her nose is so far up old man O'Connor's ass, I'm surprised she can breathe."

Across the table, a wry smile came over Dooley. He like the dissension Mary had caused. Dooley reemphasized his point and closed with, "We don't need another partner, especially a woman."

Dooley asked for the check and cringed when he saw the total. He carefully deducted the tax before figuring his 10 percent tip for the waitress. He signed the credit card receipt and walked to the exit. Murphy's two junior partners, Shawn O'Leary and Rob Herdling, looked at each other and exchanged words before leaving.

Shawn said to Rob, "I'll take care of it," as he pulled out his wallet. It was always embarrassing to dine with Dooley. Shawn went back to the waitress, shrugged his shoulders, apologized, and handed her an extra ten dollars. The four protégés caught up with Dooley and they all walked briskly back to the office.

O'Connor studied the members of the board at the table. He began making strokes on his legal pad, trying to guess what each partner would vote. He knew his motion to make Mary a partner would be close; probably down to one vote either way. He needed six of the nine members' votes. In the "for" column, he listed himself, Murphy, and their four junior partners, O'Leary, Herdling, Lally, and Stafford. In the "against" column he listed Dooley and Cossell and Farrell. Six to three the motion would pass. After all, Murphy said he had his support and his junior partners should follow. And he knew how his junior partners felt because they had discussed the motion before the meeting.

He noticed Dooley whimsically leafing through Mary's dossier while one of the junior partners recited his PowerPoint presentation about an altogether different topic. Dooley smirked and tossed the dossier aside, shifting his head side to side as if disgusted by it. This infuriated O'Connor. He knew Dooley was trying to press his buttons, so he pretended that it did not draw his ire.

At four-thirty the final PowerPoint presentation came to a merciful end. Murphy cleared his throat. The chairman said, "Any motions? Or should we call it a day?"

O'Connor wavered. Was this the appropriate time for his motion? He looked at Murphy who urged him on with his eyes. At the last second, O'Connor said, "I would like to make a motion. I am petitioning that Mary McDougal be offered a junior partnership with the firm."

Nodding acceptance, Murphy replied, "Motion for the election of Mary McDougal to junior partner accepted. Do we have a second?"

The members all looked at one another. Who would second the motion? Murphy had said that he would support the initiative, but never committed to seconding the motion. The junior partners all stared at one another. It was like a gun fight where no one would draw. O'Connor began to feel unsettled. Dooley cracked an evil smile. O'Connor began to wonder how it could go down like this. He thought the vote would be close, but at least get to the voting process.

"Will anyone second Mr. O'Connor's motion?" Murphy repeated. One could hear the second hand on the clock over the doorway. The room was silent.

Murphy lifted his gavel, but then Dooley's junior partner, Jim Cossell, interjected, "I second the motion."

Dooley slammed his fist on the table and his face turned beet red. O'Connor breathed a sigh of relief.

"A twenty-minute break and we'll vote," Murphy said, trying only a little to hide the smile on his face. He so loved the politics of it all.

These last twenty minutes would make or break the vote. Dooley tried to rally his troops to his side. O'Connor did the same. Dooley grabbed his junior partners and took them into his office. He was screaming at Farrell and Cossell through the closed door. "How could you second that motion? What are you, an idiot? If no one had seconded the motion, it never would have gone to vote. What were you thinking?"

Cossell stood firm. He didn't retreat, as many in his position would have. He waited for Dooley to end his tirade before explaining himself. "If we vote this thing down today, then we're done with it. He'll never bring it up again. We have the four votes to defeat this. By not seconding, Mr. O'Conner could bring it up again next quarter. If defeated, he will have to wait another year. Let's put an end to this charade once and for all."

Dooley took a couple of moments to consider his journeyman's reasoning. It made sense. "I hadn't thought of that," he said. "Still, you should have talked it over with me," he warned.

They left the office to seek the other junior partners, Murphy's men. Dooley and his posse wandered through the labyrinth of cubicles and offices, scrambling to find Murphy's protégés. There was no need to address O'Connor's boys, as all knew where they stood. The only votes that were not clear were those of Murphy's junior partners.

Dooley suspected where Murphy would go with his vote. He was convinced that O'Connor had persuaded him at lunch. He had to make a last ditch appeal to persuade one of Murphy's boys. He found them departing from the kitchen area. "I've been looking for you two," Dooley confronted them.

Three steps behind them, O'Connor emerged as well. "Why not try and persuade me?" he said in a satirical manner. Annoyed, Dooley escorted the two junior partners down the hall, looking back to make sure O'Connor did not follow. O'Connor just stared as the three men entered Dooley's office.

Dooley made his last-minute appeal for these two votes and both nodded as he made his points to them. Dooley decided to stick to three main points. "Gentlemen, you know I like Mary. But we can't just hand her business that she hasn't earned like we have. Secondly, let's face facts—there are already too many partners and adding another will cut into your annual bonus disbursements. And finally, what if she starts going through women's problems, like they all do. We all deal enough with that stuff at home. Then we'd have a part-time board member. This is a full-time job, gentlemen. Please don't put the firm at risk with this decision. I know I can count on you," he said, patting them on the shoulder as they left his office.

The members returned to the boardroom. Dooley caught O'Connor outside the room. "How was your lunch, O'Connor?" he asked smugly. "I took your two junior partners out with me to catch up on things."

Surprised, O'Conner wondered if he had been "one-upped" in office politics 101.

Murphy called the meeting back to order. He explained the rules for choosing a partner. "We must have a 60 percent majority on this motion and voting will be by secret ballot." He handed out the poll tickets that Rosarita had printed. He placed a glass bowl in front of him. Each member would vote, fold his ballot, and place it in the bowl.

O'Connor quickly made his mark in the "for" box, folded his ballot, and watched as the other members cast their votes.

He felt sick.

Dooley finished almost as quickly. He had obviously checked the "against" box. Shawn O'Leary had actually finished his ballot first. But instead of casting it right away, he proceeded to color in the corners, doodling. When he finished, he rose from his chair, walked to the head of the table, and dropped his ballot nonchalantly. He whistled lightly as he returned to his chair. He looked straight ahead and clasped his hands together on the table. He smiled, nodding once toward Dooley and once to O'Connor.

Soon the others had all cast their ballots.

Rosarita stood outside the boardroom. She was ready to spread the word to the other employees. She leaned up against the glass and peeked between the shut wood blinds. She could hear Mr. Murphy counting the ballots out loud. Her heart pounded loudly in her chest, partly because she did not want to get caught eavesdropping and partly because she was hoping that her friend—a woman—would succeed in breaking up the "all boys club."

Murphy pulled out a couple of ballots. "One, excuse me, I mean *two* for partnership," counting out loud. He put his hand in to remove more ballots. He grabbed three, but one fell back in. O'Leary could see his ballot in the bowl, with the markings on the corners. "Two against," Murphy proclaimed.

Dooley stewed. "On with it, Murph! Enough with your theatrics. We'd like to get home to our families tonight."

Dooley didn't even have family, not even a pet. Murphy ignored him and proceeded in the same fashion. He might have even slowed his counting just to antagonize Dooley. He pulled out four more ballots. "One for, one against. One for, one for." He sighed, knowing it would come down to the last ballot. The count stood five for, three against. To gain partnership for Mary, she needed one more ballot.

Shawn O'Leary's vote lay at the bottom of the bowl. He was the only one that already knew the outcome. "Damn, I wish I could place a bet on it," he muttered.

Murphy reached into the bowl and grabbed the last strip of paper with the decorated corners. Unfolding it, he looked around the room. Dooley and O'Connor were leaning forward, hands clenched on the table. Murphy started, "One . . . "

8

DAY TRIP

Mary and Maggie had a light meal. Mr. Wiggles sat in the window, licking his lips at the pigeons that had landed on the sill. Maggie knocked on the window to scare the birds off. "You leave those birds alone!" she said, scolding Mr. Wiggles.

Mary had decided to stay the weekend with her mother. She knew none of the drama that was transpiring at the office in her name. Maggie had cooked some homemade chicken pot pies. The two women dined and made small talk about neighbors and the weather. Both seemed happy to ignore the cancer topic, so they just enjoyed their small talk and mother-daughter bond.

Mary cleared the table and Maggie cleaned the dishes. They changed into their flannel pajamas, and Maggie topped hers off with a green and red housecoat.

Mary sat back on the sofa and flipped through the television channels.

Passing over a black and white film, her mother lurched forward, choking on her tea. "Turn it back. Turn it back. That's Joots. Baby Gumm," she yelled while looking at Mary in a perplexed fashion. "Oh, you know, Judy Garland."

Mary turned the channel back to the film. It was *The Wizard of Oz.* "You want to watch this?" Mary asked quizzically.

Her mother began a diatribe on the biography of Judy Garland. "She was the best, you know. This was made when she was young. You shoulda seen her in *Meet Me in St. Louis.*"

Mary replied, "I've never heard of it. It's a movie?"

"Yes, it's a movie. Don't be ridiculous. That's the problem nowadays. There's a lot more movies, but no good ones. She met this awful fella, who got her into drugs, but she really was a better singer than actor. Boy, she had talent. Her daughter Liza, now that's another one."

Mary could see her mother was back to her old self. When it was over, Mary went to the kitchen and scooped ice cream into two bowls. She topped it with canned whipped cream and maraschino cherries, making it look like it had come straight out of an ice cream parlor. She handed a bowl to her mother and the two women slowly ate their ice cream while watching the 10 O'clock News.

When the news ended, Maggie excused herself for the evening. Mary tried to watch TV and relax, but her mind wouldn't allow it. She needed a plan. She began asking herself questions. How many days? Alternative medicines and cures? Had her mother obtained a second opinion? Mr. Wiggles? Her thoughts raced. What else needed to be done? The lease, funeral arrangements; she was wracked with guilt for even thinking these last questions. Hospital? Hospice? Nurses? In-home care?

Mary stood up. She needed to walk and get some fresh air. She put on her coat and took the elevator downstairs. She walked aimlessly, finally arriving at the neighborhood bodega. She ordered a small coffee, cream, two sugars. The clerk said, "Two dollars," from behind his bulletproof glass while pointing to the self-serve coffee.

Mary made her coffee, put a lid on it, and proceeded back to her mother's apartment. She walked slowly, taking half strides, sipping her coffee. She looked in store windows and tried to keep her mother's health outside of her thoughts. It wasn't working. She decided that she would call her mother's doctors and ask more questions.

Mary spent the rest of the weekend with her mother. They always ate at home. Mary's mother said eating out was a waste of money and that her cooking was better anyway.

The next day they took the A Train to Manhattan and then a subway to the Upper East Side. They visited the Guggenheim Museum first. Mary liked the exhibits. Her mother was not a fan of modern art. She looked at some of the exhibits and quipped, "They call this art?" Mary stifled a laugh and shushed her mother. She knew that her mother would probably not like the Guggenheim, but Mary had not seen any of the new exhibits.

The next stop was the Frick House Museum, which was more to Maggie's taste. The Frick family had left the home to the city. It was a beautiful manor with more traditional art. The mansion was located across from Central Park. There were sculptures by Riccio and paintings by Vermeer, Saint-Auben, and Antea. While looking at a floral painting, Maggie said, "This is more like it. That Google place you took me to was awful."

Mary chuckled. Mary noticed that her mother was growing weary. Usually her mother would be the last one in the museum, especially after paying the hefty entrance fee. Mary told Maggie that she was tired so that her mother would not feel guilty. Maggie agreed and they started home. On the subway ride home, Maggie closed her eyes and fell asleep. When she awoke, Mary pretended that she had not noticed she had been asleep. Mary leaned over and put her hand on top of her mother's hands. The subway came to their stop and they walked back to Maggie's apartment.

The following day they awoke early and walked to St. Margaret's for nine o'clock Mass. They both were very pensive. Maggie wrapped rosary beads around her hands in prayer. They took communion and Mass ended soon after. They both stayed after Mass for some additional personal prayer.

Maggie left the pew first. She tapped Mary on the shoulder and whispered, "I'll be right back." She made a left at the altar and knelt in front of the Blessed Mary. She took some money out of her purse, put it in the offertory box, and lit a candle. She proceeded to say a quick prayer, genuflected, and returned to Mary in the pew.

Outside the church, Father Bob and Deacon Flaherty were still making small talk with the parishioners. They saw Maggie and started up the steps to greet her. "How are you feeling? Is everything okay?" Father Bob asked.

Maggie scoffed, "Oh, is that Terry Hanley spreading stories about my health? I'm fine, Father." Maggie thanked him for a great homily and said she would see them tomorrow.

They walked to the bakery down the street. Mary grabbed a number at the counter. The place was jammed with the after-church crowd. The air was warm and the aroma of the fresh baked goods filled the air. Mary grabbed the Sunday paper and they waited.

"Forty-two," yelled a plump lady behind the counter. Maggie ordered half a dozen doughnuts, two jelly, two glazed, and two Bavarian creams. She knew Bavarian were Mary's favorite. The lady behind the counter filled the bag. Maggie paid the cashier and the two women left for home.

Mary started the eggs and her mother made the toast. The doughnuts would be their dessert. Maggie got out the orange juice and four glasses: two regular juice glasses and two Waterford crystal glasses. They would drink their Christian Brothers sherry out of the Waterford. It was their family tradition.

After breakfast they cleaned up. Mary told her mother that she would be returning to work in the morning. Her mother was eager for Mary to go back. She would miss her company, but did not want to get Mary in trouble at MOD. Mary told her that she would be back later in the week to join her at her oncologist appointment. Her mother argued to no avail. Mary insisted that she would join her at every appointment from now on.

9

THE VOTES ARE IN

Murphy dipped his hand into the bowl and retrieved O'Leary's ballot. He unfolded it and said, "I have an announcement to make: Mary McDougal will be offered partnership at MOD."

O'Connor couldn't contain his elation and jumped out of his seat. He walked exuberantly around the table and shook hands with the other partners.

Dooley, however, pushed his chair back loudly. "Idiots," he muttered as he stormed out of the room.

Murphy said, "I'll take care of the necessary protocols. Meeting adjourned!"

O'Connor shook O'Leary's hand and held him still. "I thought for sure that Dooley had gotten to you," he said.

"Well, he actually had me convinced," O'Leary said, "until he made a crack about women. I have four daughters. I'd never be able to look at myself in the mirror if I had voted based on Dooley's logic. I mean, what if some asshole held my daughter back like that?"

The board members continued to chatter about the decision as they left the room. The junior members elected to discuss the matter over liquid refreshments at Clancy's. O'Connor and Murphy remained in the room. O'Connor shook his friend's hand, thanking Murphy for his support. "She's going to be a great addition, and it's time for a woman to be part of our team."

"Why are you still trying to sell her?" Murphy asked. "Are you trying to rationalize the decision to yourself? I wouldn't have voted for her if I didn't think she was qualified. I'd have voted for a woman years ago if we had a woman that was the right fit."

"I'm sorry for rambling," O'Connor said. "I just wanted you to realize how much your support means to me."

O'Connor almost skipped out of the board room, and Murphy started making a list of things to do. Letterhead, the firm's logo, legal, office directory, website. He shook his head and smirked. The "all boys club" wasn't exclusive anymore.

Rosarita had sequestered herself in the kitchen. When Dooley had stormed past her out of the boardroom, she knew the final tally must have gone in Mary's favor. She began to spread the news around the office. Usually employees tried to sneak out a little early on Fridays to start their weekends. Not today. The drama was playing out in the boardroom. Rumor, innuendo, even a few wagers encompassed the office. Mary was well-liked and the staff was happy with her pending promotion. Most of them agreed that no one deserved it more.

Rosarita ran from cubicle to cubicle and the word spread like wildfire. A general giddiness filled the office and hallways. Except for Dooley, who left MOD for the weekend in a fit of rage. Rosarita contemplated calling Mary, but she decided to respect her friend's need for privacy while she tended to her mother. She would wait to see her reaction on Monday.

10

REALITY SETS IN

Early Sunday afternoon, Mary prepared her makeup bag and luggage. She looked around the apartment and asked her mother if she needed anything. Maggie said, "No. Don't worry about me; I'll be fine. Thanks for everything."

They hugged at the door. Their embrace lasted longer than their typical goodbyes.

Mary caught the subway to midtown. She arrived home at three in the afternoon. She realized that she hadn't picked up her mail in a week. She opened her mailbox with a key and letters fell to the floor.

Mary sorted through the mail as she unlocked her apartment. The sun peeked into the apartment through two-inch antique metal blinds. Dust had accumulated on the flat surfaces of the blinds and furniture. Mary stroked her finger across an end table and examined her finger. *Yuck,* she thought.

She spent the rest of the afternoon cleaning her apartment. She cleaned in a slow, methodical manner, trying to keep her mind occupied. Dusting, vacuuming, scrubbing, and mopping. By six o'clock she was exhausted. She sat in her second bedroom, which served as a home office, and began to go through her mail more thoroughly. She paid all her bills online, printed them, and filed away the invoices. She shredded anything with her personal identification numbers on it. Retreating into her living room, she watered the plants. She put her stereo on low and lay on the couch.

At least the apartment *smelled* clean now. Mary pulled an afghan that her mother had crocheted for her across her body and took a book off the coffee table. She read two chapters of the book, but quickly grew disinterested. She grabbed a magazine and leafed through it instead.

Shortly thereafter, her stomach growled. She pulled herself off the couch and walked to the kitchen. She opened the freezer to explore what gourmet meal she would be microwaving. She brought a steaming turkey and broccoli Lean Cuisine back to the living room. The meal didn't really have much taste to it, with the exception of the tiny apple pie dessert.

Mary finished her meal and lay back on the sofa, covering herself with the afghan again. She flipped through the pages of the magazine, but nothing interested her. She rubbed her fingers along the fabric of the woolen afghan. The red, yellow, and blue blanket had been crocheted for her when she was a child. It wasn't very large—just big enough to cover a twin bed or single person.

She couldn't get her mother off of her mind. What had Dockendorff said? Sixty to 120 days. What does that mean?

She got on her computer and researched the disease: pancreatic cancer. No surprises here, except for links to foreign countries with claims of miracle cures. She got her purse and retrieved the oncologist's business card. Staring at it, she decided to call. Sunday night at seven-thirty? No problem.

The answering service picked up and recited the doctor's normal office hours. The service said that Dr. Dockendorff was on-call that night, and they would page him if necessary. Mary asked for him to be paged. She hung up, not expecting a return call. But she felt better that she had done something.

An hour later the telephone rang, startling Mary out of a sound sleep on the couch. She answered the phone in a hoarse voice. Dockendorff was on the line. Mary fumbled her words. She had not expected the doctor to call, at least not tonight. Dockendorff was compassionate. He listened. This wasn't the first family member he had dealt with. He listened to Mary's questions and answered as best he could.

Mary started, "What is my mother's time frame, I mean life expectancy?"

"Sixty to ninety days is my best estimate. There are no guarantees, though."

"Aren't there any alternative medicines or treatments?" Mary asked.

In a calm voice Dockendorff answered, "Your mother is a fighter. She has tried all the recommended treatments and done remarkably well for a woman her age. She has a real zeal for life. But the cancer has spread to her lymph nodes and there is no chance for recovery. At this stage we just treat for pain if needed." Silence filled the phone line. Mary was paralyzed. Dockendorff added, "I want you to meet with one of my nurses this week without your mother."

Mary repeated some of her questions. Her mind did not comprehend the doctor's answers.

"The nurse will be able to give you a better outlook of what your mother's condition will be like in the coming weeks. There are no promises—just suggestions and lots of love and prayers."

"H-how much time do you think she has?" Mary asked in a quiet, somber voice.

"Ms. McDougal, like I told you at the office—your mother has sixty to ninety days."

Ninety! Mary thought. *I thought he said 120!*

The doctor continued. "That's my best estimate. There are no exact numbers. Each patient is different.

But your mother's condition is advanced, and once the cancer has spread to the lymph nodes, it can progress in a rapid, deteriorating manner. Once you meet with my nurse, you'll have a better idea of what lies ahead," the oncologist said in a compassionate and clear manner. Mary could tell that he had given similar answers to many patients and their caretakers throughout his career. It didn't make it any easier for him, just a part of his job that he detested most.

"Thank you, doctor," Mary sighed. "I'll make the appointment to meet with your nurse."

She hung up the phone. She put her head between her legs. Tears trickled down her cheeks. She felt nauseous. She ran to the bathroom and vomited.

Sprawled on the tile next to the toilet, the waves of nausea eventually subsided. She rested her head on the cold porcelain of the toilet seat. Mary's controlled world was in a tailspin and she did not like how it felt. She needed control.

Standing up, she wiped the tears from her eyes, cleaned her face, and leaned closer to the mirror. Her hair was a mess, her eyes bloodshot, makeup smeared, and the sides of her abdomen ached from vomiting. She made her way back to the living room and sank onto the couch. She had never felt so alone.

Mary grabbed the phone again and hit speed dial number nine. A voice at the other end of the phone answered. "Luigi's." Mary began to place her order, but the voice finished it for her. "Small pie. Basil and fresh tomato. Twenty to twenty-five minutes, alright, Ms. McDougal?"

Mary was a "regular" at Luigi's, though she rarely set foot in the restaurant. Her name, phone number, and regular order were programmed in their computer. That was the organized control that Mary preferred in her life. The pizza would be great comfort food.

Half an hour later, the deliveryman hit the intercom and Mary buzzed him up. She tipped him five dollars for the twelve-dollar pie. She folded a slice and took a big bite. The oil dripped over the flap and slightly burned her cheek.

The pizza helped settle her stomach, but she needed something for her nerves. In the kitchen, she uncorked a ten-dollar bottle of cab sauvignon. She poured the glass and took a sip. She finished her first glass of wine and turned on the television. Three slices of pizza and a bottle of wine later, she fluffed up the pillow on the couch, laid her head back, and covered herself in the afghan. She succumbed to slumber a few seconds later.

Mary slept restlessly. She awoke to another bout of nausea. Before she could reach the bathroom, she doubled over and began vomiting. Was that blood in her vomit? She wretched in pain, alone in the darkness. She fell from the couch, twitching on the floor, both hands grasping her neck. She was choking on her own vomit. She felt her face burn as it turned blue from lack of oxygen. Through her alcohol-induced haze, she knew she did not have much time left if she could not dislodge the regurgitated contents from her throat.

Mary tossed back and forth, finally sitting upright on the couch. She coughed violently and dislodged a piece of pizza crust from her throat. The involuntary reaction caused her to knock over her second bottle of wine. When had she opened that? The bottle spilled all over the coffee table and carpet.

Mary wondered if she was having sympathetic symptoms for her mother. All the research she had conducted on the Web stated that nausea and vomiting were common side effects of the disease. Was her mother vomiting at that moment on the floor of her apartment? The "blood" Mary had seen in her vomit was just red wine. But what about her mother?

She considered calling her. But a five o'clock wake-up call probably wouldn't be appreciated. Mary would call her when she got to work.

Mary cleaned the mess in the living room, and then she prepared herself for her "catch-up" day at the office. She took extra care getting ready this morning. Her shower was longer. The water felt cleansing. She had felt dirty from getting sick, and the fats and oil from the pizza oozed from her pores. She let warm water fall into her open mouth and she swallowed it. She was dehydrated. Her mouth and body needed water.

Mary turned off the nozzle and stepped out of the shower. She toweled off and brushed her teeth. When she began to apply her makeup, she did it painfully slow. She wanted to look her best since she had been gone most of the prior week.

With a final swipe of her mascara pencil, she was ready to start her day. Mary took an Alka-Seltzer to settle her stomach. This was her favorite cure for a hangover.

She put on her coat and started her commute to MOD. The crisp outdoor air felt great. It reinvigorated her. She picked up her pace with each step. She would arrive at seven o'clock. Normal Mary time.

"Morning, Ms. McDougal. Glad to see you. Been on vacation?" one of the doormen asked as he opened the door for her.

Mary shook her head. "I wish," she said as she hurried into the building. The other doorman pressed the elevator button, the door opened, and he hit her floor number. "We're glad to have you back," he said.

"Glad to be back," she shouted hastily as the door closed.

The elevator doors opened and Mary walk into reception. She looked down the hall and could see Rosarita. Her head protruded above the tall façade. A man was on his knees to the left of Rosarita. As she approached, she noticed that the back of his overalls read "Midtown Glass."

Rosarita jumped out of her chair and gave her a big hug. "Is everything okay with your mother?" she asked, looking straight into Mary's eyes as if trying to divert her attention.

Mary replied, "No. But I'm okay. I'm going to meet with some professionals this week . . . and make a plan."

Rosarita grabbed both of Mary's hands and said, "If there's anything I can do, please, please let me know."

Mary thanked her and knew she was being sincere, even though she was acting a bit peculiar. Mary proceeded down the hallway to her office. She hung her coat on the back of the door and turned around to see a bouquet of flowers on her desk. She cocked her head. Did someone think her mother had died? No, the arrangement looked festive—it wasn't a funeral arrangement. She put her nose to the flowers. It was composed of fresh irises, roses, and larkspurs encompassed in fresh greens and baby's breath. The flowers stood high in a crystal vase and the sweet scent permeated her office. They served as a nice dichotomy to the dead of winter outside.

Mary pulled the card from the flowers and opened the envelope. It read, "Congratulations." She didn't understand. Congratulations for what?

She heard a man clearing his throat at her door. "Mary, I'd like to have a word with you," O'Connor said quietly. Then he simply walked away.

Mary walked out of her office and followed Mr. O'Connor, glancing back at the flowers on her desk. They walked to the lobby. Rosarita had a big smile on her face. "Come with me," O'Connor said to Mary as he opened the glass double doors to MOD.

Mary felt this was odd, but followed him outside, allowing the doors to swing shut behind them. O'Connor turned her around like a child spinning another in a game of Pin the Tail on the Donkey. She saw Rosarita through the clear doors.

"Well, how do you like the new sign?" O'Connor asked.

Mary was perplexed. She had seen the man working on the glass as she arrived at work, but she had not noticed a new sign. She looked at the firm's logo on the window above the doors leading to the lobby. Her eyes then shifted to the right, to the list of partners. She was about to tell O'Connor that she didn't notice anything different when at the bottom of the list she noticed a new name.

Mary F. McDougal.

Rosarita walked through the double doors. "I'm so happy for you," she said.

Mary looked again and read her name. She blinked repeatedly, trying to convince herself this wasn't a bad joke or a dream. Speechless, she reached out and hugged O'Connor. Then she hugged Rosarita. She fumbled for something to say, but was at a loss for words.

Finally, she mustered, "I-I can't believe it. I didn't know what the flowers were for . . . and I didn't see the new sign. When did this happen? Nobody told me." Mary began to blush.

O'Connor looked her in the eye, grabbed her by her shoulders, and said, "Nobody deserves it more. You've earned it. Congratulations! Now get back to work. We've got a lot to do . . . partner."

Partner.

It sounded so sweet to Mary. She had worked years for this moment. She took her cell phone out and took a picture of the new sign. Walking back into the office, she glanced back at it again, reading it backwards through the glass. As she walked back to her office, a couple of early-bird employees shouted, "Way to go, Mary!" She wiped a tear from her eye and walked back into her office, burying her face in the floral arrangement.

The sweet smell of victory.

Then she noticed the pile that had grown in her inbox. The envelopes were rubber-banded to keep them from toppling over. She placed the arrangement on her windowsill to set them in the sunlight—where everyone could see them. The morning sun glistened off the petals.

Partner.

As the other employees made their way into the office, they all tipped their heads in and expressed their congratulations. This went on all morning.

Murphy arrived about 7:45. There had been no sign of Dooley. Mary didn't realize that he hadn't stopped by until right before noon. That's when Dooley rapped quickly on the door, tipped his hat, and murmured, "Congratulations." Then he continued his trek down the hallway.

Dooley's quick, snide snub didn't bother her a bit. She glowed in victory. Several of the junior partners asked to take her to lunch to celebrate. Mary told them she would have to take a rain check since she needed to play "catch-up."

Amidst the "congratulations," Mary read through her pile of mail. She tossed a lot in the garbage, filed some others, and marked a few for follow-up. At one o'clock she finished reading her snail mail.

Next, she logged onto her computer. One hundred forty-two e-mails. Mary sighed, knowing that it would take her the rest of the afternoon to go through them all.

Sorting them in order of importance, she looked first at the red-flag messages. There were six. Not bad. She then sorted them by date, then by sender. This method had always proved best for her after taking any time off from work. She deleted all FYIs and filed some off to her hard drive. By four-thirty she had attended to all her e-mails.

At five o'clock, employees began to file out of the office. Some waved as they passed her office, congratulating her once again. Mary had no idea when she would be able to leave the office. She had to review some ledgers for the next day's appointments.

Mary stretched her arms over her head. Her muscles had grown tight sitting in the chair all day. She needed a brief break before diving into the "books."

Mary went to the kitchenette and got a diet cola from the vending machine. Her eyes were burning from staring into a computer screen all day. When she returned to her office, she smelled the flowers once again. A half hour later, she was staring out the window, through her flowers. The commuters looked so small from her twelfth floor view. They scurried like ants on the sidewalk below. Through the drizzling rain, a woman twirled a green and white umbrella. From Mary's vantage point, it looked like a pinwheel spinning below. Mary's mother had one just like it.

Suddenly Mary realized that she had forgotten to call her mother. She reached for the phone and quickly dialed the number. The phone rang and rang. Nobody picked up. Wild thoughts filled her head. Should she call an ambulance? She hung up and frantically dialed her mother again. On the sixth ring her mother answered.

"Where have you been?" Mary demanded.

"At Terry's, having a cup of tea. What's the matter with you?"

Mary breathed a sigh of relief realizing she had been a little loud with her mother. "Nothing, I was just worried about you," she said apologetically. They talked for a few minutes and Mary hung up. The phone had barely been set back on the receiver when Mary realized that she hadn't let her mother in on her promotion. Still frustrated from not being able to get in touch with her mother, she decided to wait and tell her later. Her head pounding, she laid her face into her hands, while her elbows rested on the desk.

Mary caught her breath. She had forgotten to call Dockendorff's office to set up an appointment with the nurse. She pulled her purse from beneath her desk and searched for Dockendorff's business card. She ravaged through it, knowing that the office would be closing at any minute. She turned the purse upside down and poured the contents onto her blotter: wallet, lipstick, mirror, compact, lip gloss, change, phone. Some of the change bounced off the desk and fell to the floor. She couldn't find the card.

Oh, damn! She had left it on her coffee table the previous night.

Spinning the chair to the other side of her desk, she hit the Google search bar on her computer. She typed in Dockendorff's name to obtain his phone number.

She misspelled it twice.

After the third attempt, she dialed the number on her screen and Dockendorff's answering service picked up. It was 5:39. Mary couldn't believe that she had forgotten to call her mother *and* the oncologist. She had become so lost in the day's excitement that time had just slipped away.

Time.

Guilt set in and the word "partner" lost its glimmer.

Mary called her mother back, and they chatted for a while. She had wanted to break the news of her promotion in person, but with her workload she decided to break the news. Picking up the phone, she dialed her mother. Maggie picked up the line and was genuinely happy to hear Mary's voice.

"How are you feeling? What did you do the rest of the day?" Mary asked.

"I feel okay, just a little tired. I cleaned the kitchen and did some laundry. Then I listened to the radio."

"You had a full day," Mary replied. The small talk would usually drive Mary crazy, but she realized that soon it would be gone and she missed it already.

Mary kept pestering her with health questions. "Are you in pain today? Did you take all your medicine? Are you getting enough rest? What can I bring you?"

Mrs. McDougal finally had enough. "Nuff 'bout me now," she said in a slight brogue. "What about you? I won't be needin' any pampering' now."

"I've got some exciting news, Mom. I was promoted to partner at MOD," she said with a girlish glee.

Her mother screamed with delight, and Mary proceeded to tell her how O'Connor surprised her with the door and flowers. Mary could hear how choked up her mother was, which got her choked up as well.

"I want to see the door," Maggie said.

"But, Mom, it's no big deal," Mary said, embarrassed. She agreed, however, to let her mother see the door—but not during business hours. Mary did not want to be seen as conceited or flaunting her accomplishment. They made plans for Mary to stay over on Friday night. They would go to the city on Saturday to shop, have lunch, maybe take in a movie, but definitely the "door" would be on the agenda.

When she hung up the phone, Mary continued to work until seven. She needed to create a plan for the rest of the week. First thing on the plan was to call Dockendorff's office and set up a meeting with the nurse.

She highlighted the entry and put a big asterisk on each side. She would not forget again.

When she walked out through the glass doors, she took one last glance at her name on the window. The victory was starting to taste bittersweet.

11

INVENTORY

Turbulence caused the C-5 Galaxy cargo plane to sway back and forth. The unwilling passengers looked at one another in the dimly lit cargo hold. Captain Lopez and his two aides, PFC Aguilar and Sergeant Johnson, were en route to the Royal Air Force base at Carnegie. Usually they would have taken a commercial airliner, but the American dollar was strong against the British pound and tourism was peaking, making seats extremely hard to come by. They didn't even have the luxury of boarding an army transport.

Lopez and his team had been sent by the General Accounting Office to do an inventory on an old hangar at the RAFB that the U.S. Army had closed years earlier during a string of closures approved by Congress.

One aide, Aguilar, struggled not to puke when the old plane hit the turbulence. Lopez told him, "Hang in there, we should be landing any time now." With that, the pilot's voice came over the speaker and informed them that they had begun their descent. The airplane received permission to land and finally touched down.

Aguilar was as white as a ghost. "Don't think I could've lasted much longer, sir," he said as he rose unsteadily to his feet.

They deplaned and made their way to a waiting Jeep. The driver saluted and welcomed them to the U.K. He escorted them to the base commander's office. They sat in a waiting room for several minutes until a corporal waved them in. Lopez and his team saluted the base commander. He then explained their mission and handed his orders over to the commander.

He took the orders and began to read them and bellowed, "Welcome to Carnegie, Captain!"

Lopez said, "Thank you," and introduced his aides. "This is Sergeant Johnson and Private Aguilar."

Wellington nodded to acknowledge the men. The commander flipped through the papers and said he had been briefed. "The hangar hasn't been used or touched since the early 1960s," said Commander Wellington. "I'd like to use the building for storage, and I'd appreciate anything you can do or recommend to expedite the process."

"With all due respect, Commander, my orders are to conduct an audit," Lopez replied. "I have no authority or say in the disposition of the equipment or the hangar."

The commander sighed. "I understand, mate. Bureaucracy and all that." He gave orders to his subordinates to escort the Americans to the hangar.

It had begun to drizzle outside, and a fog had set in. Lopez wanted to start right away so they could return stateside as soon as possible.

They rode approximately two miles to the interior of the base before they reached the deserted hangar. The red sheet metal was rusted at the seams. Hovering above two large doors a sign read, "United States of America, Mail Depot." The sign had yellowed over time, and rust bled through the bottom of the sign where the bolts held it in place.

The British airman parked the Jeep and rummaged through his keys for the one that would open the hangar. He tried several before finding the one that fit the old lock. He turned the key with some difficulty. A large chain protested as he struggled to open the large doors. Lopez ordered his men to assist him. Two on each side, they pried the doors opened.

Lopez entered first and a cobweb met his face. He wiped it off and turned the corner, feeling along the dark walls for a switch that would turn on the lights. The hangar was not more than four thousand square feet. Lopez could make out the shadows of bins, machines, and sorting boxes through the darkness. Finally, he felt a lever and pulled it down.

A hum filled the air as generators kicked in. Fluorescent bulbs flickered slowly to life. The pale yellow light startled some rats, mice, and others critters and sent them scurrying. A thick coat of dust coated everything in the hangar. "Lovely," Lopez mumbled.

The British escort chuckled and said, "Well, I'll be leaving you chaps to your work. I'll drop your bags at the guest barracks. The commander has asked for you to dine with him at 1900 hours." He saluted Lopez and sped away in his Jeep.

Lopez ordered his men to get moving. "Start by separating the tools, machinery, office furniture, and miscellaneous items." The men put gloves on and rolled up their sleeves.

Lopez booted up his laptop computer and opened an Excel file for the audit. Aguilar and Johnson began sorting. It was dirty work. Aguilar sneezed each time he disturbed the dust when he moved a large object. "What a waste of time," he muttered. "This stuff is all junk. It's more than fifty years old and ain't been touched in the last thirty."

He was right, Lopez thought. The entire hangar would have remained a fossil of the war if it had not been for the recent closure ordered by Congress and the president. "Shut up, Aguilar," he said with a smirk.

"Unless you want a recommendation to join the Poland or Turkey audit."

The two men worked for hours separating the inventory, which was difficult since only half of the lights were functional and the sun had started to set. Lopez concluded that they would have to wait until morning to continue.

The British airman arrived and delivered them to the guest barracks. The men looked forward to a meal with the commander. They knew they would eat better at his quarters than the rest of the British troops or any of the Americans that shared the base. They showered, put on their dress uniforms, and prepared for dinner.

The team arrived at the commander's house and was immediately offered cocktails. "Enjoy yourselves," Lopez said to his men out of the corner of his mouth. "Just not too much."

Commander Wellington had invited his second in command to join them. They enjoyed a relaxing night together, talking about sports and arguing in good spirits about which was rougher: football or rugby. The soldiers retired to the dining room where they feasted on steaks, shrimp, asparagus, and some beef barley soup. After dessert, they smoked cigars and drank cognac. The enlisted men were like kids in a candy store.

"So this is how officers live," Aguilar said as he exhaled a puff of arid smoke.

"Commander," Lopez said hesitantly, not wishing to poison the festive atmosphere with business. "We're going to need some assistance at the hangar. Can you spare any men or equipment?"

The commander chewed the end of this cigar thoughtfully. "I can spare two enlisted men, a forklift, and some additional lighting," he said. "I want to do everything in my power to keep the ball rolling. The additional resources will be at the hangar at 0800 hours."

Lopez and his men thanked him for his hospitality and his assistance and they departed to the guest barracks.

After a restful night's sleep, the team woke at 0530 hours. Lopez wanted to get an early start. He and his men showered, dressed, and ate breakfast. They didn't care for the stale British coffee. The British loved their tea and the mess hall didn't get many requests for coffee.

After breakfast the men arrived at the hangar promptly at 0700 hrs. Lopez did not want the commander's men to be there earlier than his own. Lopez tried to start the old boiler in the corner. The previous day the hangar had been cold enough to hang meat. The boiler groaned, rattled, and gurgled until it finally kicked in and started to heat the hangar.

At 0800 hours, a truck pulled up with two British enlisted men and the requested materials. A second truck pulled up and lowered a forklift. Lopez ordered the men to start using the hand trucks to move the items into his requested categories, segmenting them into quadrants. After that they would begin their inventory. Lopez began filling in the cells on his spreadsheet to list the equipment, descriptions, quantities, and serial numbers. He blew into his hands. The building was still a bit chilly, and he could see his breath.

The British and American military personnel worked well together. They moved all the equipment in tandem. The crew was able to see much better with the floodlights the men had brought with them, which also provided some heat.

The men had separated all of the materials per Lopez's instructions. Much of the equipment was wooden. Lopez smiled. A different era, he thought. Canvas duffel bags, cotton mailbags, wooden tools, boxes, cleaners—everything had to be accounted for.

"Junk. All junk," Aguilar complained again. "What a waste of time and money. This stuff wouldn't even sell on eBay."

The crew had finished over half of the audit and broke for lunch at 1130 hours. They rode to the mess hall. Their lunch venue proved not to be of the same variety as they had indulged in the night before. U.S. military food had improved over the years. The British were not so lucky. The men ate sparingly, moving their food around their plates more than eating it. The two

Brits quipped, "Not so hungry, lads?" as they gobbled down their meal.

After lunch the five men proceeded back to the hangar. Lopez unlocked the doors. It had finally warmed up. "Let's get a move-on, men!" Lopez said. "There's a C-4 departing at 0500 tomorrow morning and I want to be on it!"

The men agreed to start picking up the pace. Several hours later all the contents of the hangar were inventoried, with the exception of four mail sorting machines.

Lopez inspected the bolt supports that fastened the sorting machines to the floor. The bolts would not budge. The Brits left and returned to with some heavier tools to loosen the bolts. With a grunt and a big thrust, the larger of the Brits, Private Norwood, managed to loosen the first bolt. Lopez inspected the remaining bolts that held the machine in place. He ordered Aguilar to spray WD-40 on the remaining bolts. The men worked hard at unfastening the bolts and eventually all of them came off the first machine.

Lopez took a look underneath the machine. He wiped off years' worth of dust, oil, and residue from the engraved label to read the manufacturer and serial number. Carson's Manufacturing, Sheboygan, Wisconsin. But the tin had been ripped apart at some point in time on the tag, so the serial number was missing. Lopez entered it on his spreadsheet as "unavailable."

The Brits loaded the mail sorter onto the forklift and set it down on some pallets, where the Americans banded it down. The crew worked diligently on the remaining two machines, proceeding in the same fashion and order.

Lopez took a deep breath. They were almost done. He was relieved that they would likely make the early flight the next morning. Lopez took a seat on a stack of empty mail duffel bags labeled "Inbound—U.S. Domestic Mail." He rested his feet on another pile of empty duffel bags labeled "U.S. Military—Field Mail." It served as a makeshift recliner. He propped the laptop on his thighs as he made some adjustments in the remarks column.

The last of the mail sorters proved to be the most problematic. It was positioned against the southern wall of the hangar and had been subjected to the most rust and corrosion. Lopez arose from his duffel recliner and walked over to assist with a crowbar.

With two men on each of the giant wrenches, they still couldn't pry the bolts loose. After a momentary rest, Lopez called out, "On three. One, two, *three!*"

The team grunted in unison. The first bolt came loose, and the crowbar slipped. Lopez fell to the ground. Aguilar helped him to his feet and Lopez picked the crowbar back up. Once the stubborn bolt had been unfastened, the team was able to tear the machine away from the corroded wall.

A *Life* magazine and several letters fell to the floor. Dust rose into the air. Lopez coughed. He leaned over and picked up the yellowed parchment from the past. "You gotta be kidding me," he brooded as the Americans walked over to look at what he had found. Each letter had been stamped by the machine with the date December 21, 1945. The mail had slipped between the machine and the wall of the hangar.

Lopez ordered his men to finish putting the sorting machines on the pallets. When they completed the task, they threw tarps over the machines. Lopez thanked the Brits for their assistance, turned the generators and heat off, and chained the doors. Lopez put the unsent mail in his computer case and accompanied his men to the guest barracks.

After dinner Lopez lay on his bed and opened his briefcase. He looked at the ancient mail. The *Life* magazine had been read in France and was supposed to be shipped back to the States. A letter was addressed to a Mark Greenbaum in Hoboken, New Jersey. The last envelope was dirty and discolored. It had been sent from Belgium by a PFC James McDougal to a Bronx, New York address. Lopez wondered if any of the recipients or senders were even alive. He put the mail into a Ziploc bag for protection and then back into his case. He began typing his report to his superior officer, detailing the audit, inventory, and their special find. He asked for instructions on how to proceed with the found mail.

The men rose early the next morning and met the cargo plane for their ride home. The pilot said the ride would be smooth and would take approximately ten hours. They arrived at Fort Bliss, Texas, thirty minutes early. Captain Lopez excused the men until 0100 hours the next day. It was late, and they had worked hard.

Lopez returned to his house and unpacked. He walked to the refrigerator to get a beer, and then he logged on to his computer. He wanted to be prepared for the next day. He took two big gulps of beer and entered his security credentials into the computer. His mailbox kept reading "receiving mail." Something was up.

Forty-one new e-mails uploaded into his mailbox— all received within the last ten hours. The morning would not be pleasant. Thirty-nine of the e-mails were in reference to his found mail. The various senders were the Military Historical Society, commanding officers, private mail reviewers, USPS postmaster, and military lawyers. Lopez wondered what he had gotten himself into, but he was too tired to worry about it at the moment.

The next morning Lopez awoke early to start deciphering the list and see what his next plan of action would be. "It would have been easier if I had just thrown the mail into the garbage. No hassles," he lamented. "But what's done is done."

Lopez sorted through the e-mails. The military attorneys insisted that Lopez turn the mail over to his commanding officer, Major Spellman. He would be asked to keep it at the regional command office in a safe until it could be determined whose property and responsibility it was. Lopez was relieved. He would happily turn the mail over to Spellman.

Later that morning, Lopez sat across the desk from his commanding officer. Spellman emptied the Ziploc bag. "Damn," he said as he inspected the contents of the time capsule.

The U.S. Army historical department met with Spellman later that day. They tried to take possession of the letters and magazine, claiming the posts had historical value. But the lawyers intervened, saying they needed time to research whose property the mail was. The U.S. Army's private mail courier, on the other hand, wanted nothing to do with the posts because they offered no value.

Major Spellman's superior officer ordered him not to give the mail to anyone until a final determination could be made as to whose rightful property it was.

The e-mails continued to fly.

And so did the number of days.

12

NURSE CRAGEN

Mary arrived at MOD for her second full day as a partner. She still had to glance twice at her name on the door.

At eight o'clock Mary stopped everything that she was doing and dialed the oncologist's office. The receptionist transferred her to Nurse Cragen's line. Three rings later she got the nurse's voicemail. Mary left a message asking her to call back.

Mary dipped her head into her hands on the desk, trying to get her thoughts back on track. Moments later her phone rang. Dockendorff's office number was on the caller ID screen. "Mary McDougal," she answered.

"This is Nurse Cragen from Dr. Dockendorff's office."

"Thank you for getting back with me so soon."

"Mary, I'd like to make an appointment to speak with you privately about your mother."

"OK," Mary hesitantly replied.

"How about four p.m. tomorrow, then?"

Mary quickly glanced at her calendar and confirmed the appointment. "Great, I'll see you tomorrow."

"Looking forward to it," Cragen responded.

At noon on Wednesday, the junior partners made Mary fulfill her promise to join them for lunch. They ate in the private back room at Sonny's Grill. After lunch, she told Rosarita that she would be leaving early and would be back first thing in the morning. She finished some of the paperwork on her desk, activated the "out of office" on her computer, watered her floral arrangement, and left for her meeting with the nurse.

She hopped the subway and made her way to Dockendorff's office. She checked in with the receptionist, and then sat down in the waiting area. Mary flipped through the pages of some old magazines. She found nothing interesting, so she walked over to gaze at the aquarium. The fish were beautiful. Mary knelt to get a better view and became lost in the variety of colors. She was jolted from her reverie when a hand was laid gently upon her shoulder.

"Ms. McDougal?"

"Oh!" Mary gasped, but quickly composed herself. "Nurse Cragen?" She rose and brushed off her knees.

"Please. Call me Mary," she said. The two women proceeded to the nurse's office.

Nurse Cragen had been with Dr. Dockendorff for over five years. She was a seasoned nurse and counselor who had taken the nurse/social worker position after her own mother had passed away from cancer years earlier. The office had always outsourced this position, but Cragen had convinced Dockendorff to bring the position in-house.

Nurse Cragen showed Mary to a chair and closed the conference room's door. "I had the pleasure of meeting your mother during one of her last appointments. She's a strong woman. I'd like to take this opportunity to meet with you to discuss her upcoming condition and care in the near future. We'll work together, in her best interests. OK?"

Mary nodded her head in agreement.

"Do you fully understand and accept your mother's diagnosis and condition?" Again, Mary nodded, yes. "That is good. Because a lot of relatives are in a state of denial and that only makes it harder on the patient and family."

"My mother has 120 days. It could be longer, you know," Mary answered emphatically.

Cragen briefly opened and reviewed the folder. She knew Mrs. McDougal had sixty days at best. She surmised that Mary was somewhere in the middle of acceptance and denial of her mother's condition. "Call me Nancy," Nurse Cragen urged Mary. She would have to have her fully accept the situation before their next appointment if they were to make any progress on care for her mother.

Nancy opened her desk and took out a chart. She flipped to the tab marked "pancreatic cancer." Under the heading it listed the four stages of pancreatic cancer. Nancy looked at Mary. "Mary, you do realize that your mother is in stage four of the disease, don't you?"

Mary paused to read the lines next to stage four—terminal. Sixty to 120 days life expectancy, once cancer has progressed to the lymph nodes. She stared at the text.

Nurse Cragen reached out to touch her arm. "This can be very emotional and difficult," she said. "There are no lies here. What's important is that we are on the same page about your mother's diagnosis and future care."

Mary sighed and nodded her head. It was a rude awakening. She had told herself that her mother would be alive at least six months, but the chart told her otherwise. She would have to make the best of the short time they had left together.

The nurse continued to speak, but her voice seemed muffled and distant. Nancy put the chart away and pulled out another one labeled, "What to expect." This chart detailed everything that might happen to a patient, physically and emotionally.

"There are ups and downs every day that you need to be prepared for," said Nancy. "Fatigue, loss of bowels, dementia, vision problems, acute pain. These pamphlets will summarize everything we've gone over." She put them in an envelope for Mary to take home. An hour had passed and they weren't even through half of the material.

Nancy saw that Mary's face had gone white. "Are you all right?" she asked. She walked over to a small refrigerator and took out a bottle of water. She handed it to Mary. Mary opened it and took several sips. Her mouth was bone dry.

"We need to focus on your mother's medical plans for the next sixty days," Nancy continued. "Your mother lives alone?" she asked.

Mary didn't answer. She wasn't prepared to answer these types of questions. She felt like an idiot. After a long pause, Mary answered, "Yes."

"Your mother will be all right for the next two to three weeks, but I want you and home health care to check on her. Have you given any thought to your mother's living arrangements after the next thirty days?" Mary shook her head. "Well, you should look into all of your options: home health care, home nursing part-time, home nursing full-time, hospice, home hospice."

Hospice, Mary thought. How final that sounded.

"None of these decisions have to be made now, but the sooner you have a plan, the easier it will be for everyone involved," Nurse Cragen went on. "Now, what about counseling?"

"My mother will have no part of it," Mary replied.

Nancy glanced at her.

"Oh, you're talking about me." Mary felt foolish. She cleared her throat. "I don't think that will be necessary."

Still, Nurse Cragen tucked a pamphlet about counseling into the envelope. She looked up at the clock. "Oh my goodness. It's six o'clock! I'm sorry, but that's all I have for you today. We need to make a follow-up appointment to finalize some arrangements."

Mary set up an appointment with her for the following week. She noticed the nurse putting one last form in the envelope. It was labeled, "Do not resuscitate."

Outside the doctor's building, Mary took a deep breath and leaned against the brick façade of the building. There was too much to think about, but this was no time to be lackadaisical. If she procrastinated in making any of the decisions, the pressure would only grow greater. She had two to three weeks to develop and execute a plan for her mother's care. It sounded so businesslike, dispassionate.

She gathered herself and started for home. She would put together an action plan over the next two to three days. She did not look forward to compiling it, but she knew it would be necessary. The DNR form lurked in her mind as she took the subway home. How would she bring it up to her mother? Organ donor? Living will? All the forms had such a final tone to them.

She arrived home, picked up the mail, and proceeded upstairs. She read her mail and cooked dinner at a snail's pace. Anything to avoid opening the envelope.

After cleaning the dishes, Mary sat at the table and stared at the envelope. She uncorked a bottle of wine and poured herself a glass. She sipped it. She sipped it again.

Finally she spilled the contents of the envelope onto the table. She rummaged through the pamphlets to see where she would start. Like sorting her e-mails, Mary decided to review them by chronological order.

First, she would assess her mother's condition for the next two to three weeks. According to the pamphlet, fatigue and mild to acute pain might develop. She had already noticed a dramatic drop in her mother's energy level on their Manhattan weekend at the museums. Her mother had not complained of any pain, but probably wouldn't have to her. The three- to five-week stage started to worry Mary. Extreme fatigue, mild to severe pain, possible organ failure, and dehydration were the other symptoms listed.

Mary walked to the kitchen to look at the MOD calendar that her office had handed out during the holidays. Doctors appointments still needed to be made. Two appointments that week. One at Dockendorff's and one at the family physician, Dr. Donahue.

Together the two doctors would manage her mother's health care.

The six- to ten-week period was tough for Mary to digest. Loss of bowels, reading problems, organ failure, pneumonia, nausea, jaundice, heat flashes, cold flashes, academia, and the patient could be bedridden. Mary looked away from the pamphlet. She was getting emotional.

She poured another glass of wine and a glass of water. She would alternate glasses to avoid another night of overindulgence. It was February 15. Mary flipped through the calendar and realized that her mother would probably not make it to her eighty-third birthday in May.

She closed her eyes before proceeding to the next pamphlet. "Medical equipment you might need." Mary had not thought of this. Flipping through the pages, she saw equipment that was labeled "recommended" or "needed." The needed list included a walker, shower stand, cane, gauze, tape, and straws. The recommended list included hospital bed, IV trees, wheelchair, comfort pillows, adult diapers, and a DVD/TV combo. Each was available to buy or rent. Just business, Mary thought, analyzing each page.

On Thursday Mary finished work and went about her usual routine. When she got home, she once again engaged in a stare-down with the envelope that Nancy Cragen had given her. Replaying the meeting with the nurse in her mind, she took her advice to plan as much as possible.

Mary picked up the envelope and pushed aside the pamphlets she had already read. She began to read the contents of the "counseling" pamphlet. She didn't know there were so many types of counseling. There was family counseling, group support counseling, spouse counseling, one-on-one counseling, and patient counseling.

Mary's mom was extremely proud and from a different generation. Mary knew her mother would have nothing to do with any type of counseling. She would view it as a weakness of character. Mary read through the brochure and dog-eared a page about group counseling for family members of terminally ill patients.

Tossing it in her "read pile," she picked up the next brochure, "Coping During Times of Stress." The brochure advised how to cope when things got rough. It gave details on being a caregiver and how it could be one of the most rewarding times of one's life—and the most agonizing.

The brochure gave tips on how to keep one's sanity during this stage. It suggested leaving the patient, if only for an hour at a time. Another tip was for breathing exercises. Some of the tips made sense; others seemed silly or downright stupid.

The next couple of brochures were more like advertisements than information. Companies were hawking their goods or services. She hesitated before picking up the last pamphlet.

Hospice.

No coincidence, it was the final brochure in the envelope. She walked around holding it in her hands without opening it. But she knew that she was putting off the inevitable. Sitting back down, she tried to find the courage to open and read it. She tentatively opened the first page. It briefly explained what hospice was, the choices and options available. The first chapter dwelled on choices. Hospice or home hospice? What a family must decide. Mary pondered long into the night her decision and whether she would be able to live with it the rest of her life.

13

WE'RE GOING
TO SULLIVAN'S!

Mary closed the brochure. Reading about the hospice was too much for her. Gathering her courage, she closed her eyes, took a deep breath, and reopened it. She peeked at the introduction. It read:

> HOME is the best possible atmosphere for our loved ones. When curation treatments are no longer possible, Home Hospice Assistance (HHA) can provide a caregiver that will improve the patient's end-of-life experience

Mary took a deep breath. She continued reading. The brochure continued:

One on one care, with home surroundings and loved ones present, improves the quality of life and the dignity in dying, all in the comforts of a home surrounding.

It discussed the various options during the last thirty days of a patient's life. It stressed, "There are no right or wrong decisions, and one should not feel guilty about making them," it explained.

Easier said than done, Mary thought. How could one not feel guilty if they chose the hospice or home hospice? Mary's mind began to spin. What was the best choice? What would her mother think of her? She read through the material, highlighting some paragraphs. She closed her eyes at intervals, dropped her head into her hands, and looked to the ceiling for divine inspiration.

Finally she made up her mind. It had been over a week since the diagnosis. Mary's mother had seven weeks left to live in Dockendorff's best estimates. She came up with a tentative plan to present to her mother. *How* she presented it to her would make all the difference. Her mother was a fiercely independent woman. She had worked and lived on her own since her husband left for the war. She had been independent for more than sixty-five years. Mary knew it would take a lot of coaxing, but she resolved to do it.

She would tell her mom that in two weeks, Maggie would come to live with her. She knew that her mother would not agree to this, so she would have to persuade her. Mary could not bear to think of a lonely hospice filled with strangers surrounding her mother. She would suggest home health until the move to her apartment, then home hospice for the last two weeks.

She had been looking forward to celebrating with her mother over the weekend, but would this be the right time to discuss the plan?

Mary closed the brochure and prepared for bed. But she couldn't sleep. She played the scene repeatedly in her mind. There were no right words to use with her mother. She was stubborn, independent, and liked it that way. Her mother was not a big fan of change. What choice would she have? She wouldn't be able to do it on her own. A vision of her mother barricading her apartment door kept filling Mary's mind.

Mary slept intermittently through the night. She tossed and turned. The discussion weighed heavily on her mind.

At five-thirty in the morning, "Papa was a Rolling Stone," blared from the alarm clock across the room. Mary tossed the blankets off the bed, hopped out of bed, and pressed the snooze button. She had put the clock on the dresser the night before to ensure that she would get out of bed to turn it off. She fell back in bed and pulled her knees up under the blankets. She managed to drag herself out from under the warm comfort of the blankets after the second snooze alarm and made her way into the shower.

Mary toweled off and stepped onto the ceramic floor. She stared into the mirror at the dark circles under her eyes. Terrible night's sleep.

Mary blew her hair dry and applied her makeup. She kept rehearsing the conversation she would have to have with her mother. It would not be pleasant. Mary packed an overnight bag and started for work.

It was twenty-two degrees, overcast, and windy. Because she had overslept, she had not been able to style or blow-dry her hair completely. The tips of her hair began to freeze. She kept her head down, looking at the sidewalk and thinking of the old childhood rhyme, "Step on a crack, break your mother's back." She alternated between a brisk walk and a jog.

A flash of heat hit Mary as she walked into the building. She sat down to remove her sneakers and put her dress shoes on. Perspiration and melting ice from her hair began to drip down her back. Terrific, she thought.

Coffee tasted particularly good this morning. She welcomed the warmth and the caffeine rush. Rosarita dropped into her office a little before eight o'clock and asked, "How's you mother?"

Mary explained the situation. "She's doing fine. I'm the one who's a mess. Rosarita reached across the desk and held Mary's hands.

"What are you going to do?" Rosarita asked.

"I'm going to take care of my mother. I'm going to ask for some time off to be with her until the end. It's what I need to do." Mary said with a big sigh.

Mary explained the rest of her plan and became anxious as she laid it out for Rosarita. "What do you think?" Mary asked. Rosarita said she wanted to mull it over before giving her advice. Mary explained she was going to her mother's that night, and any insight would be appreciated.

Rosarita left her office and Mary began to think about the upcoming weekend.

The day went painfully slow. Mary tried to stop looking at her watch. It made the time go by even slower. But everywhere she turned there was a clock. The computer screen had a clock. The phone had the time. There was a clock over her door. The kitchen had a clock. The grandfather clock chimed in the lobby and it seemed as though someone had turned up the volume of the chimes.

Mary decided to stay at the office for lunch and ordered Chinese food. The flowers the firm had sent her had begun to wilt. The leaves had turned a little brown and were crisp. But they still smelled good, Mary thought as she buried her nose in the arrangement. Mary took out the healthier looking flowers and put them into a separate vase. She removed one of the flowers and placed it on her desk. Reaching behind her, she took a book off the shelf titled *Masters in Accounting*. It had been given to her by her college professor. Opening the book, she laid the flower in-between the pages and closed it as a memento.

The day crept along and Mary started closing up shop. Rosarita came by again and offered her some advice. "Just explain the situation to her. That she will not be able to care for herself and all. Tell her you love her and it won't be an imposition."

Mary listened attentively but didn't think any of her suggestions would work on her mother. "That may work well on a sane, reasonable person," Mary said. "But you don't know my mother."

Rosarita smiled and wished her good luck. "Call me if you need anything." As Rosarita left, Mary sat pensive in her chair. She logged off of her computer, grabbed her coat and overnight bag, and caught a bus to Riverdale.

When Mary arrived at her mother's apartment, a fresh turkey was roasting in the oven. The tasty aroma filled the apartment. Maggie had picked up some fresh vegetables too. She loved cooking for Mary, knowing that her daughter didn't eat well on her own. Every time Mary visited her, she would eat like a queen for the next couple of days. When Mary arrived, she and her mother exchanged a long hug. Their hugs had become longer and harder since her diagnosis.

Mrs. Hanley knocked on the door and said, "I was just seeing how Maggie was feeling and if she needed anything."

Mary greeted her and informed her, "I'm staying over the weekend and we should be all right. Thanks for checking on Mom"

Mrs. Hanley didn't stay long. She had basically just been checking up on Maggie. Mary was happy that at least Mrs. Hanley would be around if her mother needed anything. "Maggie, you give me a ring if you need anything," Mrs. Hanley said.

Maggie replied, "Thanks, Terry."

Mary and Maggie enjoyed the turkey and each other's company. Maggie kept mentioning how proud she was of Mary's promotion. Mary kept trying to steer the conversation back to her mother's condition. They went back and forth until there was no winner. Each stuck to her guns and the conversation went mute.

That's how Mary always remembered their relationship. If her mother wanted to talk about something, fine. If not, it would fall upon deaf ears. If the subject did not suit her, she would change the subject and/or leave the room.

After dinner, Mary helped her mother clean the table. Maggie packed leftovers for Mary, placing them in plastic containers. She said, "Remember, I need these back," inferring that Mary always kept the Tupperware. Mary smiled. She always brought the Tupperware back and her mother never failed to remind her.

They sat together on the sofa and watched a mystery movie, *Hound of the Baskervilles,* and sat back on the couch for a relaxing evening. "I always thought your father and I would have a house like that," her mother sighed about the manor in the movie. Mary gave her a wry look, since the mansion was so creepy in the film.

During a commercial break Maggie said, "I'm taking you to dinner tomorrow night to celebrate your making partner. We're going to Sullivan's steakhouse, and I'm buying."

Mary knew her mother's finances and that Sullivan's was too expensive. "Why don't we go to Mario's instead?" she asked, suggesting a small Italian restaurant that was a lot less expensive.

Maggie would have it no other way. "We're going to Sullivan's, I'm buying, and that's it!" Accepting there was no getting out of it, Mary agreed.

Halfway through the movie, Maggie began to grow weary and sat deeper into the couch. Resting her legs on the coffee table, her eyes began to get heavy. Mary turned to say something, but her mother was fast asleep. A quiet snore poured from her mouth. Her mother never fell asleep when she came over. They often spoke like little girls on a sleepover deep into the early morning hours.

Mary looked at her mother. She had never seemed old to Mary before until that moment. Mary spread the afghan across her mother and went to sleep in her own bed.

Mary woke the next morning to find her mother already in the kitchen. She was like a little girl at Christmas. "The door, promotion, my daughter is a partner at MOD," she muttered to herself.

Mary liked seeing her mother happy. "I hope no one's in today. I don't want them to think I'm gloating," Mary sighed.

Her mother piped up, "You earned that promotion, Mary. Don't you be ashamed of it now."

They ate bacon and eggs for breakfast. They grabbed a couple of scarves from the closet and walked outside to the bus stop.

When the bus let them off at midtown, Mary scrambled through her purse to find her keys. There was no doorman on weekends.

She unlocked the door to the building and proceeded to the twelfth floor. When the elevator doors opened, Maggie scurried down the hallway, which was illuminated only by the exit sign lights. Mary switched the hallway lights on to give her mother the full show. Maggie beamed with pride as she read the sign on the door. She knelt down and ran her hands over the etched glass. Turning around, she urged Mary to pose by the sign so she could take a picture.

Just then, a member of the weekend cleaning crew emerged. Maggie asked the man if he would take a picture of them in front of the sign. He agreed and the two posed on each side of the window like bookends.

Mary pressed the elevator button, and Maggie took one last glance at the door. They shopped Fifth Avenue for a little while, but Maggie grew tired quickly. They returned to Maggie's apartment for a quick nap before dinner.

Mr. Wiggles greeted them at the door, running circles around Maggie's legs and meowing incessantly. "You must be hungry, there you go," Maggie said as she poured the cat food into his dish.

The long day in the city had taken its toll on Mary's mother. "Why don't we stay home and order in?" Mary suggested.

Maggie replied, "Not on your life. We're celebrating tonight,"

After a quick nap, Maggie put on a dress and Mary got dressed in a pair of dress slacks and a blouse. They arrived at Sullivan's promptly at six-thirty. The maître d' asked, "Would you ladies like to be seated?"

Maggie declined and said, "We'd like to have a drink at the bar first." Mary rolled her eyes and followed her mother to the bar. The piano man had just arrived and began warming up.

Sullivan's had been the premier steakhouse in the area for years. It was an older establishment serving steaks and seafood. The room was dimly lit and oil portraits of politicians adorned the walls. A mirrored sign that read *Sullivan's Steak and Seafood* served as a backdrop for the top shelf liquor bottles. Maggie ordered a high ball and Mary a glass of pinot noir. "I haven't been here in years," Maggie said, taking a deep breath and raising her glass. "I'd like to make a toast. To my beautiful daughter Mary, partner at Murphy, O'Connor, and Dooley." A big smile overcame her and she clinked her glass with Mary's.

Mary replied, "I'd like to make another toast. To my beautiful mother, the best mother a daughter could ever have." They clinked their glasses in another toast.

The bartender leaned over asking, "What are you ladies celebrating?"

Maggie went on with the story of Mary's promotion. "My daughter here has been promoted to a partner at MOD. Dats the Murphy, O'Connor, and Dooley accounting firm, if you didn't know," she said in a proud brogue. She puffed up like a peacock in her barstool. Mary thought to herself that she'd tell the pope himself about the promotion, if she could only get an audience with him.

The maître d' escorted them to the dining room. The booths were plush, overstuffed red leather. Electric candles hung from the walls with an accent light over the table. The waiter came by to see if they needed another drink. Mary politely said "No," but Maggie beefed," We'll have a Dom Perignon."

Choking on her wine, Mary tried to intercede, but the waiter had already taken off. Mary cleared her throat and chastised her mother, "What, are you crazy ordering a $170 bottle of champagne?"

"You only live once. We're celebrating. Don't you worry about a thing, I'm paying."

Sullivan's was a classy place. Many of the patrons wore expensive clothing and fine jewelry. Men often donned a coat and tie, women dresses. The waiter came back with the Dom Perignon wrapped in a red linen napkin. He showed Maggie the label and proceeded to open the champagne. The waiter poured a small amount in her glass for Maggie to sample. After her approval, he poured them both a glass, and they toasted again. The waiter returned shortly with menus.

They quietly looked over the menu and Maggie said, "What are you having? The surf and turf sure looks good," Maggie said while looking over her menu at Mary.

"It does," Mary answered. The surf and turf had a market price next to it on the menu. Code for "most expensive entrée on the menu," Mary thought. She looked at the menu trying to pick out something that would not be overly expensive.

Maggie said, "Mary, please enjoy tonight. Order whatever you feel like. Don't worry about the cost. Please, for me." She reached out across the table and held Mary's hand, looking into her eyes.

Mary saw that her mother needed a willing accomplice in her exuberance. "Okay, Mom," she replied.

Maggie waved down the waiter. "Two jumbo shrimp cocktails for appetizers, please," she said. Mary grinned. They held hands over the table and laughed loudly. "I'm so proud of you," Maggie said again.

The waiter brought the appetizers to the women. He asked if they were ready to order. Maggie nodded and ordered the surf and turf. Mary ordered filet mignon. Sitting back and taking it all in, they were out of their normal element but having the time of their lives. They gorged on the colossal shrimp, dipping them in Sullivan's special cocktail sauce and washing it down with champagne.

The waiter returned with the entrées on his arm. He removed the stainless steel top off of each entrée, and the steam rose into the air, filling the area with the aroma of their meals. Maggie joked that she was glad that she wasn't rich because she'd never be able to eat like this and fit into her clothes. Butter dripping from her chin, Maggie devoured her lobster tail.

Mary cut into her steak. The juices flowed onto the plate from her incision. Then they melted into her mouth. The women exchanged satisfied grins. They joked that Sullivan's must have a partnership with a local heart hospital.

Mary was full after the bread and butter and the shrimp. She forced the entrée so as to not disappoint her mother. Making smaller cuts into her meat, she finally finished her fillet.

They sat back like lazy lions after a kill. Cleaning the table, the waiter asked "Coffee or dessert?" Maggie asked for the dessert tray.

Mary couldn't believe her ears. Her mother was usually a nibbler, never eating her entire meal. "You'd think you were going to the gallows in the morning," Mary joked.

The waiter returned with the tray. He described each dessert in detail, adding to the aura of the gluttony. Maggie insisted on Mary having a dessert. At this point, how could Mary argue? She reluctantly chose a crème brulee, thinking it would be the lightest of the fare. Her mother chose the cheesecake with a strawberry topping. Maggie also ordered two Irish coffees. Ten minutes later, the waiter reappeared with the desserts. The crème de menthe dripped over the whipped cream, topping the coffee. "Dat's Jameson Whiskey in the coffee, right?" she questioned.

"All we serve, ma'am," the waiter replied.

They sipped their coffees using a spoon to taste the whipped cream until it cooled. Their stomachs were both full, but they managed to top them off with the desserts. The waiter asked if they wanted anything more. Mary sat quietly praying her mother would finally end the feast. She said, "No thank you, just the check." Mary sighed a breath of relief.

The waiter brought the check in a leather valet. Mary held herself back. She wanted the check. Her mother probably didn't spend that much for an entire month's groceries, maybe two months.

Maggie reviewed the check, carefully verifying the math. Pushing her glasses back up the bridge of her nose, she said, "The waiter did a good job. What's a good tip these days?"

"Twenty percent for good service," Mary answered. Mary tried to catch a glimpse of the bill. Her mother peeled money from her wallet in her pocketbook. She leaned over more to see the check. The price was $345, plus tax and tip. Mary swallowed, knowing how painful the bill would be for her mother. But Maggie couldn't have cared less. She slowly peeled bills from a bank envelope in her wallet. "And there—three one-hundred dollar bills and a fifty. I think that'll cover it," she said.

The women wedged their way out of their booth and walked to the lobby. They took a taxi home, and Mary paid the fare. Mary's felt pretty tipsy, so she was wondering how her mother was holding up. At the door of the apartment, Maggie fumbled for her keys in her pocketbook. Once she found them, she struggled to put the key in the lock. Mary took the keys from her and opened the door. Maggie laughed and conceded she might be a little drunk. When she entered the apartment, Maggie began dancing with Mr. Wiggles and told him about Mary's promotion and their fine celebration.

Mr. Wiggles meowed incessantly. He was hungry and scampered to get away. "Be that way," she said as the cat ran away. Mary laughed at her mother's over indulgence.

They changed into their pajamas and watched the early news. Both were tired and would retire early. Mary began to think time was running out. She needed to confront her mother on her future care. They needed a plan.

Maggie thanked Mary for letting her treat and said, "Goodnight."

Mary got up and gave her a hug and thanked her. Her mother staggered off singing and muttering, "My daughter's a partner in the firm."

Mary would have to talk with her Sunday morning about her plan. She did not look forward to it.

14

LIGHTS, CAMERA, ACTION!

Major Spellman returned to work the next day. He threw the morning paper onto his desk and reviewed his morning briefs. He turned on his computer, entered his security codes, and began to look at his e-mails. The hot button item was the lost mail he was in possession of. He was amused by all the fuss that was being made of this. He leaned back in his office chair and chuckled as he read some of the e-mails. The judge advocate general was now actively involved. Several attorneys voiced their opinions back and forth. Each had a different viewpoint. One argued that the mail was property of the U.S. Army. Another attorney surmised that the mail was property of the sender until received by the recipient and that the U.S. Army was merely a non-liable courier for the post. The third attorney stipulated that there was not a guaranteed time of delivery and that the transaction, though delayed, was still in progress. In other words, finish the transaction by delivering the mail.

Spellman read from other parties that were involved too. The USPS offered to assist locating the recipient. The Historical Society of the Army wanted the mail pieces to use in a WWII exhibit.

Put it in an exhibit, Spellman thought. Deliver the damn mail to whoever the hell is supposed to get it!

He was caught in a unilateral, self-induced army drama. All he had to do was keep the mail in his safe and he would be able to sit on the sidelines while the bureaucrats hammered it out. This time he didn't have to get involved. Sitting back in his chair he enjoyed his coffee until his phone rang.

Corporal Myers was on the other end of the phone. "Sir, are you busy, I think you better come out here."

Spellman got out of his chair, feeling the urgency in Corporal Myers' voice. Spellman opened his door and said, "What's the matter, Karl?"

Myers jumped up and took Spellman out to the waiting area. Several reporters and a cameraman sat there talking amongst themselves. As Spellman entered the room, they jumped him exclaiming, "Are you Major Spellman?" "Where is the lost mail?" "Is it true one of the letters is from General Patton?" "What is the status of the mail?"

Taking a step back, the major was in shock. He was furious about the ambush. Who had let these reporters onto the base? The cameraman's lights shone into Spellman's eyes. "Turn that damned thing off," he told them. "Is this really necessary?"

Spellman's staunch philosophy, as a lifetime army man, was to keep a low profile. He followed orders and despised "suck-ups" that loved the limelight. He genuinely discouraged any attention. The current situation gnawed at him. Escape was his first priority. "I'm not answering any questions at this time. No comment."

The major retreated back to the safety of his office. In a turn of events, Spellman had turned from spectator to an unwilling participant in the fracas.

The corporal kept the reporters and cameraman at bay and followed the major back into his office. Apologizing, he said, "I don't know who let them in and how they found out."

Spellman stewed. He was enraged. How could this happen? He was six months from retirement. He didn't want, nor need, the attention. As long as the reporters were in the waiting room, he was a prisoner in his own office.

Corporal Myers asked, "What shall I do?"

Angrily Spellman answered, "Just wait a damn minute and let me figure this out." Spellman needed to formulate a plan to rid himself of the paparazzi crowd outside. He also needed to contact his superiors to let them know about the leak.

15

THE DISCUSSION

The McDougals had planned their usual Sunday morning. Shower, Mass, bakery, and their breakfast together. Staring at the clock, Mary knew they would be late for Mass if her mother did not awake. Opening her mother's bedroom door ever slightly, she could see that she was still asleep. Too much partying last night, Mary thought. Then again, perhaps her mother's new energy level or lack thereof was to blame. She made herself a pot of coffee and waited for her mother.

An hour passed and Mrs. McDougal emerged from her bedroom. "Why didn't you wake me earlier?" she asked.

Mary answered back, "I thought we'd just go to late Mass."

"You know I like the morning Mass, Mary. Next time make sure I'm up." Mrs. McDougal looked a little perturbed and proceeded to get in the shower to get ready. She did not like to attend the late Mass. There were too many crying children in the later Masses and, besides, she was a regular at the early Mass. It was a routine she had practiced for over forty years and did not like to deviate from it.

They walked to Mass and the sun shone upon their faces, giving them a sense of warmth. They unbuttoned their jackets, as the weather was about ten degrees higher than the prior day, unseasonably high.

After Mass they exited the church. Father Sanchez asked, "Is everything okay? We didn't see you at morning services," noting that Mrs. McDougal hadn't been at the earlier Mass.

"We just slept late," she answered with a smirk. The McDougals spoke with Father Sanchez and some other members of the parish on the church's steps before leaving for the bakery.

Enjoying the weather, they walked a bit slower than usual. After picking up bagels and doughnuts, they returned home. Mary grew anxious knowing that she would have to bring up the conversation she had been dreading. Having made her choices, she was comfortable with the plan. Knowing her mother, she was sure that she would fight tooth and nail not to change her lifestyle.

They ate their late breakfast, cleaned up, and retired to the living room to read the Sunday *New York Times*. Silence filled the room, except for a shuffling of the newspaper. They exchanged sections of the paper as they finished them. The newspaper was extra thick on Sundays.

They had been reading in the living room for three hours until Mary could not take it anymore. She had procrastinated bringing the conversation up all weekend. It was time to face the music.

"Mom, I need to talk to you," she said.

A voice from behind the "real estate" section of the paper said, "What is it dear?"

Mary leaned forward on the couch, staring at the floor, frustrated. "Mom, I need to speak with you," she repeated.

Her mother nonchalantly lowered the paper. "What is it?"

Mary cleared her throat. "We need to discuss your health and well-being for the next two months."

There was an uncomfortable, long, pregnant pause. "I was afraid that's what you wanted," her mother replied in a little voice. Mrs. McDougal rose from the couch, a cup of coffee in her hand, and walked to the window. Sipping from her coffee, she stared out into the distance. She did not focus on anything, but rather stood there in a trance-like state, pretending she was somewhere else.

Mary sat on the couch and observed, planning her next words. Standing up, she walked over to her mother. From behind her, she gently put her hand onto her shoulder. Her mother, a little startled, reached back over her shoulder and held Mary's hand. They both just stared out the window, knowing that it would soon not be the same life they had both known and loved.

"Can we talk, Mom?" Mary asked, as she put herself between her mother in the window. She nodded yes, and they sat at the dining room table.

"I was thinking. I spoke with Nurse Cragen at Dockendorff's office, and that maybe you should come live with me in a couple weeks."

Abruptly her mother replied, "What do you mean, live with you? I have my own life here. What am I supposed to do with everything here?" she said, raising her hands to accentuate her position.

It had begun. The conversation they both had dreaded. Mary had to convince her mother, or there would be no easy way of doing it. She tried to recollect her meeting with Cragen, and all those comforting words in the pamphlets eclipsed her the exact moment she needed them for her mother.

Mrs. McDougal brooded at the table, mumbling to herself. Mary couldn't come up with any words. The conversation had not started on a good note. Silence filled the room again, until Mrs. McDougal broke it. "I always thought that I would go quickly. Maybe a heart attack in my sleep or something. I never wanted to be a burden to you, Mary. You have your own life. You're a partner in your firm, for God's sake. Why don't you let me be?"

"Mom, I love you. You won't be a burden. We'll make the best of the situation. Please, Mom, I don't want you to be in some hospice, with people you don't even know. I want to take care of you. We can enjoy what time we have left, together." Mary looked to her mother for an answer.

It would not come. She needed to downplay the move. It was too much for her mother to take at one point. She thought hard. "It wouldn't be for another two to three weeks anyway. We'll take a bunch of your things from here, so you'll feel at home."

Mrs. McDougal, though extremely hard-headed, knew the time would come where she couldn't be on her own with this disease. She thought to herself for a moment and said, "Well, let me think about it for a while."

Mary knew her mother was stonewalling. They had to come to an agreement, here, today. Mary would have to be more forceful. Reemphasizing her position, she asked her mother again for a commitment. "Mother, we need a plan. We can't wait until you're feeling too ill. Please."

Her mother did not want to be stuck in a hospice either. She had an internal fear of being hooked up to machines to die in a small room with some nurse that barely spoke English. She also knew how hard Mary had worked and did not want to be the burden. She spoke of not being interference to her work. She felt cornered, but also knew Mary was not about to let her off the hook.

Mrs. McDougal looked at Mary. She slipped back in time remembering her birth, first communion, first birthday, grade school, high school, and college graduation. "I'm so proud of you," she said, choking up. They fell into an embrace. Both choked back tears. Mrs. McDougal broke off their hold, looked at Mary, and said, "I want to make it clear. If I become a burden that you can't handle, please, please tell me and find someplace else for me to go. Caring for a sick person is not an easy thing. You have never done anything like this before, Mary. Are you sure?"

"I've never been more sure of anything, Mom. I want to be able to care for you and spend as much time together as we can."

Her mother waited before answering, "Okay. I'll move in, but on my timeframe. I want to be on my own as long as I can."

Mary shook her head, and the deal had been reached. Mrs. McDougal appreciated all of Mary's concern and help. Her independence would have to submit to Mary's insistence on this issue. Mary had won this battle, but she began to think of the commitment she had just made and whether she was up to it.

Mary began to pack and Mrs. McDougal cleaned the apartment. They didn't speak to each other. The agreement they had come to would be a challenge for both of them. It would test their love for one another in their new roommate situation. Packed, Mary said, "I've got to go and catch the next bus."

"Goodbye, dear," Mrs. McDougal muttered. Mrs. McDougal sat down on the couch and slowly stroked Mr. Wiggles in total silence, making long, slow motions over the cat's head all the way to his tail, stroking his back with each stroke. Mr. Wiggles enjoyed his massage. His fur felt gentle to Mrs. McDougal. The cat's fur soothed her mind after the conversation with Mary. She continued petting Mr. Wiggles for half an hour straight until she fell asleep, exhausted, on the couch.

Mary stared into space on the bus. Relieved the conversation was over, she still felt tense. Her neck was tight and she had an unsettled stomach. She wondered if she was too hard on her mother. Her mind was all astray. What was her mother doing right now? What would she do tonight? How was she feeling right now? Her mother consumed her thoughts.

Walking to her building, she opened her mailbox. On the elevator, she sifted through her mail. It was full of brochures with advertisements for medical equipment. She had been put on a mailing list of some sort. At first she felt angry that someone had sold her name to these companies, feeling that they were jackals ready to pounce on easy prey. As she thought more about it, the solicitations just made it easier. Sorting through the mail, disregarding what equipment she thought wouldn't be applicable to her mother, she made a pile of the brochures that contained equipment that might be needed for her mother's care. She dog-eared certain pages. Sitting alone in the dark except for an aroma candle, she fell into deep thought about the arrangements that would need to be completed before her mother moved in.

Mrs. McDougal sat alone in her apartment. One hand stroked Mr. Wiggles, the other flipped through an old brown photo album. Yellow cellophane tape held the corners together. She had to be careful, as some of the dividers had fallen apart from age. Flipping each page slowly, she removed some of the pictures to see the date on the back. She felt so alone. Mr. Wiggles gave great comfort to her in this time. In the morning, she would start to go through the apartment to see what she would bring to Mary's.

Each McDougal sat alone, each in her own apartment, in a solitary state, contemplating what was to come in the next few weeks.

16

ACRONYMS

Mary arrived at MOD Monday morning. She had a blank look in her face as she picked up her floral arrangement and put it in the garbage can. Dried, rotted flowers, many crumbled, fell to the floor surrounding the trashcan. Looking at her schedule for the day, she was depressed. Although she had had the conversation with her mother, she felt the dejection resonate from her. Her independence was soon to be gone, and Mary felt it too. The pressure from the oncoming move wasn't twenty-four hours old and already it felt like an albatross around her neck.

Pondering to herself, she thought that she should feel good about it. The conversation about moving was over. They had come to a mutual agreement. Why the low, down feeling? she mused.

The clock struck nine a.m. Mary needed to call Nurse Cragen. The secretary at Dockendorff's put her through to Cragen and the nurse asked a few questions.

"Have you spoken to your mother about her future care? What was the outcome? How do you feel about it?" and scheduled her for an appointment the next day at four p.m. to discuss implementation of their plan.

Answering the questions was rough for Mary. The McDougals were extremely private people and opening up about their personal lives was vey difficult.

The following day, Mary left early from MOD at three-thirty p.m. to go to Dockendorff's office to meet Nurse Cragen. After checking in with the receptionist, Nurse Cragen arrived several minutes later and escorted Mary into a conference room. "How are you today, Mary?"

"Good as can be. I guess," she replied. The small talk pained Mary.

After exchanging pleasantries, Cragen placed a folder on the table. Setting it down, she cupped her hands together on top of the table. She paused and asked Mary, "How are you really doing?" Cragen could tell Mary was stressed.

Mary explained, "Over the weekend we had the conversation and made the tentative plans. My mother agreed, but we have no timetable."

Cragen nodded her head, listening to every detail. She opened the folder and began taking notes. "March first through fifth should be the days you should plan on having your mother move in. It is essential you have a timeline in place. At that stage, she will still be in fairly good physical shape. All, that is, except her energy level might not be what it was. You may see some advancing dementia or Alzheimer's. The fatigue may exacerbate this," Nurse Cragen declared.

Mary agreed that the timeline seemed feasible. "That seems doable." Cragen told her it was good that they had made their plans earlier rather than later. Mary stared at the calendar on the wall behind Cragen: less than ten days. She felt as if some days were in fast forward and others in a slow-motion state.

Nurse Cragen took some more notes and then asked Mary, "Does MOD support you in your decision to care for your mother?" Mary nodded, yes. "Have you and your mother decided hospice or home hospice?"

Mary then explained to her, "Home hospice is our intent."

Nurse Cragen told Mary, "It is important to keep the office notified of any change in plans. The secretary will notify home health of the pending change of address for your mother. Have you started looked into certain medical equipment for your mother's stay at your apartment?"

Mary told her, "I reviewed some of the mail solicitations that I received. At first I was a little miffed at the solicitations."

Nurse Cragen reminded her, "You did elect to sign up for the mailings at our first meeting."

At that moment, Mary slightly recalled signing papers. Nurse Cragen pulled out her own set of brochures and gave recommendations on which devices were essential and what companies were easiest to deal with in the area. The meeting seemed like a blur to Mary. It all seemed so surreal, as though she were watching it all happen to someone else.

Nurse Cragen left the table to make copies of certain papers for Mary. Handing the papers to Mary, she asked, "I know this is tough, but you have to remain focused on your mother for your sake. The next ten days will go extremely fast and you need to get as much done in preparation for your mother as possible. Are you sure you're up to this?"

Mary said, "Yes," and they continued on.

Nurse Cragen then asked Mary, "Have you talked to your employer in detail about the situation?" She then started spewing off acronyms like FELA, LOA, and BLT.

Mary nodded her head yes and then realized that she didn't have the faintest idea what she was talking about. Stopping Nurse Cragen mid-sentence she said,

"Can we go back a bit? What do all those abbreviations mean?"

Nurse Cragen apologized and slowed the conversation down. She reviewed the acronyms. "FELA stands for Family Emergency Leave Act. LOA stands for leave of absence, and BLT stands for bereavement leave time."

Mary's stomach tightened and she felt queasy. She hadn't even thought of these things.

Nurse Cragen urged her to be up front with her employer. "Most employers are understanding of the situation and will work with you. Your mother will need full-time care for her last two to three weeks," she stated.

Mary sat silent. She had so many more questions, but was overwhelmed. Nurse Cragen waited for a moment and spoke a little louder to get Mary's attention. Coming out of her trance, Mary listened.

"Mary, you need to go to a counseling session. There's a support group that's not for cancer patients, but families of cancer patients. The group is free and meets every Monday, Wednesday, and Friday at seven p.m. at the neighborhood community center." Urging Mary to attend, she added, "It will help you with the feelings you're having and the feelings you will come to have, as well as getting ideas about preparation and care."

Mary told Cragen, "I will consider going."

They wrapped up their meeting. Cragen closed saying, "We need to stay in contact. Please phone, e-mail, or call the office any time or visit, whichever you feel more comfortable with." She walked Mary out and wished her luck. She could see the state Mary was in and knew that there were no other siblings or family for support. "Please try the counseling," she reiterated.

Mary assured her that she would give it a try and walked out of the office thoroughly confused as to what steps to take next. She walked aimlessly down the street, reviewing the meeting with Nurse Cragen in her head.

Mrs. McDougal had been to Mass and had spent the rest of the day rummaging through her apartment. Foraging through the spare bedroom closet, she placed all her photo albums in three milk crates. She made different piles of clothes in the corner of the room. One pile she would take to Catholic Charities, the second pile she would offer to Mrs. Hanley, the third pile she would throw in the garbage. The night before, she had developed a strategy to pack each room for two days straight. This way she could decide where every item went and to whom. Mary would get everything sentimental or valuable. Mrs. Hanley would get her choice of what was left. Catholic Charities would receive all the rest.

She became tired, but was ahead of her set schedule. She lay down on the twin bed in the spare room and looked at the mess. Exhausted, she looked at the items she hadn't worn or seen in ten years. Mrs. McDougal grew weary, her arms hung like noodles at her side, and she was very groggy. She closed her eyes and fell asleep the rest of the day. The rest, she figured could wait till tomorrow.

Mary called to see how her mother was doing. She woke her mother, but they spoke for a while. Groggily, her mother answered the phone, "Hello," in a raspy voice.

"I'm sorry, Mom. Were you sleeping?"

"I just get a little more tired these days. I've just been packin'. Getting ready, you know."

"Why don't you get some more rest then and I'll try you later to see how you're doing?"

Later that evening, Mrs. McDougal prepared dinner. She nibbled at the food; her appetite had grown poor. When she retired to the living room, Mr. Wiggles jumped into her lap and purred. She watched the early news, but nothing of interest was on. She picked up an old photo album out of the milk crate. On the outside, in faded ink, it was titled 1944–1948. Thinking a second, she opened the album. It was dusty and the pages made crinkling noises from the old plastic pages as she turned them. All the photos were black and white.

She smiled, lost in the nostalgia. A warm feeling overtook her when she came across a page with Jimmy McDougal in his dress uniform that he had sent her. Smiling slightly, she ran her fingers over the page, as if she could touch him. A part of her died when he was killed in action. A tear swelled up and fell down her cheek. Her lip quivered as she fought hard to hold back her feelings. She became mad at herself for becoming so emotional. Brought up to hide her feelings rather than express them, she tried to suppress her heartfelt pain. Languishing there, she looked away, trying to hold on to her composure.

17

GOT A JOB?

Fifty years earlier, James McDougal and his best friend Timothy O'Leary were on a job site. Laying brick by a new building in midtown, they had been best friends since early childhood. Each had graduated high school from Tollentine in the Bronx, June of '44. Jobs were not aplenty and Jimmy's father urged him to take a job with the bricklayers. His father had wanted to get him on with the NYPD, but there was not a new class scheduled until the next year. He made the case to Jimmy that times were tough and he had an inside connection at the construction site.

Jimmy hesitated at first, wanting to try getting a white-collar job. Jobs were easy to get at factories supplying the troops fighting WWII. Construction jobs had all but stopped because the steel was needed for the war effort. Only two construction sites still existed in Manhattan.

"You may get a paper cut with those types of jobs that you're looking for, son. A real man will toil and get his hands dirty," his father would say.

After a month of searching, Jimmy relented to his father's wishes. He took the subway down to see the shift foreman that his father was friends with. In between shifts, the two met in the little box he called an office. The construction of the building was already behind schedule and the foreman, Mr. Reardon, explained to Jimmy in a husky voice that if he wanted the job, "you need to be here tomorrow morning."

Jimmy thanked him and expressed his gratitude. Inside he was disappointed. He had wanted to work in an office and dress in a suit and tie. He inquired, "Are there any other jobs available here?"

Reardon asked him, "Why?"

Explaining, "My friend Timothy needs work too."

Reardon agreed. "If he can be here tomorrow also then he's hired. We gotta get this job back on schedule."

Excited, Jimmy took the train home to find Timmy. He ran up the six flights of stairs to Timmy's apartment. He knocked in a rushed manner, and Mrs. O'Leary answered the door. "What's with all the noise, Jimmy? Are you late to a fire, son?" she questioned.

"I need to speak to Timmy, Mrs. O'Leary. Is he here?"

"I sent him to the market for milk and bread," she replied.

"Thanks," Jimmy said, and he dashed down the six flights to find Timmy. He ran down Sedgwick Avenue to the grocers. Timmy was just exiting the store.

"What's the rush, man?" Timmy asked.

Doubled over, Jimmy tried to catch his breath. His stomach ached from the lack of oxygen. He struggled to catch his wind, trying to talk, but unable. Timmy put his hand on Jimmy's back and ushered him over to a bus stop bench and told him to sit there and catch his breath before he tried to speak.

Finally, Jimmy caught his wind. He explained that he had met with his father's friend, a foreman at the construction site. "You can have a job too if you can start tomorrow."

A big smile came across Timmy's face. He had been looking for work all month long and needed a job desperately. "I'd start right now if that's what it took."

Mr. O'Leary had passed away the year before, and Timmy's mother had taken two jobs just to pay the rent. Timmy was going to drop out of school to get work, but his mother and Father Gallagher convinced him to stay in school and graduate. Father Gallagher would help

Mrs. O'Leary with some groceries so that they would have enough to eat during the week.

Jimmy was glad that his best friend would be with him if he had to take the construction job. Jimmy and Timmy walked home laughing and talking about their new job. Upon arriving back at the apartment, Jimmy said, "I've got to tell Maggie the news." He found her downstairs, babysitting some of the neighborhood kids.

She congratulated him and gave him a kiss on the cheek. "Congratulations," Maggie wished him.

"Thanks," Jimmy said. "It's only temporary 'til I can get one of those suit jobs, you know."

Maggie's dress fluttered in the breeze. Jimmy just looked at her. Her soft brown hair, blue eyes, and schoolgirl smile left him, for the moment, speechless. They agreed to meet up later in the afternoon.

Jimmy and Timmy proceeded to go to the department store. They would need clothes for the next day. The following morning they met up at 6:45 a.m. An early start, but they didn't want to be late and get on the boss's bad side. Their apartment doors were directly across from one another. The O'Learys' opened first. Mrs. O'Leary handed Timmy a brown sack. She had made him lunch and a thermos of coffee. The McDougal door opened next.

Mrs. McDougal looked out and greeted Timmy and his mother. "C'mon, James, you can't be late," she loudly whispered, not wanting to wake up the other tenants.

The women smiled and watched as the boys disappeared down the stairs.

Excited, the two walked at a brisk pace. They caught the subway to midtown and talked of their upcoming construction careers. Timmy spoke, "I'll probably be promoted quickly."

Jimmy joked, "I should just call you 'sir' now and get it over with, I guess. You haven't even worked a day, and you're talking about promotions."

Timmy conceded, "I might be a little premature."

Arriving at the job site, they checked in with the secretary at the shack. Reardon emerged and brought the boys over to meet the supervisor. He introduced the boys, "This is Jimmy McDougal and Timmy O'Leary, the new men on site," and left them.

Sweeney, the Supe, as he was nicknamed by the crew, looked irate. He smelled of liquor and hadn't showered in days. Taking no pity on the boys, he ushered them over to some steel brackets and boxes, showing them the steps and freight elevator. He ordered them, "Move the material to the third floor." He walked away muttering something under his breath. The boys shrugged it off and started moving the material. Their illustrious construction careers were underway.

The whistle blew and the boys sat down for their lunch. The other workers sat together in the shade of the first floor. The boys sat outside in the sun, resting their backs against a load of wood. They were the new guys, not accepted by the rest of the crew yet. They would have to earn the respect of the other workers to gain acceptance into the pack. Famished, they gobbled up their sandwiches. Each was exhausted, but wouldn't speak about it. Squinting, they looked up at the project through the glaring sun.

Reardon emerged from the shack. He sought out the boys and asked them how their morning had been. They both said they were fine. Reardon said, "Good," and walked away.

Sweeney sought them out next. "See, you're favored by the boss," he said in a surly tone. "We'll see about that." The whistle blew and Sweeney said, "You two with me." They followed him to the cement truck. He pointed at two shovels and had them shovel the cement into wheelbarrows. They would have to wheel the cement across the job site and empty it the rest of the afternoon. Usually the men would alternate the job hourly, because of the strain.

Sweeney was trying to run them off. He had promised the jobs to his two nephews. The nephews had shown up late for their first day and Reardon had fired them on the spot. Now Jimmy and Timmy would have to pay Sweeney's vengeance for the firings.

They worked the rest of the afternoon, and then the whistle blew. Timmy sat down and wiped his brow. Jimmy did the same. Two seasoned construction workers walked by and said, "good job" to the boys, without making eye contact. They did not want Sweeney seeing them talking to the boys. If Sweeney had seen them, they could be assigned the grunt work.

Jimmy took to one knee, caught his breath, and stood up. "Here ya go," offering his hand to Timmy, and pulled him to his feet. They had finished their first day. Exhausted, they caught the subway home. Tomorrow would be an even tougher day because their muscles would not have time to recover.

Upon arriving home to the apartment, the boys found the stairs had never been so tough for them. Their bodies ached as they climbed the stairs to home. Saying their goodbyes, each struggled to get his key into the apartment door. Jimmy took a long shower, the water as hot as he could stand, to soothe his aching body. He got dressed and walked two flights down to Maggie's. She had been waiting for him. He looked tired, but got a second wind when he saw her. Together they sat and ate dinner. Later they relaxed on the couch in the living room with her family and listened to the radio show.

Maggie questioned him about his day. She knew this wasn't his career goal, but was proud of him for getting a job. "How was it on the site? That building is how many stories tall? What did they have you do today? How's your boss?"

Jimmy told her of his day, but purposely left out the part about Sweeney. He did not want to seem like a complainer or unappreciative of his employment. About eight p.m. Jimmy's head began to nod. He tried to fight off the sleep, but the day had gotten the better of him. No longer able to fend it off, he fell asleep on the couch. Maggie covered him with a blanket and kissed him on the cheek. An hour or so later, Maggie combed her hand through Jimmy's hair. He woke. They said goodnight and Jimmy walked back upstairs to his apartment. He collapsed on the bed in his clothes and slept right on until the next morning.

The following morning, the two met at the same time and walked to the train. The excitement of the first day had worn off, and they walked at a slower pace. Their bodies were sore and could not walk at the same pace as the previous day. Upon arriving, they sipped their coffee that Mrs. O'Leary had made them. They awaited their marching orders from Sweeney. The Supe arrived in much the same manner as the day before. The stench of whiskey permeated from him.

Sweeney squinted and said, "Follow me." He took them to the other end of the job site, out of view of the shack. He did not want Reardon seeing what he had them working on. Taking the boys behind the building, he pointed at a stack of steel beams. These were cross supports that weighed 250 pounds apiece. Over 150 supports lay stacked in the yard. Sweeney pointed at the pile. "Move the entire load one hundred feet to here, so the crane can hoist the supports to the floors above." Sweeney walked away with a smirk on his face. He thought if he could get the boys to quit, Reardon might give his nephews a second chance.

Jimmy and Timmy labored until the noon hour. Their gloves were soaked in sweat and their backs were almost broken. The whistle blew, and they collapsed in the shade of the building. Some of the other workers offered uplifting words, but that was little consolation. They were beat.

Sweeney thought he had broken the boys, but they held on. After they were finished with the supports, Sweeney put them back on cement duty. They had never worked so hard in their lives. The two of them were of average build and height. They weighed approximately 160 pounds each. Their bodies would eventually bulk up with the work, but might not outlast Sweeney's vindictive orders.

The week proceeded in the same fashion. Sweeney would find the hardest job on the site and have the boys assigned to it. Timmy confessed to Jimmy, "I might not be able to take it much longer."

"Hang in there. It's almost the weekend." Jimmy tried to give him words of inspiration, but they were falling on deaf ears. If only he could get Timmy to make it through

Friday, to the weekend, Jimmy thought. The two days off would be enough for Timmy to be revitalized.

Friday came and the boys looked awful. Jimmy's father had not even seen his son since he started the construction job. He worked the night shift as a beat cop. If he had, he would have known his boy was being mistreated. Instead he sent Tom McKenna to check on his son and Timmy on the site. Patrolman McDougal had befriended McKenna at the scene of a bar fight he had been called to years earlier. He had let McKenna walk instead of locking him up, having learned their families were from the same small town in Letrum, Ireland.

Early Friday morning, McKenna sought out the boys to see how the job had been treating them. He had been on vacation, nursing a case of gout. The other laborers welcomed him back, joking about his "rich man" disease. "You're one of those high and mighty types eatin' your fine meats and wine, we see."

The gout had been labeled a rich man disease from the Queen of England's Beefeaters who often succumbed to it from their diet of excessive alcohol and red meat. McKenna joked back, "Someone must have forgotten to give me the money." He surveyed the site trying to locate the boys, finding them lugging more of the steel supports. McKenna was a giant of a figure, standing six feet six inches and over three hundred pounds. His coworkers had nicknamed him Tiny Tom.

Hundreds of men worked on the project and he questioned some of them about how long the boys had been doing this type of work. "You see those boys there? How long's the Supe had them on 'grunt' duty?"

Some of the workers confided that Sweeney had been bullying the boys all week. McKenna grew angry and sought out Sweeney. He tracked through the job site finding Sweeney on the first floor, in a corner, with a flask in his hand. McKenna approached Sweeney from behind and put his boot jarringly into Sweeney's ass.

Falling to the ground, Sweeney cried out, "Just what the hell's wrong with you? Are you trying to kill me?" he screamed. Sweeney stumbled to his feet and picked up his flask. "I'll have your job, McKenna."

Tiny Tom's face became beet red with anger. Sweeney realized that he had mistakenly pushed McKenna over the edge and backpedaled. The veins in Tiny Tom's neck pulsated and his arms twitched from his muscles contracting. He reached out and grabbed Sweeney by the neck. "I'll break your lousy neck, you bastard."

Sweeney tried to speak, but could not get any words out with Tom's grasp around his larynx. A coworker jumped in at Tom's side and begged him, "Let Sweeney go. It's just not worth it, Tom." The workman repeated his plea several times until Tiny Tom came out of his rage. He eased his grasp from Sweeney's throat and dropped him to his knees.

Sweeney fell to the ground, his hands around his neck, gasping for air. Tom looked around to see if anyone was looking. A dozen of the crew had witnessed the attack, but looked away when Tiny Tom stared their way. McKenna had to think fast. He was a fighter, not a thinker, and his brain was dizzy trying to reason his way out of the situation. He lurched forward and grabbed the flask out of Sweeney's hand. It was still half full of his morning whiskey. The flask was emblazoned with his initials on the stainless steel. "I'll turn you in to Reardon for drinking on the job, lest you forget this whole thing and treat those boys fairly," he shouted.

Sweeney had been caught numerous times drinking on the job. Reardon had warned him that his next infringement would be his last. Still holding his neck, Sweeney looked up and nodded his head in an agreeing fashion.

"Now get those boys off those steel supports," McKenna shouted at him.

Sweeney stumbled to his feet and sauntered away. The dusty footprint from Tiny Tom's boot stained the back of his jeans. He immediately took the boys off the steel supports, taking them over to the front gate. He gave them an easy job of receiving construction material.

An hour later, the boys had color back in their faces. They had been doing all the slave work and now had a pen and pad job in the shade of an umbrella. They wondered if Sweeney had been testing them all along. Never would they know that a coworker had probably saved Sweeney from a broken neck at McKenna's grasp.

After lunch, McKenna approached the boys. He explained, "I had wanted to see how you were doing, but I took some time off." The boys didn't mention the earlier part of the workweek and said they were well and enjoyed the work. McKenna joked, "When you want to get your hands dirty, come and see me. Don't want you to get a paper cut now." The three joked and talked for a while until McKenna finally left.

"See the size of him? He's the two of us combined," Timmy laughed.

"He's a good friend of me da's," Jimmy answered.

The rest of the day went well. Sweeney came back and checked on them shortly before the last whistle. He seemed almost annoyed that they were in good spirits. Sweeney would never mess with the boys again. He was genuinely afraid of McKenna, with just cause.

Friday night and the boys had a rejuvenating energy overcome them. They did not dread the Monday to come. Timmy came home and gave his mother all of his paycheck except ten dollars. Mrs. O'Leary was rightly proud of her boy. She had struggled so to keep him in school. Now with his new job, they would be able to survive.

The boys made plans. "I'll meet you later and we'll pick up the girls and celebrate our first week," Timmy said. He would get his girlfriend, Catherine, and join Jimmy and Maggie. They would go to the movies and maybe the soda parlor afterwards. The girls would be excited as they never had money for things like this.

Their summer came and went much in the same fashion. Secretly Jimmy banked a lot of his earnings, wanting to buy Maggie an engagement ring. Timmy continued to give money to his mother. Maggie got a job across the street at New York University. She had babysat and saved to make money, but a job came up in the recruitment pool, and she was hired.

The boys gained a reputation at work as hard workers. They were never late and didn't miss any days. One day at the construction site, a worker slipped off the seventh floor and fell to his death. The coworkers stared at his motionless corpse. Some turned away, gagged, or vomited. Jimmy and Timmy had known the man. He was a couple years older than them and had a wife and two children.

Sweeney pushed them back and Reardon ran over. They talked and looked up to the seventh floor where the man had fallen. Some workers from above stared down at the crowd that had gathered around the corpse.

Reardon yelled for one of the men to call an ambulance. The ambulance and some policemen showed up. It was not unusual to have a death at a construction site. Usually they were frequent. Jimmy and Timmy had never experienced this part of the job. They were unsure of their thoughts.

The paramedics put the body in the ambulance and drove off. The policeman interviewed some of the crew, Sweeney, and Reardon. It was Friday and the entire crew looked on, waiting to be told what to do. Sweeney and Reardon began talking it over. It was two p.m. Reardon gathered the men up and closed the site for the rest of the day. He said, "You can probably count on the funeral for Monday. So we'll be closed out of respect." The men all gather their belongings and left the job site. They would be paid for the time off, construction industry rule.

The following Monday, Jimmy and Timmy put on their coats and ties. They took the bus over to 207th Street Bridge to Good Shepherd Parish. The pastor gave a nice homily. The man's wife comforted their children. The organist played "Amazing Grace," but Jimmy and Timmy had a hard time concentrating. After all, this man was dead, and they were getting paid to sit in a church pew. They felt guilty and thought, "What if it had happened to me?"

After the funeral Mass, the company had buses for workers to go to the cemetery. The men piled on, perspiring profusely from the heat of the bodies and the temperature outside. The sun glistened off the polished casket at the cemetery. The mourners gathered around the freshly dug gravesite. Four gravediggers stood in the distance, leaning on their shovels underneath a shade tree. The priest read some prayers as the mourners bowed their heads. The boys seemed lost in the moment. They had never experienced this. Most of the crew was seasoned and had seen plenty of death on the job site. No one had spoken of the dangers of the construction trade. It was more or less understood as just being part of the job.

A bagpipe sounded at the end of the service. The pallbearers grasped the brass handles and raised the casket over the hole in the ground. Together they lowered the casket hand over hand, holding the rope until the casket hit bottom. Mourners filed past the grave throwing flowers onto the casket below and took turns expressing their condolences to the family.

The boys walked back to the bus, not really knowing what to make of it all. The image of the flowers dropping from the mourners hands falling onto the casket at the bottom of the freshly dug hole burned in their minds. The men all got back on the bus back to the Good Shepherd. At the church hall, there was food and refreshments. The family went through the motions of talking to those that had shown their respects. Jimmy could not keep his eyes off the man's widow. She looked so gaunt and pale, dressed in her black dress and veil. It all seemed so meaningless to him. What purpose did it all serve? Who would care for this woman and her children? he wondered.

One of the crew suggested they all should be going and proposed a group of them go to Muldoon's Pub. All of them yearned for a lighter mood. The weight of the day, sun, and long-winded priest had made their mood quite somber. They ordered pitchers of beer and talk switched from reflection to more lighthearted conversation. It tasted great after the long day and heat. A couple of hours passed and, a dozen pitchers later, the men were actually quite jovial. Some started to depart. They walked outside Muldoon's and, upon exiting, they squinted. The sun reflected off of the cars and beamed into their eyes. They shook hands and went off their separate ways.

It was getting late in the afternoon, and the boys began walking up the street. Jimmy stopped dead in his tracks and began looking into a storefront window. Staring back at him was an image of Uncle Sam. "Uncle Sam wants you," was written above his head with his finger pointing directly at Jimmy.

Timmy asked him, "What are you doing?"

Jimmy spoke dramatically, some from loss of words, some from the excess of beer. "Maybe we should do something worthwhile with our lives."

"What do you mean?" Timmy asked.

"I mean, that guy fell seven stories, and for what?" Jimmy said, his voice a little slurred. "At least we'd make a difference over there."

Timmy looked perplexed. Jimmy said, "Let's see what they have to say," as he opened the door to the recruiting office and Timmy followed him in.

Inside the recruiting station were twelve seats and two desks, with the recruiting officers in place. Six men were in chairs, and Jimmy and Timmy sat down in the waiting area. An officer came over and greeted them, "How are you two fine men doing today?" and handed the boys a questionnaire on a clipboard and a pen.

The boys looked at one another, as though each one should talk the other out of it. Neither said a word and the two began filling out the forms. An hour passed and the boys grew tired, their eyes heavy.

The recruiting officer walked over and asked, "Are you together?" They answered in unison, "Yes," and he escorted them over to his desk. He explained," The U.S. and its allies are winning the war and the country needs young brave men, like you, to achieve the ultimate victory." He asked them leading questions about their bravery, heart, and patriotism. The boys agreed with all his subtle lines and their egos soon followed his lead.

The recruiter then went into detail about the army's buddy system. He assured the boys that he could keep them together throughout their service. Asking them closed-ended questions he continued, "If I could promise to keep you two together throughout your service in the army, would you be willing to join up now?" He looked pointedly at both of them, handing them a pen to sign the form.

Flinching ever so slightly, Jimmy was first to say, "Sure thing." Timmy followed suit. The "Young Irish," as the construction crew had dubbed them, had just signed up for service in the U.S. Army.

They signed their papers and the recruiter paraded them across the office in front of the other waiting men. "Here's two young men that are damned proud to serve their country. I want to show you two of the army's newest and finest." He shook their hands repeatedly before telling them that their papers would arrive shortly thereafter in the mail.

The boys left the office and walked on the street outside. "I can't believe what we just done," Timmy exclaimed.

"Me neither, me neither," Jimmy repeated. They would soon give up their construction livelihood for the just cause, heroes in the making.

They spoke on the bus of whom and when they would tell. Timmy said, "I'll tell my mom the next weekend."

Jimmy agreed and said, "I'll tell my parents and Maggie over the same period." They would have to time it right so that no one in the apartment got wind of it beforehand.

The boys labored through the following days, second-guessing their decision to join the army. Timmy didn't even know what they got paid in the army and wondered if he would have enough money for his mother. Jimmy thought more about what Maggie would say. They had been boyfriend–girlfriend since they held hands on the way to school in the first grade. Jimmy would then have to tell his parents. His father intimidated him and his mother would wonder if he were of diminished capacity making such an erroneous decision.

They worked all week, citing the weekend, when they would come clean with their families. Friday the whistle blew and the boys began the commute home. They struggled with how to break the news and, for Jimmy, who to tell first. Jimmy decided he would tell his parents first. His father worked the eight p.m. to eight a.m. nightshift. He would tell him after dinner at six-thirty p.m. Saturday night. Timmy agreed to tell his mother at the same time. Jimmy would then tell Maggie that night.

Friday slipped away and Jimmy tiptoed around the apartment on Saturday. He did not want to wake his father prematurely and draw his ire. The family sat down to dinner at six-thirty p.m. This was their usual mealtime when his father worked. Mr. and Mrs. McDougal talked a little, but Jimmy remained silent most of the meal. He had butterflies in the stomach. His meal went mostly untouched. Jimmy's mother asked if he felt all right. His father looked at his plate and asked if he was going to eat his corned beef. Jimmy answered, "No," and his father leaned over and put his fork into the meat on Jimmy's plate and put it on his own.

At the conclusion of the meal, his mother backed up her chair to start cleaning the table. Jimmy stopped her and said, "I need to make an announcement." He cleared his throat and said, "I've joined the army. I'll be leaving for boot camp soon."

Silence filled the room. Jimmy's mother looked to his father, trying to draw his attention. His father looked clearly at her and stood. Jimmy didn't know what was to happen. His father reached out his hand to Jimmy and said, "Good luck, son, I've never been prouder of you."

His mother came over and hugged him. They all sat back down and Jimmy explained how he decided to join the army after the unfortunate accident at his work. His parents told him that they loved him and they asked about Maggie.

At that point, a loud scream came from across the hall at the O'Learys'. Patrolman McDougal jumped back up on hearing the hysteria. Shouting and screaming continued and the McDougals opened their door to see what was causing the commotion. Across the hall the door opened, with Timmy emerging from it. He looked at the McDougal family and said, "I wish that had gone better."

Mrs. O'Leary was not too happy with Timmy's decision. "If you want to go and get yourself killed, that's fine. Good God, I've raised a complete idiot," was one of her comments during her tirade.

Timmy entered the McDougals' and they spoke for a while. Timmy and Jimmy explained the buddy system and that they would not be separated during their service. Timmy wanted to let his mother calm down before returning to their apartment. He asked Jimmy, "Got any plans for the night?"

Jimmy explained, "I still have to tell Maggie."

An hour later, Patrolman McDougal readied for work. In the kitchen he shook both of the boys' hands and said, "I'm proud of the both of you." Jimmy began to get nervous. He would soon have to tell Maggie, shuddering, thinking of the disappointment on her face.

Walking down the steps slowly, he descended to Mary's apartment. She was in a great mood, speaking a mile a minute about her first week on the job at the university. "You should see the desk I work at. It's grand. The dean is a great man. He's so nice to me."

Jimmy pretended to listen as he gathered his thoughts. How would he tell her? Her mother was an earshot away in the kitchen. Jimmy balked at the moment of truth. He could not bear to tell Maggie and see her happiness turn to sadness. He excused himself from the table and made an excuse that he had to run back upstairs. He planned on consulting his father on how to break the news.

Jimmy walked back upstairs to find Timmy all excited looking for him. Life's pending adventure was a step closer. Jimmy's father came out and asked them, "What's all the noise about?"

Timmy had just picked up the mail in the lobby and explained, "Our papers are in."

Jimmy's father watched and admired their youthful exuberance. He also knew that they had no idea of the horrors that their adventure would lead them into. Not wanting to spoil their moment, he went to the refrigerator and retrieved three beers and joined them in their celebration.

Shortly thereafter, Jimmy said, "I have to tell Maggie the news." His father and Timmy understood and in unison wished him "Good luck." He met Maggie and the two walked downstairs to the street and went for their usual walk. They asked each other more about their day, but aside from that, they did not speak much. It was mid-September now. Summer had passed so swiftly. Both had graduated from Tollentine and had started new jobs.

Now fall was in the air. The nights were a little cooler and the leaves had started their transformation from green to an early stage of yellow, orange, and brown.

They walked along the water at a slow pace, holding hands and admiring the changing foliage. Maggie knew something was up. Jimmy usually spoke much more and his silence worried her.

After a mile down the path, Jimmy looked at her. His eyes were dull and not enthused. He explained, "Timmy and I joined the army and our orders arrived and we're leaving in a week and a half."

She listened and rolled her lips inward to compose herself. She lurched forward and grabbed Jimmy close. They hugged tightly along the riverbank in each other's arms. He further explained, "I feel I'm doing the right thing by joining the war effort. The war's almost over. A year or two tops, and I'll be back home." Maggie listened and held him again. Jimmy told her, "Don't worry, I'll be careful." He added, "Timmy will watch my back, you'll have nothing to worry about. I promise to write as often as I can, but I'll miss you terribly."

Maggie never spoke a word, holding back her tears and feelings of helplessness.

18

ENGAGING CONVERSATION

They walked another quarter-mile to a forgotten spot that was the halfway point on their stroll. Maggie so loved their walks. Three to four times a week they would take this walk together, no matter what the weather. Sun, rain, snow, they would walk hand-in-hand and talk about their day and of their future together. Sitting down on a park bench, they looked out on the river. A large sycamore tree was rattling as squirrels jumped branch to branch overhead. They laughed, seeing the squirrels dangling in their trapeze act above. It was getting dark, and they both took deep breaths, knowing that they should be heading back soon.

Jimmy got up from the bench and walked over to their sycamore tree. On the sycamore there was a heart with "Jimmy and Maggie" etched in the middle of the trunk. Jimmy had carved this in the bark six years ago, when they were twelve. "Remember this," he said as he pointed to it. The letters and heart had turned black and faded over time.

Maggie leaned forward on the bench with her head on her hands, elbows on knees, and smiled. "Of course, I do. I look for it every time we walk."

"You do? I do too," he said. He dug into his pocket and pulled out an old pocketknife his father had given him as a child. As he carved into the letters in the heart, the black turned to freshly cut wood again. "Let me freshen this up a bit." Letter by letter, including the arrow through the heart, he slowly refurbished their marking upon the tree. Maggie watched and a warm feeling came over her as their heart came to life again.

Jimmy stood back, admiring his work. "There, nothing like a fresh coat of paint."

Maggie stood up and walked behind Jimmy, putting her arms around him, and they just focused their eyes upon the tree, swaying back and forth together, side to side. Jimmy unclasped Maggie's hands from around his waist and turned her around so that they were facing one another. He pulled her close and they joined in a long, passionate kiss. Maggie melted in his arms, and they professed their love for one another. Maggie thought to herself she could live in this moment forever.

Jimmy grabbed her hand, and they walked off on the grass back to the riverside path. He took Maggie over to the bench and sat her down. He knelt on one knee and grasped both of Maggie's hands in his. Bowing his head first, he looked up at her and said, "Maggie Tierney, I want you to be my wife." He half nodded his head and looked his eyes straight at hers, awaiting a response.

Maggie sat in utter bewilderment. She had not been ready for this. They had been boyfriend–girlfriend since grade school and had always spoken of their future and marriage as one and the same. Her mouth got dry and hung open, lost for words.

Jimmy kept staring at her, waiting for a response. Finally he said in an inquiring tone. "Well?"

Maggie was still in a state of disbelief. Her mind was in a whirlwind. She snapped out of her state with his question and replied, "Of course, I would love to be your wife."

The smiles spread from ear to ear on their faces. Maggie began to feel dizzy and blushed a deep red. They kissed again until the squirrels knocked a branch down, falling near them, breaking their embrace. "I think they're applauding our engagement," Jimmy joked.

They laughed and walked back to the apartment. It was dark now, and both had to get ready for work the next day. Jimmy kissed her goodnight and said, "I can't wait for you to be my wife."

Maggie blushed again and said, "Me either."

They looked at each other, not wanting to break the moment. Their eyes fixed on each other as Maggie's mother finally said to her, "Close the door."

They both readied for bed, not telling either of their parents. Each lay in bed looking blankly at the ceiling, reflecting on their magical night.

The next morning Jimmy chomped on the bit, waiting for Timmy to come out of his apartment. He waited until they were outside and told him, "Maggie and I got engaged."

They punched each other in the shoulder in boyish jubilation. "Why didn't you tell me you were going to go and do that?" Timmy chided.

"Didn't know I was myself until last night. It just hit me, sort of," Jimmy answered.

Timmy offered, "Congratulations."

Jimmy swore him to secrecy until he could tell his parents. Timmy agreed and asked, "Where'd you get the ring?"

Jimmy looked pointedly at him and confessed, "I didn't get one yet."

Timmy said, "It ain't official until Maggie gets a ring, you know."

Jimmy didn't know what to make of Timmy's remark, and the "no ring" situation began to trouble him. Jimmy would now be on a mission to get a ring for Maggie. He had saved a couple hundred dollars that he had banked. He notified Sweeney of his enlistment in the army and that Tuesday would be his last day. He would take off the last few weekdays to be with Maggie and get his affairs in order before basic training. Timmy would work the entire next week, wanting to give his mother all the money he could before he left.

Friday came and Jimmy rose early. He had slept in on Wednesday and Thursday to let his body recover from the week at work, but today he wanted to be at the bank when it opened. Mrs. McDougal made him some bacon and eggs and asked, "Why are you up so early?"

He said, "I have things to do." And gave her a peck on the cheek and was off. He was first in line at the bank when it opened and withdrew the money he thought he would need for a ring. He spent the rest of the day with Maggie running errands.

Saturday came. Jimmy had never shopped for fine jewelry before and had no idea of the cost of an engagement and wedding ring. Taking the subway downtown, he started for the diamond district. He did not realize many of the stores were closed for Jewish Saturday religious services.

He visited the stores that were open. Jimmy quickly became aware that all the rings he was interested in were not in his budget. Gold had skyrocketed during wartime. Looking for hours, Jimmy became disappointed at what was available to him. He lingered at the store windows and sadness came over him, knowing he could not afford any ring he had looked at. Store after store he visited to no avail.

Totally depressed, he loitered at one store, Hirschbaum Jewelry. He was fixated on the wedding bands in the window showcase. Leaning into the storefront window, he cupped his hands around the side of his head to reduce the glare from the sun on the storefront window. An old Jewish man, dressed all in black, approached him. The man used a cane and walked slowly with a limp. The man fumbled in his pocket to remove keys and slid them into the door next to the store. He looked over to Jimmy, wished him good day, and asked, "Can I help you?"

Jimmy explained, "I'm looking for a wedding and engagement band."

The man introduced himself, "I'm Solomon Hirschbaum, owner of the jewelry store." He asked Jimmy, "Can you come back Monday so that I can help you further?"

Jimmy pleaded that he had enlisted and was leaving for basic training one week from Monday and needed something that day. Mr. Hirschbaum sighed, but empathized with Jimmy's plight. He explained to Jimmy, "I can not work on the Sabbath." He thought further about the situation. The Germans in Poland had imprisoned his family. Here, this boy was going to fight those evil forces, the ones that had imprisoned and slaughtered his relatives and people. He fought long and hard and reasoned it was God's will for him to help the boy. He unlocked the store and began to show Jimmy all the wedding bands.

At first, Jimmy was thrilled. As time went on, he began to be depressed, as none of the rings were in his price range. Mr. Hirschbaum left to him to look at some more rings and rolled the shade down the front window and door. He did not want to cause a scene for being open on Sabbath. Walking behind the counter, he sat on a stool and the two discussed some other options.

Jimmy saw one ring in the corner of the case that caught his attention. It was a Claddagh ring. Hitting him like a ton of bricks, he realized he had found his solution. The Claddagh ring was an ancient Irish ring that was used in the early 1700s in Ireland. The gold ring had two hands clasping a heart, with a crown on top. The two hands stood for friendship, the heart and crown for loyalty and fidelity.

Solomon was ecstatic. "I've had that ring in the case for years and had forgotten about it," he said. The ring would serve as an engagement ring and a wedding band. Tradition held that, given on the engagement, it would be worn on the right ring finger with the heart facing inward. That signified the wearer of the praying heart was promised, but not yet won. During the wedding ceremony, the ring is removed from the right hand and placed on the left hand, with the heart facing inward.

This signified that the world should know that two hearts were forever joined.

Mr. Hirschbaum and Jimmy came to an agreement on a price. He put it in a fine leather case and shook Jimmy's hand. "Safe travels and good luck" he wished him. The two parted company. Jimmy left the diamond district without a diamond but his goal complete. He headed for home and planned on how to give Maggie the ring.

Arriving at the apartment, he could not sit still. "Should I give it to her tonight or tomorrow? How should I give it?" Questions ran through his mind. Jimmy decided to ask Maggie to dinner and give it then.

He picked her up around six p.m. and they walked down to an Italian restaurant named Girardi's. Jimmy ordered. "We'll both have the spaghetti and meatballs." The waitress left and Jimmy asked, "What should we do this week?" Maggie had gotten vacation time from the University of New York and the two planned to spend as much of the week as they could together. They split a bottle of red wine and enjoyed their spaghetti and meatballs.

While finishing his meal, Jimmy bit into his last meatball. He feigned wincing in pain, grabbing his mouth. Looking down and away from Maggie, he shook his head back and forth in an ached fashion. Maggie got up and sat in the booth next to him, seeing if he had chipped a tooth or cut his mouth. Jimmy looked the other direction away from her.

She held his upper arm and insisted, "Let me have a look at it."

Jimmy spun back toward her, his tongue in his cheek, pushing his cheek out. Maggie insisted on seeing the inside of his mouth. Jimmy put his hand up to his mouth and with his tongue pushed the ring through his lips into his hand. Taking the ring out of his mouth while grabbing Maggie's left hand, he slid it onto her finger.

Maggie pretended to be angry at Jimmy's feigned injury, but broke into a broad smile. Jimmy asked to get out of the booth. Maggie got up to let him out and sat back down.

Jimmy got out of the booth, knelt on one knee, and proposed again. "Maggie, will you be my wife?"

Other patrons had noticed the commotion at the table and were staring intently. Maggie looked around and all the tables were staring at them. She blushed and begged Jimmy, "Get up. You're makin' a scene."

"Not until I have an answer," he responded.

She repeated her request for him to get up, but he was steadfast, waiting for an answer. "Of course, I will. Now get up and quit making a spectacle of us," she screamed through her closed teeth.

The restaurant broke out into applause. Maggie had never been so embarrassed. She was extremely private and hated attention. Jimmy sat back down on his side of the booth, fully content at the outcome.

Minutes later, a bottle of champagne arrived at their table, compliments of an anonymous patron. Mr. Girardi, the owner, came over and offered, "My congratulations. Your meal is on the house."

They had dessert and spoke of their pending nuptials. Maggie was eager to tell her parents. "I want to tell Mom and Dad the news."

Jimmy wanted to go out on the town and celebrate, but honored her wishes. They walked back up the Sedgwick Avenue to their apartment building. Mrs. Tierney was cleaning up after dinner. Mr. Tierney was sitting on the couch listening to the radio. Jimmy had asked his permission years ago to marry Maggie. Mr. Tierney said he had no objections, just as long as they were old enough.

Jimmy went in and sat with Mr. Tierney and Maggie went into the kitchen with her mother. She began helping her mother dry dishes, although at shoulder height, trying to get her mother's attention to the new ring on her hand. Mrs. Tierney was none the wiser and kept cleaning. Maggie could take it no longer. She put the dish down and stuck her hand right in her mother's face. Her mother's eyes got as big as the dishes themselves. At first she looked at the ring and just hugged Maggie. They whispered a few things to each other and walked out into the living room.

Mr. Tierney was talking to Jimmy when he noticed the women both staring at him. "Did I do something wrong? What are you to looking at?"

Mrs. Tierney held up Maggie's hand. Mr. Tierney nodded approvingly and leaned over to Jimmy and said, "Welcome to the family. Like you weren't family already?" He stood up and Maggie ran to his side. They hugged and all talked about the coming wedding.

Next would be the McDougals. They walked up the two flights and stood at the door. Maggie asked Jimmy, "What's the matter?"

Jimmy responded, "How are we going to do this? I've got an idea." He straightened his shirt and pushed on the doorbell. He waited two seconds and did it again. Another two seconds and again he pushed it. "I will get their attention," he said.

Mrs. McDougal came running to the door to see who was so impatient. She opened the door to see Jimmy and Maggie standing there grinning. "What are you two doing?" she exclaimed.

"I'd like to introduce you to my fiancée, Maggie," Jimmy said, while holding out Maggie's right hand. Mrs. McDougal's jaw almost hit the floor. She reached out to hug them and pushed them into the apartment.

"What's with all the noise?" Jimmy's father yelled.

"I've got something to show you," Mrs. McDougal cried.

"Oh me God," he said and reached out for Jimmy's hand and hugged Maggie with the other. "Look what we have here," he said happily.

Jimmy went across the hallway and got Timmy. They invited Maggie's parents up and celebrated into the night.

All was fine until Mrs. Tierney asked, "When's the date for the wedding?"

Jimmy blatantly answered, "Next Saturday, if the church is available."

Maggie, the Tierneys, and the McDougals stood stupefied. No one knew how to respond. They all looked at one another looking for an answer.

Maggie turned to Jimmy and said, "That's a week from today. We can't plan a wedding in a week."

Jimmy replied, "Oh yes we can. I leave a week from Monday and I want you to be my wife before I leave for basic."

Mrs. McDougal and Mrs. Tierney were now deep in conversation. The men sat back and became spectators in the debate.. "We got to get the church, invitations, flowers, food, dress," Mrs. McDougal said.

"Now what about the church hall and the suit?" Mrs. Tierney replied.

The conversation went deep into the night. One arguing for, one arguing against, one saying there wasn't enough time, one saying there was plenty of time. When all the debating was said and done, a decision was come to.

19

PACKING IT UP

A week had passed for Mrs. McDougal. She continued her packing of all her worldly possessions. Mary called her mother two to three times a day. At first her mother was annoyed at the frequency of her calls. But as the days passed, she came to enjoy Mary's concern for her welfare. The memories and nostalgia from a life past emerged from her closets. She came across pictures, trinkets, clothing, and letters of yesteryear, some as old as sixty years, a lifetime of memories. Some brought back happiness, others sadness, and she would find herself laughing or crying, depending on the item she had uncovered.

Mrs. McDougal continued to go to Dockendorff's office for her scheduled appointments. The doctor would take blood, weigh her, and test all her vital signs. He became a bit more concerned after Mrs. McDougal had lost nine pounds in a week. Her blood count was low too. He started giving her vitamin E injections to help her immune system fight off any viruses.

After her scheduled appointment, she met with the nurse. Cragen asked her, "How are you feeling?" She weighed her and evaluated her mental status. The nurse also asked how Mary was and "when are you planning to move in together?"

Mrs. McDougal felt as though nurse was pushing a little too hard. She felt like Cragen was invading her personal space and privacy. The nurse could feel Mary's mother's resistance and backed off her questions. Mrs. McDougal left and Cragen proceeded to call Mary at her office.

Mary had been in a meeting. She knew something was wrong when Rosarita appeared outside her door waving a pink message slip. She excused herself from the meeting with a client and took the slip, thanking Rosarita. Mary returned to her office and wrapped up the meeting. She returned Nurse Cragen's call and they discussed the situation.

Cragen started, "I'm worried about your mother's mental state. I think she might be depressed or in a semi-state of denial about her condition and prognosis."

Mary reassured her, "Mom's fully aware that she is terminal, and although she may be a bit, understandably, depressed, I don't think she's in denial." Mary told Cragen, "My mother's a very private person and probably felt pressured with all the questions about her plans." She further explained, "She's always been independent and non-reliant on outsiders."

Cragen reiterated her concerns, but felt better after Mary's assessment. She turned her focus to Mary. She asked, "How are you holding up? How's your mother's moving in with you going to affect your relationship and her mental state?"

Pausing for a second, Mary admitted, "I do feel anxious about the upcoming move." She also told her, "I did get a chance to attend a couple of the counseling sessions."

Cragen asked her, "Have they been helpful?"

She explained, "The counseling session is difficult for me. I confided to a stranger, a woman I had never met, some of my innermost feelings about myself and my mother's condition." The two had commiserated for hours at a coffee shop after the meeting. "It just didn't feel right to me."

Cragen didn't buy into the dialogue of the conversation. She did explain to Mary, "I think it would be helpful if you keep attending the meetings and speaking to your new friend. It will help you cope with the situation. Sometimes you just need to talk to someone. Explain what you're going through. You can always call here to talk to me or phone your friend also," Cragen said compassionately.

Mary took a few deep breaths to compose herself. Cragen then asked further about the schedule for her mother's move in. Explaining their plan, Mary informed her that the move was scheduled for the following weekend. The days were whisking by. She thought to herself that there was so much more to do. The nurse wrapped up the call telling Mary that it seemed that she had everything in order. Mary never felt so disorganized in her life. It seemed as though her life was out of control, a train without a conductor.

The nurse offered her advice and said, "Here's my cell phone and home number." First, Cragen was not only a dedicated employee, but also a real person with a human touch. "If you see any of the telltale signs of depression please get in touch with me."

Hanging up the phone, Mary reviewed her timeline and her list of things to do. There was so much to do and so little time. Her mother was moving into her apartment in less than seven days and she felt a sickly stress come over her. Her stomach turned and she left the building to seek out some fresh air. Walking down the street to the bodega, she bought a can of ginger ale to settle her stomach. The cool breeze felt good on her face and she took deep breaths of it to soothe her mind.

Mary had some friends come by with their SUV that evening. She gave them her futon, a chest of drawers, lamp, and a nightstand from her second bedroom. They weren't the best of furniture, but Mary had insisted that her mother bring all her old furniture from her place. In Mary's mind, this would make her feel more at home.

After her friends left, she began to rummage through the closet in her bedroom. Cassettes and eight tracks in one box, elementary, high school, and college yearbooks, a typewriter, and other items cluttered the closet. She began relocating the junk into her bedroom so that her mother would not feel crowded. Before she knew it, the clock read midnight. The room and closet were almost there, ready for her mother's arrival.

Mrs. McDougal awoke before dawn the next day. She had difficulty sleeping throughout the night anymore. Not that she didn't sleep a great deal more than when she was healthy, just not contiguously. She showered and attended early Mass. Returning home, she looked over what she would bring to Mary's apartment. She insisted to herself that she would travel light. She did not want to crowd Mary's space. She packed a large suitcase and a medium-sized travel bag.

Mr. Wiggles sat on top of the bed, wagging his tail and meowing. He knew something was up. Mrs. McDougal had had a conversation with Mrs. Hanley the prior night. Unbeknownst to Mr. Hanley, Mr. Wiggles would be moving in with the Hanleys, a new addition to their family. Mrs. Hanley had offered to take care of the cat. This put Mrs. McDougal at ease, knowing Mary's apartment did not allow pets. Mrs. Hanley knew her husband hated cats, but she could not refuse her sick friend.

"I'm leaving in one week, Terry. I'll miss you and the times we had together. You have been a great friend," she said solemnly.

Mrs. Hanley replied, "Me too," and they hugged each other. Mary's mother offered some of her small appliances to Mrs. Hanley. She gave her a blender, toaster, and the few pots and pans. "I won't be needin' these where I'm going," she said, her head stuck in the cabinet.

20

TO THE RESCUE

Major Spellman was extremely displeased. He had ordered his captain to safeguard the mail and did not feel as though he had to explicitly tell his subordinates not to discuss the matter with anyone. The "shit sandwich," a euphemism of the army dialogue, was his to be feast upon. First he notified his superiors of the breach and received a terse response. His commanding officer, Captain Flanders, informed him that he would be contacted by the army's Public Relations Bureau very soon.

The captain questioned, shouting through the phone, "Spellman, have you lost control of your subordinates and the situation at hand? Have you lost the ability to command?" Spellman stumbled on his words while holding the phone and the screaming Flanders away from his ear. "I hope there will be no further breaches. Do you understand?"

"Yes sir," he responded.

Captain Flanders slammed the phone in Spellman's ear. Spellman sat back, rolled his eyes, and thought about it. At least he wouldn't have to deal with it anymore, he thought. He ordered his corporal to go to the mess hall and get lunch. That way, he wouldn't have to face the reporters and cameramen outside his office.

Lunch arrived and Spellman ate at his desk. He opened the door a couple of times, just an inch, to peer out and see if the crew was still there. To his regret, they still sat in the office stalking him.

Shortly after lunch a jeep pulled up outside his building. A major and a captain jumped out of the back. The driver stayed in the vehicle. They entered the building and checked in with the corporal at the desk. Spellman's phone rang, announcing his visitors.

"Major McConnell and Captain Turner to see you, sir," the corporal chimed.

"Show them in."

The corporal opened the door and escorted the men into Spellman's office They introduced themselves. Major McConnell had a recognizable face. Spellman had seen him before on television giving a press conference. Captain Turner was new to the department. Spellman briefed them on the situation.

McConnell confirmed, "You still have the mail in your possession?"

"Yes sir."

"Can I see it?"

Opening the safe, Spellman handed it over to him.

"We've got to put this to bed as soon as possible," McConnell said affirmatively. He then asked Turner if he had any suggestions.

The PR officers asked Spellman, "Can we borrow your desk?"

He complied, wanting to assist in any manner he could to rid himself of this nuisance. Turner typed into the computer and had McConnell look over his shoulder. They researched a similar situation that happened twenty years earlier, with mail found from the same era. They decided to put together a strategy to dispel the growing notoriety the story would bring.

"We'll keep it short and to the point," Turner added. McConnell agreed.

Then Spellman asked, "What are we going to do?"

McConnell told him, "You're going to do nothing."

At first Spellman felt resentment at his remark, but then decided it was much better with his little to no involvement. Turner took over and described what would happen next.

After explaining the strategy to Spellman, McConnell said, "Are we ready?"

They were.

Spellman phoned his corporal and had him escort the two reporters and cameramen into his office. The corporal showed the group in. Turner sat behind a desk and Spellman and McConnell stood behind him. Spellman readjusted his collar knowing he was about to be filmed. Turner and McConnell were perfectly calm. Spellman began to sweat as the light from the camera shone upon his face. If the situation became escalated, it might blow up in his face. He hoped his PR comrades had come up with the right strategy.

Turner quickly took control of the meeting. He introduced all the army personnel in the room, their respective ranks and title. Then he asked, "How can we help you today?"

The reporter jumped in and said, "We have it from reliable sources that mail has been discovered from WWII and that this office has possession of it. Can you confirm this? How much mail and where was it found? Have the recipients been informed of their property?"

The lights grew hotter from the cameramen and hit Spellman directly in the eyes. He squinted, and the perspiration began to form on his brow and underarms.

Turner looked at each of them slowly and pushed his gold-wired glass frames up his nose. He cleared his throat and made eye contact with all of them. He had been taught this in his training. Never look down or away. It would be viewed as dishonest. "I can confirm the existence of undelivered mail in our possession. It has been turned over to Major Spellman here for safekeeping. It is in his possession under lock and key," he said, while looking over his shoulder at Spellman. He turned back and continued, "Two of the three recipients have been located. One will have his mail delivered this week. The other recipient is deceased, and we are in the process of finding her rightful heirs. Upon confirmation of their relationship, the second piece of mail will be delivered."

"What about the third piece of mail?" the reporter, cutting him off, said.

Turner answered in a calm, stoic manner, "If you had let me finish, I would have explained." The reporter sat back, balking. Turner continued, "The third recipient has not been located. Upon locating her, we will promptly have the piece of mail delivered. The army is working in conjunction with the Lost Letter Department of the USPS to find the recipient."

"Can we see the mail?" asked another reporter.

"Due to privacy concerns and respect for all parties involved, we cannot let you see any of the post. Any other questions?" The reporters and cameramen looked at one another but said nothing. "Then if there are no further questions, Corporal Myers, will you please show these fine members of the media out?"

The corporal opened the door behind them and escorted them out. Looking deflated, the reporters left one by one followed by the cameraman. Their hot story had been cooled down effectively by the captain. The door shut and Turner came out of his role-play.

McConnell said, "Good job" to Turner and slapped Spellman on the back of his shoulder. "See, that wasn't so bad, now was it?" he said, laughing, gathering their belongings. "It's been a pleasure, Major. If they contact you again, please give them my contact information," McConnell chimed. He handed Spellman his business card and the two officers left.

From the window, Spellman loosened his collar and watched them get into the Jeep. They scooted away and Spellman sat back in his chair, a free man. His tormentors and the PR department gone, he sat back and relaxed.

The major finished work and went to his home on base. Reclining back in his chair, he turned on the TV and put on the nightly news. He leaned forward as the human interest story came on. It was titled "WWII-Lost Letters." They had left it as a teaser, right before commercial break. After the advertisements, the reporter told the tale of the lost posts and then there was some brief footage of their meeting. In all, the entire coverage lasted less than a minute, after the editor had cut everything. "Shit, that's it," Spellman yelled out, as he finished off his beer.

The next day Spellman wrote a report detailing the outcome. He made sure to thank the PR department and carbon copied them on the e-mail. He was advised not to do anything with the mail until further directed. His crisis now settled, he felt relieved that the frenzy had subsided. Hoping his involvement was over in the matter, he threw a newspaper at the television in frustration and headed to the refrigerator for another beer.

21

THE WEDDING'S ON

Long into the night, the McDougals and Tierneys discussed Jimmy's announcement. The discussion went from impossible to plausible. Patrolman McDougal and Mr. Tierney had long since finished the beer in the apartment and listened while their wives discussed the situation. The improbable task of pulling off the wedding, looked a bit more probable, as they discussed what would have to be done. Jimmy and Maggie offered their opinions whenever their mothers gasped for air in their discussion. They had always imagined a large wedding, with family and friends in attendance. With Jimmy's basic training departure nine days away, it would be impossible to accomplish. If they would proceed, it would have to be greatly downsized.

Maggie began looking at Jimmy. Her love for him had never been deeper. She watched as he tried to get a word in, between their mothers. He tried, "Mom," before looking to Maggie's mother, "Mrs. Tierney." The women kept speaking to one another, not even realizing he had spoken.

The men laughed and Mr. Tierney chided, "You're fightin' a losing battle there, lad."

Stealing away, the couple walked to the other side of the room. Maggie whispered, "I love you, Jimmy. I can't wait to be Mrs. McDougal. It doesn't matter how big or small the wedding is, and maybe it should just be the two of us and our parents."

Upon hearing Maggie's statement, the two mothers fell silent and stared at her. For a brief moment the silence encompassed the room, a temporary stalemate. Resigned to their son's and daughter's decision, they joined forces and began making a list of things that needed to be done for a smaller wedding and set upon making an invite list.

Jimmy and Maggie looked away and laughed. Their mothers were deep in planning mode and were talking longer and faster than ever. Their fathers were now fast asleep in the living room. Mr. Tierney lay across the couch and Patrolman McDougal was asleep in his chair, his head resting on his chest. He snored every minute or so and would startle himself awake. Jimmy and Maggie slipped outside the apartment door and walked downstairs, speaking of the evening and recollecting the moments. They laughed and teased how their mothers would probably be nonstop talking until the sun rose.

"Did you see your mother's face when I suggested it just be us? I thought she was going berserk," Jimmy exclaimed.

Maggie laughed and returned, "How about our fathers sleepin' while those two were fighting who was going to get the next word in?"

The couple decided to take their usual walk down the riverbank to the old sycamore tree. It was two a.m. now, and they grew tired. The air was sharp and Maggie grew cold. She leaned her head onto Jimmy's chest as they sat on the park bench. An owl hooted in the distance, and some ducks splashed in the water. Tomorrow, after Mass, they would approach Father Gallagher, to see if the church was available and if he would marry them.

"What do you think Father will say?" Maggie asked.

"Of course I will marry you," Jimmy answered.

They walked back and entered the apartment, where their mothers were still planning the wedding. The engaged couple looked at one another and wondered if their mothers had ever realized they had left.

Maggie woke her father and silently tapped her mother on the shoulder. "We ought to be going," she whispered.

Her mother said, "But we've got so much to do." Then she realized the time and made arrangements to meet Mrs. McDougal the following day after Mass. "I'll see you for brunch and we'll get this under wraps," she said while Maggie gently pushed her toward the door.

Sunday, both of the families were exhausted. They all attended noon Mass. Following the Mass, Jimmy and Maggie approached Father Gallagher on the bottom of the church steps. They waited until almost all of the other parishioners had left. The McDougals and Tierneys watched from atop the steps in the distance.

Jimmy asked Father Gallagher, "Have you any plans for next weekend, Father?"

He responded, "No. I might take in one of the football games if I have the chance."

"Would you be willing to marry Maggie and me then?" He told the priest of his scheduled departure and the urgency.

Maggie, holding Jimmy's hand, also pleaded, "Would ya please marry us, Father?"

Knowing the couple since they were born, Father Gallagher had performed all of their sacraments. "I remember both of your baptisms, first holy communions, and confirmations." Father Gallagher asked them, "Have you respect, affection, and love for one another?"

The each answered in tandem, "Yes."

The couple was holding hands in front of the church on the steps in front of him. He reached out and put a hand on each of their shoulders and said, "Then how could I say no? What time would you like to be married?" he asked.

"Two o'clock," Mary quickly replied.

"Then we'll plan on a two o'clock wedding for next Saturday. I can catch a football game any time," the smiling priest said.

Their parents watched from the steps and could tell by their reactions that the wedding was on. Patrolman McDougal turned to Mr. Tierney and they shook hands. The mothers walked over to the church office. It was usually closed on Sundays, but they had run into Mrs. Dugan at the Mass and spoken to her at the conclusion. She opened the office for them and looked at the logs for the following week. The church was not booked.

Mrs. Tierney reserved the church hall for the reception. Two of the biggest obstacles have been taken care of in less than an hour. The wedding was on!

The families all walked back to Sedgwick Avenue from the church, St. Nicholas of Tollentine. They felt good about the church and the hall, but there was still a lot of planning left to do. Catering, flowers, invites, and a wedding dress. The families walked back to the McDougals' and had brunch. The previous night they had agreed to limit the wedding invites to forty people because of the time constraint. Twenty guests a family would go fast, and the families began to choose their guests with great scrutiny. Some of their friends and relatives would expect invitations and be disappointed or insulted if they did not receive one.

Their mothers started talking about the wedding dress for Maggie. They planned to meet in the morning and go to the garment district to shop. Later in the day, they would go to the florist. Jimmy and his father were tasked with the caterer and fitting Jimmy for a new suit. Mr. Tierney would be in charge of the invitations. He had a friend that was a printer and was pretty sure he'd do a rush job for them. All agreed that they would hand-deliver the invitations in the neighborhood, not wanting to chance the invites arriving late. With their tasks assigned, all members of the families were ready for their Monday duties.

Monday was successful. All had accomplished their tasks with the exception of the women. The dresses were too expensive. Maggie wasn't that fussy and did not want to be a financial burden to her family and suggested just wearing a white dress. Mrs. Tierney came up with an idea. Mrs. Tierney was a seamstress and would sew the dress, if they could find material. The women decided to drop in a local fabric wholesaler in the garment district. Rolls of fabric were tossed all around the building, in no sense of order. A man behind a desk looked up from his paperwork long enough to know they were not tradesmen and asked what they wanted.

"Wedding dress material," Mrs. Tierney replied.

Having excess inventory from his summer weddings, he led them over to a damaged role. He offered it to them at a real favorable price to rid it from his stock. "I'll give you this whole roll for forty dollars."

The women inspected the roll, which was slightly water damaged. "I can make it work," Mrs. Tierney replied.

"Would ya take thirty-five dollars?" Mrs. McDougal haggled.

"Sure," he replied, wanting to rid himself of the damaged roll. The women huddled and took the deal.

The families had dinner at the Tierneys that night to discuss how each had fared at the given task. They were quite relieved that there had been no hiccups. The only thing left was the delivery of the invitations, sewing of the dress, and the entertainment. Looking at one another, they realized the entertainment hadn't been assigned. It was short notice and a decision would have to be made. Patrolman McDougal offered up some of his friends from the precinct. They had a three-man band composed of a drummer, a squeezebox, and a singer. Not much, but it would have to do. He would see them tonight at work and see if they were available. The wedding was on.

22

MOVING DAY

Attending the counseling session, Mary sat next to her new friend for support. The group sat on folding chairs in a circle. Twelve attendees were present. After each person introduced himself, the meeting facilitator took over. He explained, "There are a couple of new people attending. I just want to explain the rules." He pretty much said it was an open discussion and forum. One could speak about any topic and the group would offer their device on how to deal with it.

One woman spoke of her resentment for her father. "My father has been diagnosed with terminal lung cancer and continues to smoke. I hate the tobacco companies and loathe my father's smoking, especially with the oxygen containers and the risk of an explosion."

The group listened intently. One member of the group offered a "tough love" approach, saying, "Put him in hospice if he continues to smoke with the oxygen." Others were more sympathetic, saying he had an addiction that he could not kick in the limited time he had left and said to just let it be and enjoy what time they had left together.

Lastly, the facilitator brought up the danger of smoking with the oxygen. "You have to consider he's not only endangering his own life, but that of yours and anyone nearby."

"Hadn't thought of that," one lady grudgingly said. He added there were no right or wrong answers, just open discussion to cope and live through an individual's cancer crisis.

The next group participant spoke of his sick child. "My boy has leukemia, and the pain during his treatments is unbearable. He has weekly injections into his spine and has suffered immensely. He also suffered the further indignity of losing his hair at ten years old. Last year while attending school he had to wear a knit cap because he did not want anyone to make fun of his baldness. In early June of last year the chemotherapy made him feel cold, and he needed to keep warm without his hair." He broke down and cried recalling the incident.

A woman next to him leaned over and patted him on the back, joining in his sobs. "What's his name?"

He answered through his sobs, "Charlie." He went on to question the good of painful treatments and whether the continued treatments were for him or for his son. "Am I keeping him alive for my own selfish feelings? Charlie asked me the other day if he had to continue treatment." The room fell silent. He wiped his eyes with a handkerchief and blew his nose. Group members offered their support and suggestions. The man sat back and listened to each response and looked relieved at their support.

Mary's stomach was in knots. She desperately wanted to share her issues with the group, but she was an introvert around new people. Feeling as though the words wouldn't come out of her mouth, she tried in vain to speak. Her new friend laid a comforting hand on Mary's knee.

The group looked around for the next volunteer. All remained quiet as Mary tried to amass the courage to partake. Mary got up the guts to share her situation. She explained, "My mother has terminal pancreatic cancer and has a month or two to live. I have decided to have her move in but have much anxiety over her staying with me. We're both headstrong and I don't want her last days filled with bickering or resentment."

The group all listened intently to her situation. Some spoke of similar circumstances and that her fears were natural. Others offered words of encouragement and told her to remain brave. Still others offered other advice. Mary began to settle down and even joined in further discussion. Relief from her anxiety had come. At the conclusion of the meeting, she met with some members and spoke privately. They exchanged phone numbers to call each other for advice or support.

The facilitator took Mary aside and commented, "Thanks for participating. I think it helps you and others. I hope you'll be able to make it to some future meetings." He knew that the health care and living situation would be very taxing on her mentally and physically. He handed her his card with the hotline number on it. It was a twenty-four-hour national Cancer Crisis Center hotline. "Someone is always there to listen and help you if you need it," he said. He wrote down his personal number and urged her to use it. "We've all been through something like this and we're here for each other," he said solemnly.

Thanking him, Mary put his card in her purse. She walked back over to several group members still talking and said "Goodbye." Leaving, she felt more at ease and was able to look at the days to come with better clarity.

She walked back to her apartment and phoned her mother, awakening her from a dead sleep. She answered the phone groggily. Mary apologized for waking her up and said she felt bad for disturbing her and would call tomorrow.

Her mother was angered by Mary calling so late and said, "No one calls anybody at this hour, are you crazy or something?" and hung up the phone. Mary sat back on her couch and felt bad for disturbing her mother and pondered about their pending living arrangement.

Moving day had arrived. Mrs. McDougal rose early and went to morning services. She bought a dozen doughnuts and some coffee to go on her way home. All her pans and dishes have been given away or were packed, so she treated herself. It was only eight-thirty a.m. After finishing her breakfast, she sat, almost posing, and the minutes seemed like hours, watching her clock tick away, waiting for her daughter and friends.

Mary rose early too. She had already been to the supermarket to pick up groceries that her mother liked. Fig Newtons, half-and-half, decaffeinated tea, ice cream, wheat crackers would make her mother feel more at home. Rising at six a.m., she had already gone to the supermarket, cleaned the apartment, reorganized the pantry, and emptied the last load from the second bedroom closet. The apartment was ready for Mrs. McDougal, but was Mary?

Sipping on some hot coffee, she eagerly awaited her friends to arrive to help her with the move. Her friends owned a cargo van for their carpet business and had offered their assistance. Putting on a jacket, Mary looked down from her terrace above. The air was crisp as she watched the cars speed by below. Leaning over the rail, she looked down to see if they'd arrived. It was close to nine-thirty a.m., and it would be a twenty to thirty-minute drive to her mother's place.

The phone rang and it was her friends, Doug and Lisa, announcing their arrival. She spoke to them and saw their van pull up on the street below as she waved to them from the terrace. They had driven their van and a SUV, so that everything would fit. Mary locked up the apartment and took the elevator down. Waving to Doug in the van, she opened the SUV and hopped in with Lisa. They made their way up the West Side Highway to the Henry Hudson Parkway. Twenty-five minutes later they were in Riverdale, her mother's home for the last thirty years.

Mrs. McDougal had grown up on Sedgwick Ave in the South Bronx. She had never wanted to leave that area, but a five-alarm fire had forced her to move in the early 1970s. Barely surviving the blaze, she had been rescued by New York's Bravest by cherry picker from her top floor apartment.

They arrived at her apartment, and Mrs. McDougal opened the door and promptly announced, "I'm ready." She apologized, "I'm sorry I have nothin' to offer you except for the doughnuts, that is."

Lisa and Doug said, "Don't worry, we're fine."

Mary kissed her mother and took her friends into the master bedroom to look at what they would be moving. She pointed, saying, "The bed, end tables, and chair. Outside in the living room are four boxes and the two suitcases."

Mrs. McDougal had a large cross that hung in her bedroom in her hands. She did not want it to break and insisted on carrying it. Doug looked the furniture over again and took out a measuring tape. He measured the dresser twice. He looked puzzled at it again and said, "I think we're going to have to make two trips." Everyone looked a little disappointed. Mrs. McDougal started packing a box, not wanting to be a nuisance. Mary told her it wasn't a big deal.

Lisa assured, "We set aside the whole day for the move and everything's all right. If it takes two trips, it takes two trips."

Mary's mother felt that she was being a bother. Doug and Lisa said, "Let's get a' moving," trying to diffuse the situation. The couple and Mary walked downstairs to get the vehicles. Parking outside in a loading zone, they put the hazards on. Doug grabbed a dolly and Lisa the hand truck. Stretching the bungee cords, he wrestled with the dresser and put it on the dolly. "Grab the mattress top so that I can rest it against the side of the van so the dresser won't get scratched," he said.

The women struggled with the double bed mattress top as they dragged it to the elevator. Mrs. McDougal kept asking, "What can I do to help?"

The three answered, "Nothing, we got it."

Mary's mother felt expendable. The "useless" feeling entombed her. They placed the mattress up against the metal interior of the van, then the dresser. Next up, a box spring and headboard. Then they wedged the boxes in between the dresser on the other side of the van.

Mrs. McDougal became depressed and walked next door to Mrs. Hanley's. Together they had some tea, and Mrs. McDougal said her last goodbyes to Mr. Wiggles. She even got some sympathy from old man Hanley. Seeing her disposition, he mumbled, "Don't worry about the cat, Maggie, we'll take care of it."

Mrs. McDougal thought to herself, the cat's a "him" not an "it," but thanked him nevertheless.

The SUV and the van were full, but the headboard and two boxes would not fit. Mary went back upstairs to get her mother and explained, "We have to make two trips."

Mrs. McDougal said, "I will just stay, if you don't mind. I'm not doing anything anyway."

Mary could tell her mother was getting cold feet and was trying to squeak out a few minutes more at her old homestead. As the three left, Mary told her mother, "I'll be back in two hours."

Mrs. McDougal remained, Mr. Wiggles in her lap, and enjoyed her tea with Mrs. Hanley.

After unloading everything at Mary's apartment, Doug left for New Jersey, his home across the bridge. Mary thanked him profusely and the two girls backtracked to Riverdale. They found Mrs. McDougal in the same spot as two hours before and told her, "It's time to leave."

She said her goodbyes to the Hanleys and gave Mr. Wiggles a long hug while snuggling him up to her face. "I'm gonna miss you, friend," she whispered into the cat's ear before resting him on the floor. Mr. Wiggles rubbed against her leg affectionately, almost sensing her goodbye.

Off they were to Mrs. McDougal's new home in Manhattan. Thirty-five minutes to midtown. The doorman assisted the women and they unloaded the headboard and boxes onto the elevator. "Need some help, ladies?"

Lisa was double-parked and asked if they needed any more help. She said, "I haven't seen my kids all day. Can you handle the rest?"

Mary responded, "We got it. Thanks a million. I'll call you next week."

The McDougals hopped on the elevator upstairs. The doorman lifted the heavy headboard into the room and assembled it for them. Mary tipped him and he was gone.

Mrs. McDougal took off her coat and left for her bedroom. "I want to be alone while I unpack."

"Okay, Mom," Mary replied sheepishly. Mary did not know what to think. An hour or so later, Mary tapped lightly on her mother's door. There was no response. She wondered if she had offended her or hurt her feelings. She didn't look, not wanting to start their cohabitation off on the wrong foot, but gently knocked on the door again.

Her mother peered out and said, "I am going to rest for a while."

Mary left her and watched some television. It was 2:40 p.m. Mary kept looking at her watch. Three, then four o'clock. She knew her mother did not have the stamina of before, and she became worried. Five, then five-thirty p.m. She could not take it anymore. Her mind began to play tricks on her. Turning off the television, she had terrible thoughts. Had her mother passed away in the next room, her first day in her apartment? Had she had a stroke? Self-doubt filled her every thought. Had she done the right thing inviting her mother to live there? Would she be happy? Maybe home health and hospice would have been better?

She could take it no longer. Leaping off the couch, she walked with trepidation to her mother's room. Stopping outside of it, she pondered what to do next. It had been three hours. Could she really be that tired? What had she said or done to hurt her mother's feeling so badly? Not knowing what to do, she leaned up against the door and cupped her ear to see if she could hear anything up against the door.

As she leaned against the door, simultaneously her mother opened it. Mary fell stumbling into the room. Embarrassed and apologizing, she looked at her mother in disbelief. Grasping for words, she looked around the bedroom. All the furniture was in place. The bed was made and the boxes emptied into the closet. Three pictures set atop her dresser. Her mother and father's black and white wedding photo sat right in the middle of the dresser. To each side were two different pictures, one of Mary wearing her christening gown in her mother's arms, another of her mother and grandparents. The bed was made with a down comforter and an orange, green, and white afghan that she had quilted years ago. Other pictures were put on existing nails that were embedded in the wall. A crucifix was directly over the bed and a Bible on the nightstand. Her older, gold-plated windup alarm clock was on the other nightstand. "I didn't think you'd mind me making myself at home," she said at a loss for words.

Mary stuttered, "Not at all," and Mrs. McDougal eased her way past Mary, still standing in the doorway.

Mary caught up with her mother drinking a glass of water in the kitchen. "I thought we'd order out tonight, Mom."

"All right, Mary," she replied. "But we're not doing that sort of thing every night. I am still able to cook, you know."

Mary left her to herself. All her dreadful thoughts, what was she thinking? she mused.

"What do you feel like?" she asked.

"Anything is all right for me, except that Indian food. It gives me indigestion," Mrs. McDougal said.

"Chinese it is then," Mary said, handing her mother the take-out menu. Mary ordered the chicken lo mein while her mother only wanted the soup and some dumplings. The deliveryman buzzed about thirty minutes later and came to the door.

Mary paid and the two had their first meal as new roommates. Mary was famished and devoured her food. Halfway through the meal, she noticed that her mother did not have the same enthusiasm for the meal. "Don't you like it, Mom? I can order something else for you if you don't."

Her mother answered, "I'm not that hungry."

Growing concerned, Mary put some of her food on a smaller plate to see if her mother would eat it. "Try some of this."

She thanked her and played around with it on her plate with her plastic fork, but did not eat that much of it. Mary noticed that she had lost more weight also. She was down to 108 pounds. Her clothes looked as though they were purchased a size or two too big. They were not form-fitting and looked as if they were draped on her. Mrs. McDougal continued to poke away at her meal, eating two bites of what Mary gave her, half of her soup, and only two of the six dumplings.

Cleaning up the table, they put their leftovers back in the Styrofoam packaging and white folded boxes and retired to the living room. Mary turned on the television and asked, "What would you like to watch?"

Mrs. McDougal said, "I don't care. I'm extremely tired and will probably go to bed soon."

Finding an old movie, *Rebel Without a Cause,* Mary remarked to her mother, "This was a good one." Eight p.m., and Mary continued to watch the movie. Her mother was fast asleep, exhausted from the move and the day's events. Mary woke her mother at about nine p.m., and Mrs. McDougal went to bed. Mary turned off the television and looked at her calendar. According to Dockendorff's prognosis, her mother had only thirty days left to live. She reflected on the day's events and thought it had gone as good as possible. She hoped their cohabitation during the next thirty days would be a bonding between them, not adversarial. Mary desired to strengthen their relationship and to find out more about her mother and their family before she departed this world.

Thinking about the week to come, Mary went to bed.

During their first week living as roommates, they would eat breakfast together every morning. Mary would work half a day at MOD and her mother would attend Mass at St. Patrick's Cathedral. There were other churches closer, but Mrs. McDougal always enjoyed St. Patrick's. Mary's MOD partners assisted with her clients during this family emergency. Mr. O'Connor always made sure to ask Mary about her mother. The afternoons were tough; Mary would arrive home and Mrs. McDougal would be tired and need some rest.

Mary had envisioned them going on field trips across the city, living a different adventure every day. What she hadn't planned on was her mother's loss of stamina, appetite, and memory. Their second day together, Mary returned home from work about twelve-thirty p.m. Carlos, the doorman, waved to Mary. He took her to the corner of the lobby to speak to her in private. In his Dominican accent, he said, "We had a slight problem today. It is your mother. She became lost or confused or something, I'm thinking."

Mary, with growing concern for her mother's welfare, asked him, "Explain, please."

"You know she was trying to get into Mr. Maxwell's apartment on the ninth floor. She keep trying her key in his door, and then she become mad when it not work. She began pounding on his door."

"I'm sorry," Mary apologized. "I'll take care of it." Mary glared at the resident listing next to the buzzers downstairs. She would make it a point to apologize to Mr. Maxwell too. He lived in apartment 9E. She realized this was her mother's apartment number in Riverdale. Mary lived in apartment 7C. Entering her apartment, she greeted her mother and inquired about her morning. She was careful not to bring up the issue at Mr. Maxwell's right away.

Her mother explained that after Mary left, "I went to Mass and then to the food store for tonight's dinner. That's about it," she replied as though nothing had happened.

Mary mused about not bringing up the issue entirely or just making light of it. She decided that she better get her mother's account. "Did you go to the wrong apartment by mistake, Mom?"

Mrs. McDougal became agitated about the question and became tightlipped. "I don't want to talk about it. That man is rude."

Mary could not figure out which man she referred to, Carlos or Mr. Maxwell, and decided not to pursue it any further, fearing to incense her mother. An hour later it was as though nothing had happened. They went for a walk and Mrs. McDougal took a long nap while Mary worked at home.

Home health made its first visit to Mary's on the third day. Two nurses came to the apartment. One would be the regular nurse, Megan. The second was a trainee assigned to her. The visit took about an hour and a half. Megan tried to endear herself to Mrs. McDougal. She complimented her, "That's a beautiful dress and necklace." Mrs. McDougal enjoyed the flattery and began to warm to her.

Seventy-five percent of the visit was about paperwork. Megan took all the information down. Mary had it all prepared beforehand, upon Nurse Cragen's advice. First there was the address change. Next it was a living will and DNR status. Then, was she an organ donor? "Is all this really necessary?" Mrs. McDougal asked. "We did all of the same forms at Dr. Dockendorff's last week."

Megan assured her, "You know the paperwork never ends. I'm sorry about the duplication, but it's necessary. You don't want to get me in trouble, do you?" She even joked that she would be asking the same question each visit. "We have to verify the information because patients may change their mind on different issues," she said.

Mrs. McDougal became a little agitated, but Megan defused it by changing the subject to her brogue accent. Megan asked, "Is that an Irish brogue I detect?"

Mrs. McDougal explained that her parents were from County Sligo in Ireland. "I thought that's what I heard," Megan replied.

The next twenty mad minutes were tests. First they took her pulse, 74 BPM. Next they took her blood pressure, 135 over 80. Megan pulled a needle from her case and drew a vial of blood. She asked, "How are you feeling? I'm not hurting you, am I?"

"I'm just dandy," she replied sarcastically.

The trainee fumbled through the clipboard, trying to keep up with Megan's requests. "Everything looks good. We'll see you three times a week, starting next week. I'll send the blood in for testing. Otherwise, I think we're done."

Mary escorted the nurses out and explained what had happened the prior day at Mr. Maxwell's. Megan said, "Keep an eye on her. It could have just been a one-time occurrence or the situation could escalate." Mary thanked her and they left.

The fourth day went off without a hitch. On the fifth day Mary returned home from MOD. She looked at the entrance to the apartment building with trepidation. Carlos just waved and wished her a good afternoon. Each day she saw him, she feared what might have happened while she was gone. She felt relieved by his greeting at the elevator going upstairs.

Opening the door to the apartment, she smelled gas. Mary ran inside and found the burner on, but nothing on the stove. Quickly she turned the burner off and ran to the French doors of the terrace balcony and swung them open. She hurried to the dining room and unhinged the two large windows. She frantically sought out her mother, finding her in the bedroom.

Mary's mother exclaimed, "Oh, we are home early, dear. I was just going to make some tea. Do you want some?" as she strode by her.

At first, Mary was furious. Thinking it over, she questioned her mother about the stovetop. Her mother made light of it saying it was not that big of a deal. "Like you've never done it."

Mary went into her bedroom and called Cragen. She explained a few of the incidents that had occurred over their first week together. Cragen listened to all the details. "You're lucky that your mother or anybody else did not get hurt. I recommend that you not leave her unattended for more than an hour anymore. There are people we have that are called 'sitters.' They have no medical training, but simply stay at your home and watch the patient's on-goings to prevent situations like you have."

Mary acknowledged her concerns and hung up. She walked back to the kitchen as her mother sat and drank her tea. "Up for a cup," her mother said, "sit down and relax." Her mother thumbed through the newspaper and Mary observed her. She was slipping into deeper Alzheimer's. When she questioned her mother about the content of the newspaper and what she had done all morning, her mother answered all the questions quite pointedly. She commented on all the news and was quite clear about the stories. Mary's disquietude over her mother being alone grew. She could not chance leaving her alone for more than an hour again. There were moments of ambiguity and lucidity in her mother's everyday life.

Thinking over the situation, she called O'Connor to explain what recently happened. He listened attentively and urged Mary to take whatever actions she felt necessary. He asked if there was anything he could do to help.

Mary told him," I won't be able to come in for half days anymore. My mother should not be left alone."

After hearing her recount the week's events, he couldn't agree more. "How can we help you, Mary?" he asked concernedly.

"I don't know," Mary replied, confused. She was getting irritated by a situation that she had no control over.

O'Connor thought a brief second. "What if I could have a courier deliver your ledgers every day instead of you coming in?" he asked. Thinking it over, he realized it made perfect sense to him. A courier would enable Mary to stay with her mother while not leaving her unsupervised.

Mary agreed and thanked O'Connor for being so understanding.

23

AGNES

Mr. Tierney came home late Tuesday morning. He had picked up the invitations that his printer friend had rushed for them. Eagerly he opened the box and removed the tissue paper lining the top. Proudly he read the invitation to Maggie and her mother. In a baritone voice, he read, "Mr. and Mrs. Sean Tierney and Mr. and Mrs. Michael McDougal request the honor of your presence at the marriage of their children, Agnes Margaret and James Francis, on Saturday, the 17th of September, 1944 at 2 p.m. in the afternoon, at St. Nicholas of Tollentine Catholic Church, Bronx, New York. How do you like that?"

Mrs. Tierney replied, "That's lovely."

Maggie was not so pleased. "Daddy, why did you put Agnes on the invites? I hate that name," she said sourly.

Mr. Tierney replied, "It was your grandmother's name and 'tis your birth name. For it to be legal and all, you better sign your name accordinly on the marriage certificate."

Maggie became edgy. She didn't even know if Jimmy knew Agnes was her real name. She had taken up her middle name, Margaret, in first grade, and her friends and mother had shortened it to Maggie.

Walking upstairs to meet Jimmy, she held the McDougals' box with their half of the invites. Mrs. McDougal opened the door and let Maggie in. Jimmy walked over and gave her a kiss. Mrs. McDougal had made lunch. Four days until the wedding and everyone involved was a little on edge taking care of their particular task.

Patrolman McDougal asked Maggie, "What's in the box?"

Maggie told them, "It's your half of the invitations," in a soft-spoken voice.

Jimmy's mother had to get a glimpse and wiped off her hands. Maggie tried to distract her and bring up a different subject. Mrs. McDougal would have no part of it. She opened the box and began reading the top invite. Midway through reading, she looked up to see Maggie standing there paranoid, hoping she would not read out her name, Agnes. Mrs. McDougal quickly caught on why she hadn't wanted her to read the invite. She too read the invite aloud, but changed Maggie's name to

Margaret instead of Agnes Margaret. Maggie breathed a sigh of relief.

Her son listened and commented, "How formal it all sounds."

Mrs. McDougal threw Maggie a wink when Jimmy turned his head. She mouthed a whispered "thank you." Maggie didn't want Jimmy teasing her or telling anyone else.

"Let me get these addressed and into the envelopes so you two can deliver them," Jimmy's mother said. Maggie's secret was safe for now.

They ate lunch together and began making their deliveries of the McDougals' invites. The first five of the invitations were easy. Walking down six flights of stairs to the apartment mailboxes, they dropped them in the slots. They all lived in the same building. The last five would take some travel, with them having to walk a few blocks to drop off an invite and then hit the appropriate direction to the next on the list. The last of the five required a bus.

Tired, having walked all day, they retreated back home to the Tierneys.' Maggie's mother had started sewing her dress. "Get on top of the milk crate so that I can take some measurements."

Jimmy became bored and started rifling through the clutter on top of the table next to him. The Tierneys' assortments of invites were almost all addressed, except for one, which remained open. He picked up the envelope and quickly looked over the invite. Reading it, his eyes did a double take. At the same moment, Maggie saw what he was reading. It was too late.

"Agnes, who is Agnes?" he said.

Panicked, Maggie jumped off the milk crate and grabbed the invite out of his hand.

Realizing the situation, he reached out his arms and said, "Come to your fiancé, Agnes."

Maggie threw the imitation at him in frustration. Mrs. Tierney just shook her head, needles hanging from her mouth. "I need you back up here," she said, pointing at the milk crate.

"Agnes, you heard your mother," Jimmy joked.

Maggie hopped back on the milk crate and pointed at Jimmy. "You're going to regret it if you call me that again," she angrily remarked.

Jimmy smiled and dropped it. He could tell she was upset and didn't want to rattle her anymore. The night went on with little fanfare and no more mention of his beloved Agnes.

The next day the couple delivered all of the Tierney invites much in the same manner. Ten lived in the same building. The others required some walking. They didn't rush through it. In three days they would be wed. They delivered all the invites and dropped in to the florist. Maggie wanted to show Jimmy the flowers that she and her mother had picked out for the ceremony. Jimmy pretended to be interested. Inside he could care less about the flowers, but didn't want to look as though he didn't. Maggie showed him all the arrangements. She knew it didn't matter to him, but appreciated that he faked it anyway.

"Aren't these beautiful?"

"Oh, you couldn't have picked nicer ones, Maggie," he replied.

That night they went out with Timmy and his Catherine. The two couples decided to go to the Roosevelt Hotel on the east side of Forty-third Street. They grabbed a quick bite to eat and were off to the Roosevelt for a night of dancing.

Around midnight the band slowed up the tempo a bit. The four were having drinks and Jimmy grabbed Maggie for a dance. They played "I Don't Want To Walk Without You" by Jule Styne, the lyrics by Frank Loesser. It was a slow song that was perfect for them because of their fondness for long walks together.

They were tired from the rushed week. Jimmy held her tight to his chest. Maggie could feel his heart beat through his shirt against her chest. He rubbed the back side of his hand against her cheek and put his other hand behind her back. Maggie could smell his musk through his aftershave. Jimmy twisted the Claddagh ring in circles on her finger. Their eyes met as they kissed on the floor, oblivious to the crowd around them. In their moment, they were the only two in the room. They swayed back and forth on the floor to the slow rhythm of the song, lost in the moment.

The song ended and the lights came on. The band was going to take a break. Jimmy and Maggie stopped and gazed into each other's eyes. The sweat rolled down Jimmy's back and Maggie focused deeply on her fiancé. They whispered in unison, "I love you" to each other. Grinning, they kissed again and left the dance floor. After another round of drinks, the couples danced the night away, celebrating what was probably their last double date for a long time.

24

HERE COMES THE BRIDE

Friday had come. One day until the wedding. Mrs. Tierney and Mrs. McDougal took care of all the last-minute details. They would have a simple rehearsal dinner at the Fordham Steakhouse. The dinner was more of a celebration than a rehearsal. Patrolman McDougal and Mr. Tierney shook hands and slapped one another on the back the entire night. Toast after toast the fathers made. "Here's to my wife." "Here's to my new son-in-law." "Here's to Ireland." They toasted their children, their spouses, and each other.

Finally their wives put a stop to it all. "They'll be no more toastin'," Mrs. Tierney cried halfway through the affair. "Look atcha. You're half in the bag already, for God's sake."

The dinner was over, and the wedding was in the morning. Leaving the Fordham Steakhouse, they agreed that a good time was had by all. Most everyone went to bed early with the exception of Jimmy and Maggie. The two went on their walk and spoke of the future. "A house in the country, a grand manor it will be," he gloated. Jimmy walked Maggie to her door and looked at his watch. It was 12:15 a.m. "Today you will be my wife," he said as he leaned over to kiss her goodnight.

"I can't wait," Maggie said.

The morning came early, with both families rising at six a.m. Everyone got ready in a brisk fashion. Breakfast was very quiet. All had had a long night, and the morning would go by in a flash. Mrs. Tierney got into the bathroom first. The bride's mother had to get herself ready first, then her daughter. Mr. Tierney stayed out of the women's way. There was only one bathroom and he would be the last and have the shortest time in it, not even thinking about going first or arguing about it.

Mrs. Tierney packed the wedding gown and shoebox in a large two-handled shopping bag. She meticulously folded it, having spent days sewing, altering, and ironing it. The Tierney women left for the church at eleven a.m. They would get dressed in the church hall. Mr. Tierney told them he would meet them about 10:50 a.m. Mrs. Tierney tersely replied, "You'll be there at noon I need to make sure you're ready too." He stayed out of their way as they both appeared tense.

Upstairs at the McDougals, only one woman needed to get ready, but the air was just as thick. Mrs. McDougal had planned to meet the Tierneys at eleven a.m., but was running late. She ran back and forth from the bedroom to the bathroom a dozen times.

"What could she be doing in there?" Jimmy asked his father.

"I don't know, but stay out of her way," he mumbled back.

Jimmy's mother left about eleven a.m. fully dressed, running out of the apartment in her heels. Scolding them on the way out, she said, "You two don't be late. Ten-thirty a.m. latest," slamming the door on the way out.

Patrolman McDougal looked at Jimmy while sipping his coffee and the two shrugged their shoulders at each other. Nothing needed to be said; they had an hour to get ready between the two of them. No problem.

The McDougal men knocked on the Tierneys' door on their way past at 12:15 p.m. They proceeded down the stairs when no one answered. A flight down, they heard the door open.

"Wait for me," Mr. Tierney yelled down.

"Thought you'd already be there?" Jimmy posed the question.

"I'm not goin' early with those two lunatics," he replied. The three laughed and began their walk to St. Nicholas.

Mrs. McDougal and Mrs. Tierney were putting their final touches on Maggie. Mr. Tierney gently knocked and walked in. "You're late," Maggie's mother commented.

"Depends on who you ask," he laughed.

She got up from Maggie and adjusted his tie. "Don't move. It's not straight," she quipped as she maneuvered his tie back and forth. Mr. Tierney was a large, portly man with a deep voice. He was a motor man on the subway and had to wear a tie to work also. The skin on his neck fell over the lapel of the shirt. The shirt looked entombed, trapped between layers of his neck's folded skin.

Outside, the organist began to play a few lines from a hymn to warm up. The McDougal men were out at the altar speaking with Father Gallagher. Mrs. McDougal came out. People filled the first pews, waving and smiling at them. Her heels clattered on the marble floor, echoing her planned assault on them. She quickly inspected all of them, readjusting their jackets and ties. Licking her fingers, she pulled down on Jimmy's hair, like a child.

"What do you think you're doing," he said, stepping away from her.

"Come here," she said as she tried to keep a couple of his hairs from standing up with the saliva on her fingers. Turning, she tried to do the same to Patrolman McDougal.

He grabbed her hand and exclaimed, "Don't even 'tink about it."

Frustrated, she sat down in the first pew in a huff. "Then be that way," she muttered.

In the back of the church the men could see Mr. Tierney, down the aisle. He was staring straight at them, hands clasped behind his back. His attention diverted to the right and, unclasping his hands, his right arm out reached and all of a sudden a burst of white fabric appeared with Maggie engulfed in it. The processional hymn began, and all rose to their feet in the church. Their mothers, in tandem, turned to look down the aisle for the bride and her father.

Mr. Tierney walked with Maggie down the aisle, slowly. He was a giant; she looked so dainty next to him. They approached the altar, and Mr. Tierney removed her veil and kissed her. "You look beautiful," he mouthed.

Moving to her side, Father Gallagher nodded and started the Mass. Jimmy and Maggie couldn't take their eyes off of each other. Father Gallagher proceeded into the sacrament of marriage. At that point, he asked "if there is any man that knows why these two should not be married?"

The church was silent. He went forward and asked, "Who is here to give this woman away?"

Mr. Tierney answered, "I am."

The ceremony continued. "To honor and cherish," Father Gallagher continued. A tear slowly rolled down

Maggie's cheek and Jimmy let go of her right hand and gently wiped it away with the back of his hand.

After they both had answered, "I do," Father Gallagher pronounced, "I now pronounce you man and wife.".

Jimmy removed the Claddagh ring from Maggie's hand and turned it around 180 degrees. He placed it back on her hand with the heart facing inward. This signified to the world that the two hearts were forever joined.

"You may kiss the bride," Father Gallagher announced. Jimmy leaned forward and put his hand behind her head and the other around her waist.

Maggie was truly a blushing bride. They turned to face their guests and enormous smiles were across their faces. Strolling down the aisle, they looked on as the audience smiled and clapped. The organist blasted the wedding march from above, and the two walked down the aisle. The rear doors opened and the burst of light hurt their eyes. Walking down the steps squinting, they were pelted by rice from well-wishers. Patrolman McDougal and Mr. Tierney shook hands at the top of the steps. The photographer continued to snap photographs. The weather was beautiful, sunny, and sixty-two degrees. Cars drove past honking their horns at the new bride and groom.

The photographer wanted to take the bride and groom back into the church for pictures at the altar. Father Gallagher had not allowed any pictures during the ceremony, as was commonplace in the church at the time. Bride, with groom, groom and groom's parents, bride and groom and bride's parents, bride and groom and wedding party, all families, it went on forever.

Jimmy began to get annoyed and called an end to the pictures. It was now three-thirty p.m. and the guests were next door at the hall awaiting their arrival. The parents entered the hall first, to the applause of all the guests, next Timmy and Catherine, the best man and maid of honor. Finally the lead band member announced, "I would like to introduce you to Mr. and Mrs. James Francis McDougal."

Jimmy and Maggie walked in and the band played the wedding march. It all seemed so surreal to them. They had just a week of planning and now they were married. They were led to a table in front of all the guests. Father Gallagher came over and offered his congratulations. "Young Mr. and Mrs. McDougal. Congratulations."

Jimmy stood up and shook his hand and Maggie gave him an enormous hug. He was genuinely proud to have wedded them, he thought as he drank from his Irish whiskey. "Before I forget," he said as he removed two pieces of paper out of his jacket. "One for the diocese and one for the City of New York." He directed them on where to sign.

Jimmy reached into his pocket and pulled out a copy of a form from the army. "Sign here too," he instructed

Maggie. It was a benefits form in case anything happened during his service.

All legal, the reception was in full gear. Mr. Tierney started the dancing after slamming back his drink. The father of the bride and bride danced in the middle of the room. Jimmy joined in with his mother. Shortly thereafter, Jimmy and Maggie shared their first dance as husband and wife. The crowd circled around them as they joined in their inaugural dance. Timmy and Catherine took to the floor, then their parents. Next, almost all the guests were on the dance floor.

Wedded, the new couple sat down to observe the show. They held hands and joked about some of the dancing. "Look at Mr. Rourke, he sure looks suave," Jimmy laughed.

"How about your father and mother? That's a little close dancing, don't you think?" Maggie replied.

Timmy hushed all in attendance and made the best man's speech. "I've known Jimmy and Maggie since we were five years old. I could bore you with stories of past times, current times, and the future." Jimmy had prepared himself for one of Timmy's corny jokes, but his best man had prepared an honest and sincere speech. He ended with a toast to the couple, "May God bring Jimmy back safely to his new bride, Maggie. May He bless them for the rest of their lives, as I have felt blessed to have known them all of mine."

Jimmy raised his glass and the Tierneys, McDougals, and guests were left teary eyed by Timmy's heartfelt toast. Jimmy and Maggie both got up after the toast and the three wrapped their arms around one another.

After the meal, the celebration went on until late afternoon. Jimmy and Maggie made their rounds to each table to thank all their guests for attending. Mr. Tierney and Patrolman McDougal gathered the gifts and called for two taxis. The new couple had reserved a hotel room at the Waldorf Astoria. Patrolman McDougal's ranking captain had arranged a favor of a complimentary room for them. It seems the manager of the hotel owed the captain a favor, and now the room was theirs for the night. They said their farewells and embraced each of their parents and the wedding party.

Jimmy and Maggie's taxi pulled up to the Waldorf at six-thirty p.m. The bellman said, "Welcome to the Waldorf" as he opened the door to their cab and retrieved their bags. Jimmy paid the fare and they followed the bellman's lead to the entrance. Two doormen, dressed in red- and black-trimmed suits, pulled back the large brass doors. Everything shone in the lobby and they gazed straight up at the crystal chandelier overhanging the lobby. The bellman could tell it was their first time at a hotel.

"James McDougal," Jimmy said at the front desk.

Upon hearing their surname, the clerk called for the manager as he had been instructed. Taking over from the clerk, the manager said, "I understand congratulations are in order on your nuptials. Have a great stay and let us know if there's anything we can do to make it better." He was a thin man with black glasses, dressed in a gray pinstripe suit with tails. He ordered the bellman to take their bags to the honeymoon suite.

Jimmy and Maggie looked like two hayseeds gawking at the exuberance of wealth displayed at the hotel. The couch was constructed of fine fabric, with gold roping on the seams. Gargoyles looked down upon them from the walls. Following the bellman, they entered the elevator to the penthouse honeymoon suite. The bellman showed them where everything was in the room and set their bags on the luggage caddy. He wore a little red jacket, lined with black trim with brass buttons. He stood almost at attention, hands behind him like a sailor on deck, clearing his throat. "If there's not anything else," he said as he awkwardly waited for a tip. Maggie tapped Jimmy to remind him as he searched for a silver dollar to tip him.

Like children at an amusement park, they yawped at their room, discovering new amenities and surprises in each room or drawer. "Can you believe people live like this?" Maggie stuttered.

"Lookie here," Jimmy excitedly said. A bottle of champagne was on the ice in a brass bucket beside the bed. A note attached to the bucket read "From the men of the 43rd Precinct. Good Luck!"

Jimmy pulled back the curtains and took a full view of the city in front of him. The neon lights shone from below them straight into the air. Maggie came over to look out with him and he put his arms around her. They swayed back and forth looking at the scene around them. Jimmy leaned down and began kissing her neck from behind her. Maggie reached back and grabbed his head from behind. They turned to face one another and deeply embraced.

They moved toward the king-sized bed. Jimmy reached up and unknotted his tie. Throwing it aside, he took his shirt off. Turning Mary around, he unbuttoned the back of her dress. There she stood naked before him, next to the bed. Her body was illuminated from the outside lights on the marquee. She subtly smiled and lay next to him in the bed. Their bodies were warm and soon entwined. They had never made love before. Jimmy respected Maggie too much and had never pushed the issue. Virginity was sacred to Maggie and she knew it would be Jimmy to be her one and only lover. They made love for the first time and reveled in it. Looking into one another's eyes, they wrestled in the heat of passion.

After they had consummated the marriage, the couple lay back, and a chill went through them from the sheets soaked in sweat. Maggie lay in Jimmy's arms, head upon his chest. He brushed back the hair from her face and slowly, repeatedly ran his fingers through her hair.

She silently spoke, "I love you with all my heart, James McDougal. I will miss you terribly while you're gone. You make sure you come back to me."

He professed his undying love for her and pulled her head up and put his lips to hers. He put his finger on her lips and told her, "Don't worry, I'll be back soon."

They lay in each other's arms for hours. Jimmy got up and went to the bathroom and started a bath for them. He poured in some bath powder, and large bubbles emerged as the tub filled. Walking back to the bedroom, he uncorked the champagne and poured two glasses. Maggie sat upright in bed and they clinked glasses toasting, "To us." They smiled at their toast, took a sip of champagne, and walked to the bathroom.

Getting into the tub, Maggie held Jimmy's hand, so as not to slip. He handed her the two glasses of champagne and entered himself. Maggie handed him his glass and the two delighted in their champagne bubble bath. They looked at one another with great affection, endearingly, deeply in love. In two days the reality of war would separate them. But for the time being, they were lost in time, enjoying their moment.

Jimmy got out of the bath and toweled off. Unfolding a bathrobe, he held it out to put on his new bride. "Here you go. Be careful." Pouring another glass of champagne, they sat back on the couch and Jimmy put the radio on. An Andrews Sisters' hit, "Boogie Woogie Bugle Boy," played from the hotel room radio. Lying back in bed, they fell once again into the thralls of deep passion. Exhausted, the young McDougals fell asleep in each other's arms.

A beam of sunlight peeked through around six-thirty a.m. It hit Jimmy straight on the side of his face. Leaning over to look where it was coming from, he saw that the sunbeam shone through the curtains. He realized he had forgotten to pull them all the way shut the night before. Squinting, he looked around the room. A four-poster bed, green and yellow velvet floral wallpaper, and ornate light fixtures surrounded him. More sunlight began to shine through and Maggie rolled over to shy away from it.

Jimmy leaned down and kissed his new bride's forehead. "Good morning," he whispered.

"What time is it?" she groggily inquired.

"Six-thirty a.m.," he replied.

"What time do we need to leave?" Maggie asked.

"Checkout is at eleven a.m.," Jimmy said. They got up, showered, and prepared to go downstairs to the dining room for breakfast. Upon entering the dining room, they were seated. A large, robust man in a chef's hat with a white shirt, pants, and apron was on a grill behind the swinging doors in the kitchen across from their table. They ordered breakfast and the waiter gave them some coffee and juice. The eggs looked as though they were laid by a swan, they were so large. Glazed honey buns sat on a plate to their side. Breakfast potatoes, lightly browned, topped with parsley, finished off the plates.

Their short-lived honeymoon was about over. After breakfast they returned upstairs to their room and packed. Both took a long last look at the room as they shut the door. The new couple made it down to the lobby and checked out. The bellman took their bags and hailed a cab. Back to the Bronx they headed.

25

A BUS TO CATCH

Everyone at MOD, especially O'Connor, had worked with their new partner to enable Mary to work at home during her time of crisis. Even Dooley lent a hand by seeing one of her clients. She was very appreciative of their support. That weekend, Mary and her mother spent a lot of quality time together. They ate all their meals together, although Mrs. McDougal's appetite was poor. She picked at her food and often did not eat at all. Losing more weight, she had dwindled to one hundred pounds.

The next week Mary went about her accounting business at home. A courier would deliver the ledgers between nine-thirty and ten-thirty a.m. Mary would work until lunch and her mother would sleep. She would work a couple of hours more and then they would try to get out of the house. One day they would shop, another go to a movie or just run errands. They hadn't spent time like this together since Mary was a little girl. There had never been time. Her mother had worked full-time at Fordham University and would take the bus from Sedgwick Avenue. Father Clanon, Dean of Discipline, was her boss. During the summer, the school had a relaxed schedule, and Father Clanon would let her mother off a little early.

Mary remembered holding her mother's hand as they walked from store to store shopping in the neighborhood. She pondered their current situation and how their roles had reversed. Mary had attended Fordham University on a scholarship for employees' children and her mother was always extremely proud that Mary was a student there. She always claimed the Jesuits were the best teachers and never thought that she would be able to afford to send Mary to the university. "The scholarship was a blessing from above," her mother had said.

At night they would sit back and relax in the living room after dinner, talking more freely and honestly than ever, her mother having opened up to her and exposed a side that Mary had never seen. Mrs. McDougal and Mary would talk for hours. She would speak of her childhood days and earlier years. Story after story came out in enormous detail. Mary was beside herself. She had never known anything about her mother's life, with the exception of an isolated story here or there. Now her mother was finally opening up. The stories were from the heart, some happy, some sad. The tales had no chronological timeline and jumped from varying subjects with no semblance of order.

Mary listened to every detail, every word, eagerly getting to know her mother's inner self. Sometimes her mother would get lost in a story or just stop mid-sentence. Mary would first try to let her mother find herself, but often she needed to remind her what and who she was talking about. Occasionally she would not be able to recollect the story. She would become frustrated and embarrassed. "Who wants to listen to an old fool anyways?"

Mary would comfort her and try to put her back on point. She had never had a relationship with her mother like this. It was always a teaching or disciplinary role her mother had. Never one for explaining, just do it her way. Hours flew by like minutes and Mary greatly enjoyed the stories. Often they would sip a glass of wine while they talked, laughing or crying, depending on the story.

One night, her mother spoke of her first meeting with the likes of James McDougal. "Your father lived on the sixth floor, we lived on the fourth floor," she started. Mary's ears perked up. On the edge of her seat, she begged her mother for more details of their first meeting. A wry smile came over Mrs. McDougal as she recalled, "It was the Labor Day weekend. We were moving into the apartment on Sedgwick Avenue. Your grandfather and his friends were unpacking a truck they had borrowed, with all of our furniture and belongings. Jimmy and Timmy O'Leary were on the roof of the building. The men were straining to move the furniture out of the truck, onto the sidewalk in front of the building. My father and his friend picked up a couch from the curb. I was in front of the building with your grandmother, picking up smaller boxes.

"Straining and grunting from picking up the couch the men were, when all of a sudden, wallop, a water balloon came crashing down upon my father's head. He dropped the couch, screamed some unpleasantries, and looked upward. There were your father and Timmy, heads leaning over the side of the roof, looking down upon us. My father made for the stairs and ran up them like a madman. Your father and Timmy panicked. They never thought they actually might hit someone. So first they tried to hide on the roof. Next they made for their apartments. Your grandfather caught Jimmy while he was opening his apartment door. He grabbed him by the scruff of the neck and began shaking him.

"Hearing the commotion inside, Patrolman McDougal interceded. He was dressed in his policeman's uniform getting ready to leave for work. Your grandfather explained to him what had happened. By now, my mother and I were in the hallway. Jimmy put his head down when asked by his father if he had done it. Patrolman McDougal told my father he would handle it and apologized about the incident. The door shut and you could hear the belt cracking against your father's backside two floors down. He yelped in pain. It went on for a good ten minutes. Your grandfather, my father-in-law, had quite a temper. And that's the story of how I met James McDougal." Sitting back deeper onto the couch, she looked all content with her story. She put the glass to her lips and took a sip of wine. "He had a little bit of a mischievous side, especially around that Timmy O'Leary," she ended.

Mary was delighted and begged for more. "Tell me some more about Father."

Her mother thought a while and then began speaking of their next encounter. She spoke of the next day. "School started that Tuesday after Labor Day weekend. My mother and me were downstairs, ready to walk to Tollentine, that was the school run by the church. Mrs. McDougal and your father Jimmy came down the stairs right after us. Jimmy had a black eye. His father would have nothing but an obedient child, and the water balloon incident had greatly displeased him. Our mothers introduced themselves and then the children to each other. I was dressed in a navy blue jumper with a white blouse and black shoes. Jimmy was dressed in a blue tie and jacket. That's how they made us dress for school. It was the dress code. He mumbled hello, after some prompting from his mother, while staring straight at the ground. His mother made him carry my books. I felt bad for him, knowing the punishment his father had administered on him. But I guarantee you, he never did that again.

"We walked to school, the two of us ahead of our mothers. I tried to speak to him, but he was very shy. After two blocks, he finally spoke. We were six years old on our way to first day of class. He asked me, 'Do you like frogs?' I told him I did, and he asked me, 'Want to go see some after school?' I said yes. We arrived at Tollentine and our mothers, bid us farewell. They asked if we knew how to get home and we said, 'Yes.' Mrs. McDougal looked your father right in the eyes and said to walk me home. 'And make sure you carry her books,' she said.

"We finished our first day of school, and…." Mrs. McDougal became quiet. She looked around the room as though looking for something in the air.

Mary put her hand on her shoulder and said, "It's alright."

"What was I saying?" her mother asked. Mary reminded her of the story and she squinted, trying to recall that day. "All I was saying was school ended and we walked home. He tried to impress me real good, your father, he did. Jumping trash cans, hopping over cracks in the sidewalk, he tried to impress me real good."

"Well, did he?" Mary joked.

"Not much yet, but we got back to the apartment and he took me down to the river. There he skipped stones and taught me how to skip them too. We sat down on the riverbank and took off our shoes. Jimmy went into the water knee-high and scurried up a couple of frogs. He handed one to me and kept the other. We named the frogs after ourselves. I slipped and fell on my rear, getting my dress all wet. Your father pulled me out and brushed the muck off of me. That's what impressed me," her mother ended.

"What?" Mary asked.

"That he helped me clean up. He didn't want me to get in trouble and get spanked. He knew my mother would be mad if I was in the water and that I got my school clothes dirty. We walked back along the path that ran along the river, and that's when he asked me."

"Asked what?" Mary said.

"To be his girlfriend, silly," she answered. "And that was it. We were boyfriend–girlfriend ever since. Those were great times," she mused. "Life was so, so simple. We were just happy kids having a good time."

"Tell me more," Mary pleaded. Her mother finished what was left in her wineglass and said she couldn't go on. Exhausted, she retired to her bedroom. Mary sat back, finishing her glass of wine, recalling the entire evening's conversation. Laughing to herself, she pictured the water balloon hitting her grandfather and him dashing up the stairs in pursuit. Mary took out her laptop and began a file to keep her mother's memories alive. She began to type in some of their recent conversations and stories, not wanting to forget a date or detail. She typed the rest of the night. Lying back in bed, she imagined her mother and father on their first date at the river, with frogs in hand. She smiled as she lay awake, recalling her mother's memories. Mary hoped the next night's conversation would be as lively as tonight's.

Nurse Cragen called the next day to check on Mrs. McDougal's condition. Mary rambled on about how well she was doing and the conversations they had been having. She spoke fast and was excited. Cragen could feel her enthusiasm over the phone and had trouble keeping her on track about the medical issues. The nurse was worried about her mother's lack of appetite and weight loss. She wanted Mrs. McDougal to come in for an appointment with Dockendorff to evaluating her condition. "Home health can only do so much," she stated. Mary came back from her momentary lapse and agreed. They would make the appointment for the following day.

The courier arrived and dropped off Mary's ledgers. She began her work but had a rough time concentrating on it, recalling the conversation of last night. The day went by very slowly for her and she waited for their dinner and down time together.

Mrs. McDougal picked at her meal. Mary tried to encourage her to eat more, to no avail. Instead she concentrated on making sure her mother drank more cranberry juice and water. Nurse Cragen had warned Mary about watching her mother's fluids and about dehydration in patients. After dinner they began their night much like the night before. Mary edged up on the front of her seat, much like a toddler waiting for her bedtime story. She looked at her mother, wanting to hear more details of her life.

Silence filled the room. Much like a child, she looked at her mother and said, "Tell me more."

Her mother, a perplexed look on her face, turned to her and said, "Tell you more about what?"

"Stories about your life. Come on, Mom."

"Oh, I don't want to be rambling on. I'll just bore you," she replied.

After more prompting, her mother thought a bit and pursed her lips. "There was this one time, your father, Timmy, and the other boys in the neighborhood were playin' stickball. It was sometime in the summer. I remember it was one of those hot, humid days of summer. Must have been one hundred degrees and humid as can be. The boys had opened a fire extinguisher, and we all played in the cool, refreshing water until the firemen came and turned it off. We all sat there, disappointed that our fun had ended when the boys decided to play a game of stickball. The girls in the neighborhood and me were playin' hopscotch on the sidewalk and watched as the boys played. The sun radiated off the pavement and the boys were drenched in sweat playin' ball.

"I guess it was close, because they were all yelling at one another. Jimmy and Timmy were on the same team—always were, you know. Well, Timmy was on third base, and he was the winning run. There were two outs in the last inning and your father was at the plate. He looked around the street while taunting the opposing players. He rattled the stick a couple times on a smashed Coke can that served as home plate. Timmy was yelling words of encouragement, 'C'mon, Jimmy, crack it outta here,' and the boy on the other team threw the pitch. Jimmy hit the ball real hard. It flew through the air over the outfielder's head across the parked cars and crashed right through the meat markets window.

"Old man Gallipoli, the local butcher, came running out. He was kind of a portly man. Blood was all over his apron from cutting meat and he held a meat cleaver in his hand. All the boys and girls looked briefly at one another then we ran. A younger man, the apprentice butcher, came out of the meat market and gave chase to us. He was in his mid-twenties and was closing in on us. Old Gallipoli only made it half a block. He was doubled over coughing, leaning up against the side of a building.

"The young butcher chased us for two blocks. Some of us ditched into an alley, our hearts felt like they were in our mouths as they beat against our chests. Your father and me were hiding behind a couple of garbage cans when the man came into the alley. We ducked down lower and watched him through two garbage cans to see his whereabouts. Jimmy put his finger over his mouth for me to be quiet. He took a couple of steps into the alley and looked as if he was staring straight at us. We were cornered. We ducked our heads down and breathed into our hands so that he could not hear us. He looked both ways, and then left. Jimmy laughed, 'That was a close one'."

"They never caught you?" Mary asked in astonishment.

"No," she replied. "But your father began feeling guilty. Timmy tried to talk him out of it, but he would have none of it. The next day, Jimmy, Timmy, and I walked down the street to the butcher shop. Timmy and I stayed on the other side of the street. There we all stood across from the butcher shop staring right at the scene of the crime. A wooden board covered half of the storefront window where the ball had crashed through. Your father walked over to the butcher shop alone. Timmy and I were worried. Timmy tried to talk him out of it at the last second. 'Jimmy, you're crazy. No one will ever know 'cept us.' Shaking his head sideways in disagreement, he said, 'I'll know' as he walked right into the butcher shop.

"We could see him talking to the junior butcher. The young man went and got old man Gallipoli out of the back of the shop. He came out from behind the counter and put his hand on Jimmy's shoulder. They spoke for about five minutes, and he came back out."

Her mother sighed and stopped. She looked confused and started talking about her job at Fordham University. "Some of the boys would be in trouble with the dean of discipline and would wait in the office to speak to him. The boys at the university got in as much trouble as young kids. Most of it was from drinking, you know."

Mary looked bewildered. She didn't understand her mother's progression of the story. Only then did she realize that her mother was recollecting two different stories. She needed to get her back on track without embarrassing or angering her. Mary interrupted and asked, "So what did the butcher say then?"

Her mother looked a little bit disoriented, but continued, "Oh, he had confessed to the butcher. Jimmy had taken all the blame. He explained to Gallipoli that yesterday he was scared when he ran and was sorry. He asked him how much the window was to repair. The butcher told him twenty dollars. Your father lowered his head and shrugged that he had no money. He lifted his head back up and offered to work it off at the butcher shop. The next four weeks, your father worked at the butcher store. Gallipoli even took a liking to him and gave him a part-time job after school.

"Jimmy's father was proud of him for doing the right thing. His mother was too and didn't mind that the butcher would even send him home with meats for their meals. Timmy always thought he was crazy fessin' up to the whole thing. I just know your father was a righteous man. Father Gallagher even told us so when he heard what Jimmy had done." With that she yawned deeply and made her way to bed.

Mary wished her goodnight. "Sleep well, Mom" and marveled at the story. The way her mother described it, she could picture the scene. Typing away, she put it all in her file on the computer.

The next day they left their apartment for the appointment with Dockendorff. He checked all her vitals and ordered x-rays and a CAT scan of Mrs. McDougal's midsection. Afterwards they met with Cragen. Some of the tests angered her mother. She felt they were insulting, that there was a certain indignity to it. The tests she most disliked were the cognitive ability tests.

After about ten minutes of taking the tests she looked at Cragen and muttered, "I know how to add and who the hell the president is." She stood up and walked out of the examining room. "I'll wait for you in the lobby, Mary." She purposely did not look at Cragen as she left the room and walked to the lobby waiting area.

Mary apologized to Cragen, and they discussed how everything was going. The nurse briefly stepped out and needed to confer with the doctor. Mary peeked out to check on her mother. Mrs. McDougal sat straight up, knees together with her pocketbook on them, almost at attention at the end of a chair. Mary became sad seeing her mother looking so annoyed, but knew Cragen was just doing her job.

Dockendorff and Cragen returned and shut the door. He put some x-rays and the CAT scan on the table. "Your mother's tumor has grown. It has wrapped itself around the pancreas and may be in her liver. It's tough to tell from this shot. How's her Alzheimer's?"

Mary shook her head in response. "Not well. Nurse Cragen and I have discussed my mother's Alzheimer's and it seems that it remains the same."

"Her loss of appetite and dementia are consistent with the diagnosis of the cancer and Alzheimer's," the doctor added.

Some people might not have liked Dockendorff's bedside manner, but Mary did. He was very much about the facts; straight to the point, they didn't try to sugarcoat anything. "How long does she have?" Mary asked.

Dockendorff paused a second before answering, "One to two weeks, three best-case scenario."

Mary tried to compose herself and nodded in an up and down manner, acknowledging his answer.

"I have some prescriptions here that you may want to fill, depending on how your mother is feeling." He handed Mary the prescription fill sheets. Her hands were trembling as she held the forms. She blinked a few times to clear her thoughts. Dockendorff and Cragen looked at her and waited. They could see that she had fallen into a semi-state of shock.

Cragen leaned over and touched her on the arm. "It's all going to be all right. We need to stay strong for your mother. Try and compose yourself before going into the waiting room." Mary looked around the room and tried to gather her thoughts. "Dr. Dockendorff said he would like to see her again the next week," the nurse said. He wished her a good day, leaving the room and closing the door behind him. Cragen told Mary, "Start thinking about the transition from home health to home hospice in the next couple of weeks."

Mary's numbness expanded to her body. She had known all the facts of her mother's condition and accepted them, but something, or someone, pulled an emotional trigger inside of her. She reached for some tissue to dry her eyes and clear her nose. After composing herself, Mary and the nurse discussed the next couple of weeks.

Mary thanked Cragen and left the conference room. She looked down the hall and saw her mother. Mrs. McDougal made eye contact with Mary. She was upset and Mary knew it. Standing at the door, she looked long at her mother. Her mother looked back in a pleading glare, wanting Mary to assist her in escaping her tormentors. Mary walked down the hall to her seated mother and asked, "Are you okay?" Her mother tightened her lips and nodded her head yes. Mary helped her get up, holding her by her elbow, until she gained her balance. The two left in silence. Visually shaken, they left the building and went home. Mrs. McDougal slept the entire afternoon.

Mary tried to do some of her MOD work, but was lost in thought. Two hours had passed and she hadn't even reviewed a single balance sheet. Frustrated, she closed the books and set about cleaning the living room and kitchen. Trying to busy herself, she figured it might clear her mind. While it did help in reducing her frenzied thoughts, the finality of her mother's disease began to gnaw at her. She contemplated researching alternative treatments and miracle cures again on the Internet.

Four hours had passed since the exam and at last her nerves began to calm down. Her breathing patterns and pulse returned to normal. She began to think rationally again.

The door to her mother's room opened. Fearing her walking about, Mary looked to the opening from the hallway at the mouth of the living room. Mrs. McDougal walked out, and a wide, deep yawn emerged from her as she walked into the living room. "I don't think I want to meet with that awful nurse again," she angrily snapped. "It ruined my whole day. I don't have to put up with that little bitch."

Mary was taken back. Her mother never cursed and seemed quite upset and irate. "We won't see her again, if you want to," Mary assured her. Mrs. McDougal put the television on and sat back. Mary asked, "What about dinner?"

She responded, "That nurse ruined my appetite."

"It's okay. I'm not that hungry either." After a couple minutes, Mary broke the silence and said, "Maybe we'll just have dessert later instead of dinner," looking at her mother for a response.

Mrs. McDougal was overcome with a big smile at Mary's suggestion. "That sounds good to me."

Mary sat back on the couch and moved toward her. Mrs. McDougal was on the right side of the couch. Mary gently moved to the middle of the couch and laid her head on her mother's shoulder. At first her mother was a little shocked, but reached over and put an afghan across Mary. She gently rested her cheek across the top of Mary's head. No words needed to be said. They resonated in the solace and peace each brought to one another. A mother–daughter moment, they felt comfort and relished in it.

An hour and a half passed. Mary slept like a baby in her mother's lap. Awakening, Mary felt cloudy. She had been in a deep sleep. Tossing the afghan off of her, she sat up. A moment passed and she asked her mother, "What have you been watching?"

Her mother answered, "I don't even know. I really wasn't paying attention." Mrs. McDougal had been caressing Mary's back and running her hand from the top of Mary's head to her shoulders. She had been reminiscing about their earlier years. Also, she had been thinking about her own mother and father.

Mary got up from the couch and went to the kitchen to get dessert. Mrs. McDougal continued reflecting about past memories. Mary prepared a special dessert. Cutting into an apple pie, she made each piece double servings. Laughing while cutting them, she knew her mother would comment on the size of the slices, but also knew her mother wouldn't leave a crumb. Opening the freezer, she placed two large scoops of cookie dough ice cream over each gigantic slice. Putting each dish in the microwave, she warmed them for thirty-three seconds each. She put a spoon in the middle of each scoop. The ice cream melted down over the slices of apple pie. The smell had enveloped the kitchen and drifted out to the living room.

"Is that our dessert I smell?" her mother called out.

"Uh-huh," Mary said while handing the dish to her mother. Mary waited for a response. After a couple of bites, Mrs. McDougal just gave her a guilty, schoolgirl smile.

Almost finished, Mary asked, "What were you thinking about before, Mom?"

Waiting a second, her mother responded, "Oh just about simpler times, my mother and father, days in the past, you know."

"What about them?" Mary pondered.

"Just how my parents came from a village, Leitrum, a county in southern Ireland, on a boat to Ellis Island. Me da was sick and quarantined for thirty days. He had the fever, you know. My mother stayed with her sister until he got released. Times were tough. Me da had to get a job when he finally got off the island. They stayed on the floor at my aunt's 'til me da found work. A lot of places back then wouldn't hire him 'cause he was Irish and all. He told me they even had signs in the windows, 'Irish need not apply.' Can you imagine that? He eventually got on with a job at the docks down on Fulton Street. Me mother would look after my sister and me. She would stitch and mend clothes. That's how I learned. Times were tough, but we managed," she said with a sigh.

Mary hung on every word. "What else?" she asked.

"Oh, I don't know, Mary. Just that we had nothing, but we were happy. I wonder if people are as happy as we were in those days. I mean, we had no car, television, clothes, and things. We had a couch, radio, and each other. Barely had enough to eat. Glad to just have a roof over our heads. Me da left Ireland because a pack of wolves had eaten his sheep one night. They had a small farm in Leitrum, County Sligo, but lost everything that night. Me mother wrote her sister and told her about the wolves and losing the sheep. Writing back and forth, me aunt spoke about all the great things in America. She offered their apartment for our family to stay in 'til me da could find work and get a place of our own. So they got on a ship in and moved to NYC. They were on the boat fifteen days. Down in the bottom, third class. My mother said it was awful hot and had a terrible stench from all the people. I wonder how life would have been if those wolves hadn't attacked that night. How things would have been if we had stayed in Leitrum."

She looked at Mary and smiled. Mary returned the smile and Mrs. McDougal continued, "You know one thing that I've missed in life?" Mary looked at her and slowly shook her head no. "It's your father," she said in a long, slow, sad voice. "We had such plans. I remember our days together. When we were just kids, our high school years, our wedding, and his eyes looking at me through the bus window as he rode off to war."

Her eyes filled with tears. Tears of a deep loss and tears of a living memory. "I wish you could have known him, Mary. He was a great man, a loving man. That's why I never married again. I had the best, your father."

Mary reached out and held her mother's hand. "Tell me more about my father, Mom."

Her mother thought for a moment and recalled their last night together. "We were tired from our wedding and made it back to Sedgwick Avenue. We spoke to our parents. I took a shower and your father went over to Timmy's. They set up their plan to meet the next morning. The bus was scheduled to depart at eight a.m. All sixty of the recruits would meet there and be off to basic training. That meant they would have to leave at about 7:15 a.m. to make it on time. Your father decided to take a shower. We had a late lunch at around one-thirty p.m.

"The plan was for Jimmy and me to eat with both our parents at my mother's apartment. The rest of the afternoon, we relaxed and got your father packed. He could only bring one bag, so we got his shirt and pants and everything else he needed ready. We talked about our future. We wanted two boys and two girls. He wanted a girl first that looked beautiful, like me, he said. He always knew what to say, your father. I always was glad you looked like him, not me. You see, I got pregnant our wedding night."

She reached out and touched Mary's face and looked into her eyes. "Jimmy had your eyes, identical. I always knew a piece of him was there in you when I saw your eyes." She stopped and reflected. Mary coaxed her into continuing on. "We had a wonderful dinner together at Mom's. We had turkey, ham, mashed potatoes, and string beans. I can still smell the butter from the potatoes, apple butter. We said a special prayer holding hands during grace. We thanked God for all our blessings, our wedding, and to keep Jimmy safe while he was gone.

"After dinner, we cleaned up. Your father said he was going to his parents. We would be staying there that night. Jimmy's father had taken the night off, since it was Jimmy's last night. We spoke to them for a couple hours and they went to bed around ten p.m. Jimmy's father had trouble going to bed that early because he worked the nights, but he knew we needed some alone time. We stayed up late talking about are four kids. We also spoke of the 'suit job' for Jimmy when he returned. We would take our vacations at the Jersey Shore. We talked about renting a bungalow, swimming in the ocean, and barbecuing.

"He wanted the best for me and his kids. We spoke of names for our children. Margaret, Patricia, Michael Jr., Thomas. 'Twas to be our family. We talked of taking a real honeymoon somewhere. We talked about education and how our kids would go to college. He would have been so proud of you, Mary. I was tired, it was almost midnight, but Jimmy wanted to go on our walk, one last time.

"I agreed and we walked down the river path. We ran into Officer O'Hara. He was walking Jimmy's father's beat, twirling his baton. He said hello and wished Jimmy good luck, knowing he was leaving for the war. We walked real slow, trying to prolong our last stroll together. We got to our tree and stopped. Your father kissed me and put his hand underneath my shirt on my back. I was on my toes reaching up to kiss him. He moved his hand forward to my stomach and pushed me back a bit. Then he looked at me, placing his palm flat on my belly. 'I think she's kicking,' he said.

"Eyes wide open, he pushed me away and ran a little bit. He let me catch up so that I fell into his arms. 'You devil,' I told him. To this day, I don't know if he was kidding or an angel told him I was pregnant. We walked back hand in hand and got ready for bed. It was one a.m. We slept like spoons the entire night. I'll never forget his smile or his touch.

"Morning came in the blink of an eye. Jimmy slipped out of bed and took a shower. He kissed me on the cheek as he got out of the bed. While he was getting ready, I heard his mother and father get up in the other room and walk to the kitchen. The scent of bacon and eggs began to fill the apartment. I put on your father's bathrobe and helped his mother set the table. When Jimmy was finished showering, we would have breakfast together.

"There were a lot of deep, longing stares at Jimmy. None of us knew when we would see him again. If he caught us looking at him, he would just give us one of his reassuring smiles. He saw me gazing at him and whispered, 'Don't worry, everything's gonna be all right.' We spoke of the wedding and how grand an affair it had been. The Mass celebration, the food and drink, the dancing, we all vividly remembered and shared our accounts with one another. We talked about the guests and how great it was to have seen all of them. Although everyone lived nearby, all their lives were caught up in work and they hadn't time to visit one another.

"We talked about Jimmy's upcoming service to his country and how we were all proud of him. Then we joked that he would be replacing General Patton soon and bringing this awful war to an early end. At the end of the table, Jimmy reached out his hands. With his right, he held my hand, with his left his mother's. He told us, 'Don't worry, I'll be home soon. I love all of you and you'll be in my thoughts and prayers every night.'

"He looked to the end of the table at his father, rolling his lips inward, and he nodded slowly at him. No words were spoken between them. It isn't like mothers and daughters. You could feel the intense love between father and son. This is when Mrs. McDougal and I cleared the table. Jimmy and his father retrieved his luggage from the bedroom. It was time for him to leave. He hugged his mom and kissed her goodbye. He shook his father's hand and Patrolman McDougal put his arm around him then saluted him.

"I went with your father and Timmy to the bus stop. The three of us sat on the bus bench awaiting its arrival. I saw the bus coming at the top of the hill. I knew your father saw it too. His grip on my hand grew stronger. I put my other hand around his. I briefly looked over and wished Timmy 'Good luck and goodbye. Keep an eye on this guy for me.' Timmy got up from the bench. Jimmy and I stood up also, and he gave me a long kiss. The bus pulled up and half a dozen or so people that were waiting along with us got on.

"While holding hands, he looked at me and told me, 'I love you' and with that, he picked up his suitcase. He gave me another short kiss, leaned over, and whispered in my ear, 'And take care of our little girl.' He gently gave me a pat on the rear and got on the bus. Sitting by the window he smiled and put his hand on the window. The bus pulled away as I waved emphatically to your father." After a long, pregnant pause, in a hushed voice she finished, "It was the last time I ever saw him."

Mary had not been prepared for this story. She sat there, bawling, next to her mother.

26

A BUN IN THE OVEN

Jimmy and Timmy had started their army careers. Taking a bus to the recruiting station, signing in, they looked around and sized up the other recruits. About sixty of them waited to be bused to the airport. Timmy knew some of the boys from the neighborhood. There were a couple of Italian boys from Arthur Avenue and a Jewish kid from 183rd Street. The boys all joked on the bus and the mood was light. They spoke of killing Germans and Japanese, being war heroes, seeing the world. None of them had ever even fired a gun before, and most hadn't been farther than Jersey in their travels. Little did they know the horrors they would face in a few short months.

Nerves began to set in on their flight from New York to Texas. The general mood began to tense up as they began their descent. The plane grew much quieter as the chatter almost stilled. They landed in Texas shortly before three p.m. It was sunny and ninety-two degrees. As they deplaned, roll call was sounded, and they were separated into different groups. It was here that they realized the party was over. The drill instructors lacked the same pleasant demeanor as the recruiters. They were met with, "Get your scrawny little asses up there on that bus."

The screaming was horrible as each tried to get on the bus. The boys tripped over one another trying to get their bags and obey the command to board the bus. From here, they were led to a large processing area in a separate building. They were ordered to strip naked and get in line, and a doctor checked each boy for lice, tooth decay, vision, hernia, flat feet, and any physical abnormalities. Here they were issued undergarments and uniforms. They were led to twelve barbers, stationed across from one another in lines of six, who promptly shaved all their hair down to the scalp. Dog tags were draped around their necks.

They had begun their indoctrination into the U.S. Army. The drill instructors kept their inflaming, derogatory pseudonyms hurled at them. "Now you ladies are ready for the dance," barked a drill instructor. "Move it, move it," was also a popular phrase for the instructors. It seemed as though all the boys were referred to as "a useless piece of shit" often. Each boy wondered what the hell he had gotten himself into.

After the initial two-hour process, they made their way to an assigned barracks. Once again they were hollered at and shoved into their quarters. They had each been issued a footlocker, a slim wall locker, as well as half a bunk bed.

Jimmy and Timmy quickly caught on that the army didn't use the same recipes as their mothers. Runny potatoes, carrots, and a tasteless piece of meat was their dinner. After supper they ran back to the barracks. It was seven-thirty p.m. now and most of the boys were exhausted from the day's events. The drill sergeant told them to unpack their belongings and get ready for bed. Lights out at nine p.m. The barracks was filled with loud snoring by 9:15 p.m.

At four-thirty a.m. the next morning, the drill instructor came out from his room at the back of the barracks. He surveyed the sleeping boys in the barracks before lifting up a stainless steel, five-gallon pot and started loudly rattling a stainless steel soup ladle inside of it while flashing the lights on overhead. The boys jumped out of bed at attention at the end of the beds.

"Drop your cocks and grab your socks," he screamed. "Outside in five minutes." It was completely dark and the boys were still half asleep. Utter chaos took over the inside of the barracks.

He began by running them two and a half miles out, then two and a half miles back in. "Nothing like a brisk morning run before breakfast, girls," he said. He made them sprint the last half-mile. At the end of the run, some boys fell to their knees, some doubled over, and still others were puking from the run. Leaving them alone for two minutes to get their wind back, he got them into formation again and marched them to the mess hall.

It was here, at their first breakfast, where they were introduced to "shit on a shingle," otherwise known as oatmeal on burnt toast. Timmy tried to eat it, but had trouble keeping it down. He gagged from the taste. Jimmy told him to try smaller bites and to drink more coffee to kill the taste. The coffee resembled motor oil, thick and extremely strong. They were allowed twenty-five minutes for breakfast. After their breakfast, they would perform calisthenics the rest of the morning.

Following a forty-five-minute lunch, they started another five-mile run. Many of the boys ran to the side of the trail to vomit. They had completed their first twenty-four hours of basic. Before lights out Timmy confided to Jimmy, "Maybe we made a mistake joining up. Life at the job site sure seemed better than this," he complained. He asked Jimmy, "Do you think we can get out of it somehow?"

Jimmy shook his head no and said, "It's gonna get better. Don't worry about it. Get some sleep."

Their second, third, fourth, and fifth days were much of the same. Rigorous calisthenics, running, and belittling were standard operating procedure. The only uncertainties were at what hellacious time the drill sergeant would rattle the stainless steel pot or what crappy food they would be served. There was also the uncertainty of what indignant names he would call the boys that day as the drill sergeants always had new defamations in their vocabulary. It was like déjà vu other than that.

Jimmy and Timmy penned letters home on the fifth night as they lay in bed. Timmy wrote one to his mother and one to Catherine. Jimmy wrote one to his mother and father and one to Maggie. He made sure not to alarm them and told them everything was just fine. Mrs. McDougal and Maggie were a nervous wreck, not knowing what had happened to their son and husband. Patrolman McDougal pretty much knew the drill that Jimmy and Timmy would be exposed to. He made sure not to alarm the women as to their plight. He reassured them that the army was getting them in shape and training them with all the skills they would need for their service.

Jimmy did let on in his letter to his mother that he did miss her cooking. To Maggie he explained the physical demands and that although it was challenging for most, it was a breeze for a McDougal. Closing, he wrote of his love for her and questioned the well-being of their daughter. Smiling, he sealed the letter as the drill instructor said, "Lights out, ladies."

During the following weeks, the training escalated. Hand-to-hand combat simulations started. This was extremely physical, and Jimmy and Timmy were partners for many of the drills. They started by taking it easy on one another, but began taking the instruction to heart. Two other boys were doing the exercise lightly when the drill instructor took notice of them. He separated the boys and used them as volunteers while displaying the maneuvers. He took the one young fellow and squared off against him. The boy was frightened and did not know what to do. The instructor screamed at him to charge and attack him. After more prodding and screaming, the boy took a swing at the instructor, who moved to the side while grabbing his arm and flipped him onto his back. The dust came up from his body as he was slammed in the floor, all the air knocked out of his lungs. Two assistants picked up the boy and helped him to his feet. The drill instructor promptly used the boy's partner as his next volunteer and he met the same fate. Jimmy and Timmy whispered to each other that it looked like he had hurt them as the boys were moaning as they lay on the ground.

"Show no mercy to your enemy. Surely they won't to you," he uttered. After the last volunteer was removed from the ground, he displayed different techniques for killing the enemy.

Jimmy and Timmy practiced the takedown and kill. Jimmy threw Timmy to the ground, but had a problem with the final kill maneuver. After several attempts in vain, the drill instructor noticed his hesitance at finishing the kill maneuver. He made his way around to observe them from behind. After Jimmy took Timmy down, the drill sergeant got right in Jimmy's face. "Now, finish him off, damn it," he yelled, inches from Jimmy's face, battering him with saliva. The drill sergeant repeated his order, but Jimmy froze.

He pushed Jimmy to the ground and grabbed the bayonet from his hand. He dove on top of him, spun him around, and put the bayonet to his neck. All the boys had circled around them to see the display. "Now PFC McDougal is dead. Dead. He is dead because he did not take the initiative to engage his enemy. Do I make myself clear?"

The boys answered in chorus, "Yes sir, Drill Sergeant, sir."

He threw the bayonet on the ground at Jimmy's head in disgust. "Now PFC McDougal will display the correct method or we will do this exercise until he gets it right," he yelled.

Jimmy lay on the ground motionless. Blood from his nose had begun to flow after the drill sergeant had thrown him to the ground. He ground his teeth, angry from the humiliation he had suffered in front of the other men in the platoon. He did not like to be made an example of, to be embarrassed. Jimmy jumped to his feet. The instructor handed him his bayonet and blew his whistle to start the drill once again.

There was a fire in Jimmy's eyes as he lunged at Timmy, grabbed him by his arm, and twisted it. In the same maneuver, he positioned his rump and back while hurling Timmy over his shoulder to the ground. The air left Timmy's lungs, and his eyes rolled back in his head as he hit the dirt. Jimmy pounced on him and put the bayonet to his throat and simulated striking it across.

After that, an incision appeared on Timmy's throat where Jimmy had simulated the bayonet kill and blood started to emerge from it. He put his hand to his throat, feeling the cut, and blood quickly squeezed through his fingers, covering his hand, as he looked at Jimmy in bewilderment. Timmy was in a state of shock.

Jimmy tossed the bayonet on the ground and walked away. An animal in him had emerged that he had never felt before. The drill sergeant kept up his platoon saying, "There, there, now that's the way to kill the enemy and perform the maneuver correctly." He put his hand out for Timmy to grab and assisted him to his feet. He inspected the incision in Timmy's neck and told him it didn't look bad. Ordering him to wash up and report back in five minutes, he sent Timmy to the latrine. The platoon also took a break, but Jimmy stood alone by himself, staring into the distance.

That night after dinner, the drill sergeant called lights out. The boys were exhausted from the day. Timmy and Jimmy had not spoken about the exercise. Jimmy had remained silent the rest of the day. They lay in their bunks as some boys drifted off to sleep. Others whispered to one another or joked around.

In the bunk next to theirs were two brothers. The Falletti brothers were from the Bronx also. Residing off of Fordham Road in an Italian neighborhood, they were big boys with loud mouths. The older of the two, Nick, began wondering aloud to his younger brother, Michael, "I wonder if the platoon can count on these Irish pricks from Sedgwick Ave to take off their dresses if we need 'em in a fight? You know what I mean, Mikey?" as he playfully kicked the upper bunk mattress.

Mikey turned over and peered down to the lower bunk at his brother and answered, "I think they'd rather play hopscotch, jump rope, or cut out paper dolls."

The barracks erupted in hushed laughs. The Fallettis kept the verbal taunts up. Nick added, "These two couldn't fight their way out of a wet paper bag."

Young Mikey kept the drubbing up, adding, "You think they're like those downtown faggots you see, huh, Nick? Maybe they're just faggots, that's what I think."

The verbal assaults kept on as they continued to stir the barracks. Jimmy stirred in his bed and couldn't take it anymore. He sprang out of the bunk and grabbed the older Falletti brother, Nick, from his bed. Nick swung to hit Jimmy with a large roundhouse punch. Jimmy ducked and countered with a punch to his abdomen. Nick doubled over. Jimmy grabbed the back of his head with both his hands and swiftly brought his knee to Nick's face. Nick crumbled to the ground. Jimmy picked him up and grabbed him by the back of his undershirt and forearm and violently propelled him into the wall locker. Nick collapsed at the front of the locker; a pool of blood began to encircle his head as he lay on the ground unconscious.

Timmy had been engaged with the younger brother, Mikey. Both had leapt out of the top bunk bed, almost colliding in midair before landing. Timmy delivered the first blow, surprising Mikey with an uppercut to his jaw. Dazed, he tried to punch back. Timmy avoided it and punched him in his solar plexus, knocking the wind out of him temporarily. He then hit him with a jab in his eye. Mikey got up, but Timmy put him in a full nelson wrestling move that left him powerless.

The rest of the platoon was watching, either sitting up in their bunks or standing alongside for the ruckus. The lights came on and the drill sergeant in his army T-shirt, boxer shorts, and army boots raced down the middle of the barracks to the ruckus. "Who the hell is making all the noise in my barracks?" He stood between the Fallettis and Jimmy and Timmy's bunk beds assessing the scene.

There was Nick, now conscious, lying with his back propped up against the wall locker, wiping the blood from his face with his hand and the sleeve of his T-shirt. Timmy had let Mikey go and the three of them stood at attention, staring ahead. The drill sergeant looked around to see if there are was anything else he should be aware of. Jimmy, Timmy, and the Fallettis now stood at attention in front of their footlockers with the other boys in the aisle.

The drill sergeant paced back and forth and got in the face of Mark Weisberg, the Jewish kid from 183rd Ave. He was nose to nose with Weisberg, screaming in his face, "PFC Weisberg, what the hell went on here? Did you see what happened?" Weisberg stood his ground, silent. "I asked you a question, Private Weisberg. Are you trying to make me angry? Answer the god damn question."

Weisberg thought for a second and answered that he didn't have his glasses on and couldn't see what had happened. This greatly angered the drill sergeant. "Are you trying to make a mockery of me, Private Weisberg?"

"No sir," he answered.

Taking three steps, he stood in front of Nick Falletti. Blood still trickled from his eye and nose. His T-shirt sleeve was stained red with the blood he had wiped from his face. "And you, Falletti, what happened to you tonight?"

"I fell outta my bunk, Drill Sergeant," he answered in his deep New York accent. The boys held back their snickers, biting their tongues or the side of their mouths trying to contain themselves.

"Fell out of your bunk? Why, that's downright careless of you, Private Falletti. What about your brother? Did he fall out of his bunk too? Does you r mother have rails on the side of you boys' beds at home still?"

Mikey's eye had begun to swell shut. He put the same question to Mikey. Mikey answered, I musta fell outta my bunk too."

This really drew the ire of the drill sergeant, but in the same sense filled him with some respect; the boys were becoming a unit. He looked over and, out of the corner of his eye, he could see blood on Jimmy's knee from Nick's face, and Timmy's knuckles were bloody from punching Mikey. Knowing exactly what and who had been involved, he paced the wooden floor of the barracks as his polished boots echoed, as the boys stood at attention. "Since there seems to be some problem with the bunk, we'll have to have a safety drill on proper procedures for sleeping. In the meantime, since we're all awake, and no one cares to sleep, we'll go on a midnight run so that we can sleep later tonight. Out front in five," he notified the platoon.

The boys were disenchanted, but rushed to be ready. He confronted the Fallettis and told them to clean themselves up. Mikey scowled at Timmy and Jimmy as the brothers made their way to the latrine. Nick pointed at the boys and through clenched teeth said, "This ain't over you, Irish pricks."

Returning from their run at two a.m., the boys proceeded to get ready for bed once again. The four were removing their boots when the assistant drill instructor told them to report outside immediately. The rest of the platoon listened as the drill sergeant issued different orders to the Fallettis, Jimmy, and Timmy. Push-ups, running in place, marching for two straight hours. Four a.m. and they were about to drop dead from exhaustion.

He looked at them and pointed to the latrine. He handed them four toothbrushes and two pails. "Now scrub the latrine, since y'all can't sleep. I better not see a speck of dirt."

The four dropped to their hands and knees and scrubbed away. A glow in the barracks emitted from the latrine light, where the four boys scrubbed away. The silhouette of their shadows, scrubbing, was visible to the other boys in their beds. The toothbrushes swooshed as the heads hit the grout lines in between the tiles on the floor.

They finished at five a.m. and dragged themselves into bed. Their heads had barely hit the pillow before they fell asleep. A half-hour later, the drill sergeant emerged, rattling the pot with the ladle. They struggled to open their eyes in a state of shock. The foursome labored to make it through the day. The drill sergeant kept his eye on them during the entire day's training. That night, the four went to bed. An enervation had encompassed them. Their bodies ached, depleted of all energy. No mention was made by any of the platoon about the incident. Most did not want to anger the Fallettis. They were hotheads and not shy of fisticuffs. But Jimmy and Timmy had established a newfound respect within the barracks. The other boys in the platoon quickly dubbed them "The Fighting Irish."

They had finished their first six weeks of basic training. Having concluded hand-to-hand combat training, their next instruction would be weaponry. The platoon was brought into a classroom and the drill sergeant introduced a weapons expert. He stood in front of the class, a M1 Garand semi-automatic rifle on the table in front of him. He picked up a rifle and discussed basic handling of the weapon. He described how to hold the rifle to avoid shooting oneself or another member of the platoon.

A hillbilly from Arkansas, Billy Bob Wooton, commented, "Only a moron would do that." He was a self-proclaimed marksman, having shot "coons" since the age of seven.

The drill sergeant told him to, "Shut the hell up and listen or I'll use you for target practice."

He muttered, "None of you 'Yanks' could hit me, not even the side of a barn." He grinned through his missing teeth. Most of the boys in the platoon were from lower New York and had never seen a rifle or a shotgun. The few members from Arkansas and western Pennsylvania were accustomed to the long guns, being raised in a hunting culture.

Most paid careful attention as the instructor explained further intricacies of the weapon. He did a detailed how-to on assembling and reassembling the rifle. Next he explained how to clean and care for it. Interceding, the drill sergeant stressed the importance of the lesson. He detailed how a rifle might not perform in the field and the learning from this lesson just might save their lives. This brought most of the boys back to attention. The instructor resumed and the lesson took the entire morning.

After lunch, each boy was issued a rifle. The reaction from each boy was extremely different. Some were mesmerized, some scared, others indifferent to the weapon. The afternoon would be spent assembling and reassembling the rifle for five hours. By the end of the day, they were all able to perform these actions, literally with their eyes closed.

The next day they were drilled on marching with the rifle and how to hold it. Immediately after, they were taught how to use the rifle as a hand-to-hand weapon, not a firing weapon. They were taught how to put the bayonet on, how to use the rifle defensively and offensively. The allure of the weapon lost most of its magic as the boys learned to respect it as a tool.

Jimmy wrote Maggie a few times a week when time allowed. The army demanded so much of them physically and mentally. At night most boys would fall asleep from exhaustion. Some would play cards and the rest would write letters. Jimmy never dwelt on the negatives about the army in his letters. In fact, he made light of some of the absurdities. He joked that they must be in some remedial unit because they were still practicing marching after eight weeks.

Maggie would check her mailbox daily. If it was empty, she would run up the five flights to the apartment to see if her mother had already retrieved the mail. "Anything from Jimmy?" were the first things out of her mouth when she would see her mother. Maggie would write back and fill Jimmy in on all the Sedgwick Ave. gossip. Their young hearts longed for each other. They had never been apart since their first meeting in first grade. Only once, when the McDougals took a weekend vacation to the Jersey shore, did they not see each other daily.

They entered their ninth week at Camp Fenning. The drill sergeant started their morning at six a.m.

He actually let them sleep in. This week was different. He addressed them as men, not ladies, little girls, or anything else indignant. The men looked at one another, immediately recognizing his new address. "This is the last week of training together, men. We need to work on a few things, but this will be a top-fit, cohesive unit. Outside in five," he stated.

Their last week proved to be the least testing. They were ready to move on to the infantry training at Fort Meade. Infantry training would last two weeks. Upon completion, they would be deployed, but where?

The men marched in formation, past the commanding officer at Camp Fenning, following the platoon in front of them. The commander and his supporting officers saluted the men as they marched by. From here, they were boarded on a bus to the airfield for a flight to Fort Meade.

The men loaded all their gear and got on the transport plane. The mood was light, with the rumors already starting about where they would be deployed. Some thought the Pacific while others were positive it would be the European Theatre of Operations.

Infantry training proved to be much different than basic. They drilled under harsh conditions. Live fire rocketed as they crawled under barbwire with their rifles through the mud. The concussions from the blasts were enormous. Dirt and mud flew in every direction. Bullets flew by, just feet over their heads. The instructors screamed at them to keep moving. Some of the men were paralyzed in fright. Members of the platoon would slap them. Others would drag the frozen soldier, to keep the line moving. They practiced artillery and machine guns under live fire. Each member of the platoon needed to be cross-trained in case another member was injured or killed.

Maggie had gotten word of some of the atrocities of training. A boy from down the block had been injured at basic training and sent home. He had told her of the hellish conditions. She wrote Jimmy asking about some of her concerns. He wrote back and changed the topic, not addressing her questions, writing that he had met a lot of people from all across the country and how nice they all were or that the food wasn't as bad as he thought it would be.

The tenth week passed and the platoon had only one week left before deployment. Sunday morning the mail call jeep pulled up. The platoon circled around the jeep. "Pound, Henderson, Weisberg, Calhoun," the men from the jeep yelled out the names of some of the platoon members. Continuing, they followed with "O'Hern, Smith, Falletti, McDougal."

Jimmy was handed his mail. He pushed forward through the crowd to get to the men distributing it. Plucking the letter out of the soldier's hand, he retreated back to his bunk, looking at the envelope, immediately recognizing it was from Maggie. He turned it over to open it and a lipstick kiss was implanted on the back of the envelope. He unsealed the letter and lifted it out up to his nose. Maggie always dabbed her letters with a little of her perfume. His eyes slowly closed as the scent brought her image to his mind. Opening his eyes, he began reading the letter. Maggie went on about the new priest at a neighboring parish and how some of the new tenants were loud and obnoxious in the apartment building. Reading her last paragraph, he was overtaken with a blank stare. All it said was, "Your baby girl is doing fine, Love Maggie."

He thought for a minute, until a voice alerted him, "McDougal, you got more mail out here." He ran out and found another letter from Maggie. It started, "I hope you received the other letter first." She wanted to lead him on and further wrote, "I anxiously await the return of my child's father. I'm so proud to be the mother of your child."

Jimmy ran around the barracks, frantically trying to get enough change to call Maggie. "You got any change? You got any change?" he kept repeating as he ran up to members of the platoon. After hearing his pleas and being alerted to his pending fatherhood, the men all generously gave him their change for the call, refusing his attempts to give them paper money in exchange.

Jimmy sprinted to the phone booth six barracks down. He paced back and forth as another man finished his call. Clumsily he collided with the folding door as he rushed to enter the phone booth. Hastily removing the coins from his pocket, they fell all over the phone booth. His hands shook as he tried to put coin after coin into the slot. The operator assisted him with a long-distance call.

Maggie's mother answered and yelled to her husband, "It's Jimmy, it's Jimmy. Get Maggie, hurry. It's long-distance." Maggie ran to the phone and they spoke for the first time in ten weeks. They professed their love for one another and how much they missed each other. Maggie kept talking.

Jimmy cut her off, "It's true, is it true?"

"What are you talking about?" she said.

"Are you pregnant?" he jolted back.

"Of course I am, silly, didn't you get the letter about our baby girl?" Maggie answered. They laughed and cried and started talking about names and plans for their future when the operator returned. "One dollar seventy-five cents, please. Would you please deposit one dollar seventy-five cents for an additional three minutes," the operator said, interrupting their conversation. "Please deposit another dollar and seventy-five cents for an additional three minutes," the operator repeated.

Jimmy put in all the change he had and they spoke for an additional five minutes before the operator cut in, asking for more money. Jimmy spoke over her voice and said, "I don't have any more money. I love you."

Maggie answered, "I do..." but the line went dead.

"I'm sorry, sir, you went over your allotted paid time..."

Jimmy hung up, slamming the phone onto the hook, disappointed at not being able to speak longer, but immensely excited at his pending fatherhood. He went back to the barracks, where Timmy and the other men offered their congratulations. Even the Fallettis shook his hand.

Sitting up in his bunk that night, Jimmy could not sleep. He took a flashlight from his locker and put a blanket over his head, dangling it over his knees. He penned a long letter to Maggie, expressing his love and affection as well as his exuberance over her pregnancy. It was the week of Thanksgiving and he explained, "I feel so lonely without you, a deep emptiness and a hollow fills my soul. I dream about our nightly walks and holding one another's hands. Looking into each other's eyes."

The letter ended only when he ran out of paper at two a.m. He walked to the latrine as Timmy was exiting it. He put out his hand to shake Jimmy's. He put the other on his shoulder and told him, "I'm proud and excited for you."

The men were given off on Thanksgiving Day. They sat idle around the barracks, and all missed their families and loved ones. Exchanging stories of their family traditions, they spoke of friends, family, and feasts. The Falettis spoke of the special sauce their mother would make. Wooton told how he'd chop the heads off of the turkey the night before "so they was fresh."

The army had a special meal for the troops that night. Turkey, ham, mashed potatoes, gravy, cranberry sauce, vegetables, and apple pie. The special meal was much better than their counterparts, already deployed, would be receiving that evening. During the day, the men spent their time walking the base, playing basketball or football and making calls home to family. The line at the phone booth was twelve deep as men waited to call their families to wish them a happy Thanksgiving.

Friday after Thanksgiving came and the men were anxious. They all wanted to know where they would be deployed. Eagerly they sat around the barracks, like expectant fathers pacing and jawing to one another.

Lieutenant Sprocket walked into the barracks and all fell silent. When he stated he had an announcement to make, one could hear a pin drop in the room. Opening the envelope and unfolding the paper, he took out their orders and read, "By order of the United States Armed

Forces, and Commander of the Allied Forces, Dwight D. Eisenhower, under command of General Omar Bradley, you are hereby enrolled in the U.S. First Army, U.S. 106th, infantry division."

Then the barracks broke out into cheers and applause. They were going to Europe. "We move out in three days," he added. They slapped each other's backs, and the excitement rang through the barracks.

"I knew it. I told you so. We're going to fight the Krauts," one soldier yelled to another.

Their training had ended and they were Europe bound. The next three days moved swiftly at times and boorishly slow at others.

It seemed forever for them to wait, but seventy-two hours later they would be on a transport to the U.K. From there, they would receive their orders on where in the European Theatre of Operations they would be deployed.

Jimmy immediately penned his parents and Maggie to tell them the news. His parents were happy that he would be under General Bradley. They had heard that General Patton was hard on his men and suffered higher casualties. Maggie read his letter and just felt relief knowing that it was all moving forward and that Jimmy would return soon enough.

The lieutenant read about some history of the First Army and urged the man to listen to what a proud group they would be a part of. He stated, "The First Army was activated during World War I and reactivated in 1933. After D-Day, they were under the Twenty-first Army group and now command all American ground forces."

The men were excited to be part of the First Army. They celebrated that night and bought beer into the barracks, toasting Ike, General Bradley, and First Army. They were en-route to war and did not know the evil that was brewing afar. Lost in their excitement, friendship, and patriotism, the boys only knew of the gallantry exhibited in the recruiting movies. Despite an early morning the next day, the men celebrated, and conversation filled the barracks long after lights out.

At five a.m. they packed all their gear and set it outside for loading. One last chow at the mess hall before they began their flight. After breakfast, while waiting on line to board, Jimmy took a long last look at his surroundings before being nudged in the back by Timmy to get in the plane. They sat, shoulder to shoulder, for fourteen hours in the cargo plane. The flight was long and uncomfortable and turbulence caused some to get sick. The plane smelled from vomit, excrement, and body odor. Jimmy put his nose underneath the collar of his uniform trying to keep the smell from entering his nasal cavity. He foraged through his wallet to get out his picture of Maggie. It was black and white, and the edges were worn from being taken in and out of his wallet so often. He stared at the picture wishing he could be with her soon. He held the picture close to his heart and prayed for her well-being. Suddenly a red light came on overhead and the lieutenant told them to get ready for landing.

They arrived in the U.K. as the plane emerged from a deep fog and touched down. The wheels brought up water from the light rain. The date was December 10. They loaded up all their gear and were issued quarters. That night they were told they'd be moving out in the morning. Their mission was to take them to the Western Front in Belgium. Here the First Army would take root and protect the valued gained grounds that the allies had taken.

27

THE LAST RITES

Mrs. McDougal's health took a turn for the worst. She had been sleeping twelve hours a night and sometimes up to an additional four hours during the day. Her appetite came in spurts. Concerned, Mary had called the doctor about this. Dockendorff admitted that this was not unusual, but took heed of Mary's concern and proceeded to prescribe an appetite stimulator, Megestral. Mary also noticed that her mother winced in pain when she thought Mary was not looking. He also prescribed a morphine pill. Home health began to come to the apartment every other day.

Her mother refused to go down to Dockendorff's office for visits anymore. She complained that they tired her, and there was nothing they could do for her anyway.

"I'm not going to be one of their lab rats to do studies on, Mary," she blasted out in frustration.

Mary sighed and actually agreed with her mother's stance. She has been poked and prodded enough and didn't need to put up with it anymore. The last set of x-rays the prior week had shown the tumor had grown substantially. It was now attached to her mother's pancreas and had started spreading to her liver.

Mrs. McDougal did not wait for Dockendorff's prognosis. Instead she waited for Mary to meet with him. At dinner, in a monotone, depressed voice, she asked Mary, "How long do I have? Don't sugarcoat anything, please."

Mary cleared a lump in her throat, trying not to be emotional and replied, "Two weeks, Mom. I guess, that's what he had initially said," she added in a matter of fact tone.

Mrs. McDougal ran her fingers across the rosary beads in her left hand. Her hand looked terribly emaciated. The skin was extremely dry and draped over the bones in her hand. She had developed a slight tremor and the beads shook as she passed one bead after another through her thumb and index finger. "I've got plenty of time then," she answered and left the table. Later that night she asked Mary the same question, not remembering that she had asked earlier that day.

Mary gave her the same response and left briefly for her bedroom to compose herself. Returning from the bedroom she saw her mother with the lamp turned on and a shoebox on her lap, taking letters out of the box one by one and reading them. "What have you there?" Mary asked.

Mrs. McDougal smiled and replied, "All the letters your father sent me during the war. He wrote me all the time and I wrote him too." There were fifty or so letters in the box as she began to read them. Mary just looked at her to see her reactions.

While reading one of the letters she commented, "Well, I really shouldn't be telling you this, but your father and me were in the sixth grade. We musta been around twelve years old, you know. We took one of our walks down the path on the river. It was hot, I remember, right before school lets out for summer. We were skipping stones and having fun when Jimmy spots a couple frogs. I scurried knee-high into the water.

"Your father spotted a littered container in the wastebasket next to the bench. I threw some stones to scare the frogs from their lily pads onto the shore. They hopped off their pads and Jimmy chased them down and put them in the container. He sneaked them into his apartment while his mother cooked dinner in the kitchen. He kept them in his apartment under his bed, so that his mother and father would not find them. One frog let out a large croak and his mother chastised him for belching and not excusing himself.

"Earlier that week, I had been caught talking during class. There was this older nun, her name was Sister Ann Marie. She had a reputation for being one of the stricter teachers at the school. She became extremely angry when she caught me talking. She asked me, 'What was more interesting than my lecture on English?' I replied, 'Nothing, Sister.'

"She gave me a slap across my face and told me to put my hands into fists out on top of the desk. With that, she took her ruler and struck me across my knuckles. I began to cry and she told me to put out the other hand. I guess I put the other hand out too slow, 'cause she hit the second hand even harder and slapped me across the side of my head again. She then asked if anyone else would like to talk in class. I sat there crying, trying to control myself."

Mary couldn't believe her ears. "You're kidding; the nun hit you that hard for talking?"

Her mother assured her it was true and continued. "Your father was so mad that that old biddy nun hit me. He swore we'd get even. Oh, how he hated the nuns. Jimmy used to say they just needed a broomstick and a pointy hat, and they'd be a twin for a witch. The next day, Jimmy, Timmy, and I walked to school. We went to my class when the bell rang. Sister Ann Marie promptly told the boys to leave. You see, the girls were all taught by Dominican nuns and the boys by La Salle Christian brothers.

"Timmy distracted Sister Ann Marie while Jimmy circled up from behind her. She was a great big fat woman and the habit she wore draped her like a tent. Jimmy slid one of the frogs in each of her side pockets and the two boys left. She sat at the front of the classroom trying to regain order over us children. I sat in the first row with my eyes wide open pinned on the sister. I could see Jimmy and Timmy's heads looking through the small window in the classroom door. I guess the frogs began to feel a little distraught at their new habitat and started moving and jumping around in her pockets. She began to make some weird facial contortions, not knowing what was going on in her pockets.

"As she put her plump fingers into her pockets, a look of sheer disgust and fright overcame her round face. The frogs began croaking and hopping around in her pockets. She jumped around and ran around the classroom screaming for help. 'Aaaaaahh, aaaaaahh,' she screamed, running around the front of the classroom.

"All the students were laughing at the sight. Her pleas were heard down the hallway and Father Gallagher came running to the classroom to see what the commotion was about. Jimmy and Timmy doubled over laughing their heads off in the hall. They turned and ran once the principal and Father Gallagher arrived. He chased down Sister Ann Marie and held her in a corner while assisting to remove the frogs from her habit. The classroom was in hysteria. He took the frogs outside of the fire door and let them loose. Sister Ann Marie was visibly shaken.

He asked, 'How did it happen?'

"She thought for a while and then said, 'Jimmy and Timmy were in the classroom earlier. I don't know,' as she sniffled. He shook his head and left.

"Father Gallagher walked down to the other side of the school, where the boys held class. He peered into the classroom looking for Jimmy and Timmy. Timmy saw his head in the window and nudged Jimmy. Timmy whispered to your father, 'He knows it was us.'

"Jimmy answered him, 'It was worth it.'

"Father Gallagher walked into the class and spoke to Brother Robert. He pointed to Jimmy and Timmy with his finger and told them, 'You two, with me.' Removing them from class, he brought them to the Dean of Discipline, Brother Brady.

"The brother asked them, 'Were you two responsible for the frogs?' Each stuck to their story and replied in tandem, 'No.' He further questioned the boys, thinking he could break their story and alibi. Pulling a bullwhip out of his desk drawer, he slammed it onto the desk in front of the boys, trying to stir them. 'Did you do it?' he repeated.

"Each one flatly denied having anything to do with it. The boy squirmed with fear. They knew that the punishments at the school were severe. 'Wait here,' he said, leaving the bullwhip in plain sight on the desk. He closed the door and spoke to Father Gallagher outside his office. Jimmy and Timmy tried to listen, but could not hear their discussion. Their hearts beat fast and pounded against their chests. They dared not look back to see the brother and Father talking.

"'Stick with the story, no matter what,' your father said. Jimmy maneuvered himself in his chair to see a reflection in the mirror behind Brother Brady's desk. From the reflection, he could see them talking through the window behind them. At this moment he became a little relieved when he saw them actually laughing outside the door. Father Gallagher mimicked the nun's mad dash around the classroom, arms flailing. Jimmy whispered to Timmy that everything was going to be all right and not to worry about a thing.

"The door opened and Brother Brady reentered the office. He told the boys to report to him after school. He imposed a light sentence upon them, making them assist the groundskeeper at the school for a week. God, he could have whipped or expelled them. Jimmy, Timmy, and I never spoke to anyone about the incident. In fact, we flat-out denied it 'cause if anyone caught wind that we'd been involved, the consequences would have been dire."

Mary sat in disbelief at the story. "No, you haven't told me that," she said, laughing. "What else haven't you told me? So none of you ever got caught or your parents told about it?"

"No," her mother chuckled. Mrs. McDougal continued reading her letters, but she was clearly fatigued. She excused herself and went to bed.

Mary asked, "Do you need my help?" but she refused and Mary sat alone in the living room reflecting on her mother's great tale. Mary began thinking about her mother. She recalled that she had had affection for frogs since Mary could remember. All over her apartment there were frogs. There were porcelain frogs in her living room, a print with frogs, even frog placemats. She finally realized where her mother had developed the affection. Lying there underneath the lamp was her mother's shoebox with the letters. The silhouette from the shoebox shone upon the wall. Sitting there, she resisted the temptation to open the shoebox and read some of the letters. They were her mother's most valued possessions. She could not breach her mother's trust and read them without her permission.

The box began to beg her to open it. Mary began to read a book, but would quickly become distract from it. The box called for her. Finally she could take it no more. Removing herself from the room, she fought the temptation and went to bed early, still giddy from her mother's story. She eagerly waited for tomorrow. Hopefully her mother would share some more of her stories from her letters with her. Lying in bed, she laughed herself to sleep, thinking of the portly nun running amuck, with the frogs croaking and jumping.

The next day her mother staggered to the table. Mary could tell she wasn't herself and assisted her as she tried to sit. Complaining of a headache and some slight dizziness, she spent most of the morning falling in and out of sleep, a cold compress across her forehead. The doorbell buzzed and the phone kept ringing and distractions kept waking her mother and she became irate and left for her bedroom for the rest of the day. Late in the afternoon Mary checked on her, but she still lay in a deep sleep.

Her mother made it to dinner, but only managed a few spoonfuls of chicken noodle soup to her lips. She had no appetite. Mary forced her to drink some more fluids so that she would not dehydrate. Her mother barked, "What does it matter, anyway?" Mary tried to rekindle her spirits, but she walked off to her bedroom for the rest of the evening.

The next morning Mrs. McDougal emerged a new woman. She had energy and was revitalized. Mary had not seen her mother like this in weeks. She smiled; it made her feel good to see her mother well. They ate breakfast and discussed what they would do that day. Mary suggested they visit Broadway and try to see a Wednesday matinee.

Mrs. McDougal had always wanted to see "Cats" and hinted to the fact. They had reopened the show the week prior.

Mary called the TicketCenter and bought two tickets for them. They took the bus over to the theater and saw a wonderful show. Her mother's eyes were as wide as saucers as she never blinked an eye, not wanting to miss a flinch. It was as though her mother was her old self, full of energy, happy, and very attentive to her hygiene. She had applied her makeup painstakingly and put one of her best dresses on. She even wore jewelry for the first time in weeks.

After the show, they went to Duffy's. Mrs. McDougal had insisted on paying for the show. "By God, the matinees are half price, Mary, I've got dinner too!" she proclaimed. The girls enjoyed a bottle of wine and ordered dinner. Mary could not believe her mother's appetite, eating a salad, dinner, and then asking to see the dessert menu.

Mary hailed a cab and they returned home. To her surprise, her mother wanted to stay up and talk. She accepted her invitation and made coffee for them. Mrs. McDougal told Mary that she had a wonderful time, recapping the evening from the bus ride to Broadway to the dessert at Duffy's. "The show was fabulous," she professed. She looked at Mary and slowly shook her head. "It's a shame your father never got to see you. He would've been so proud. Jimmy would have spoiled you rotten, you know," she sighed.

"Tell me more about him, Mother," Mary pleaded.

Mrs. McDougal sat, pondering what to say. "Let me think," she said. "Your father, well, he was an optimist. If you or I saw rain, he would talk about the rainbow to come. 'Half-full' type of man. No three-quarters full, I mean," she laughed. "He was a dreamer, your father. Never saw him mad, less someone spoke or treated his family or friends ill. He and Timmy had this dream. They each wanted to open a bar and grille downtown. They'd serve drinks and food to the Wall Street crowd. Thought they'd make a killing with the money and all down there.

"They had this crazy idea. Timmy wanted to have an aquarium behind the bar where all the bottles of liquor were. In it, he wanted all kinds of tropical fish. All types and all colors, swimming away for the customers to gawk at. Now Jimmy, he had a different idea, but along the same lines. Instead of all them fish, he wanted a shark. He said the thing would only grow to the size of its surrounding environment. I don't know if he was right on that, though. So Jimmy said they could have a feeding hour at six-thirty p.m. every night. Happy hour would be five to six p.m., and they would feed the shark at six-thirty p.m. This way, he figured, the customers would hang around to see the shark in its feeding frenzy. He wanted to put live fish in the aquarium for it to chase and devour. Crazy he was.

"Timmy liked the idea. The two would talk hours on end about the different drinks and food they would serve. They would argue about the menu and what to name the place."

"What did they want to call it?" Mary asked.

"Oh, Timmy wanted to name it after them, Timmy and Jimmy's. Your father wanted to name it the Sharky's Downtown. We'd talk about the outside sign with a big shark on it and the slogan, 'Take a Bite out of Life.' He was a dreamer, all right. Later, before he left for the war, he talked about getting a suit job."

Bewildered she asked, "Suit job?"

"You know, not laborin' but in an office and all. He wanted us to live in the suburbs in a house with a lawn for you kids. He had all these ideas, dreams, they were. But I would listen to him talk about these things for hours. Sometimes we'd take a walk and stop on the hill by our tree. I would lay my head on his lap and he would talk about us growing old together. I would listen with my head on his lap, picking petals off a flower, just listening to him."

She sighed heavily and told Mary, "There's not a day I don't think about him. An idea for tomorrow, Mary," she blurted out.

Mary turned her head in a quizzical fashion. "What's that?" she asked.

"Let's go down to the old neighborhood. We'll go to Tollentine for early morning Mass, then we'll go to Fleischmann's Bakery. We'll get some rolls and butter. Then we'll go over to Sedgwick Avenue and see if that old bench and tree are still there," she excitedly said. She looked to Mary for approval.

Mary was eager to please her mother, but did not know if the old neighborhood was safe anymore. Mary looked at her mother. She was like a child on her birthday looking for a present. "Okay," Mary answered. "It sounds like a plan, as long as you're feeling up to it."

Her mother told her not to worry, that she would be fine. She got up and wished Mary goodnight. She kissed her on the cheek and said, "I love you" and walked off to bed. Mary hoped everything would work out for the next day.

Mary awoke at six a.m. Mass at Tollentine on weekdays was at eight a.m. Walking to her front door, she opened it and picked up the newspaper. Pouring herself a cup of coffee, she looked at the day's weather forecast. Unseasonably high, seventy degrees, sunny, five-mph winds. She did a double take. The weather couldn't be better for their outing, she thought. Waiting until six-thirty a.m., she waited for her mother to rise. Nothing.

At 6:45 a.m. she peeked in. Walking in slowly, she touched her mother on the shoulder. No reaction, no movement. Mary froze. The worst of fears began to overtake her. She stepped back looking for any sign of life from her mother. What seemed like an eternity later, she saw the blankets rise as her mother took a breath. Mary's anxiety lowered, all but a little. She stepped forward and touched her mother again. This time, her mother just mumbled, "Let me be."

Mary became depressed, but understood. She sighed and put the blanket back over her mother's shoulder. Backpedaling slowly out of the doorway, she closed the door and let her mother rest. Maybe they would have breakfast there, skip Mass, but still make their river walk to the bench and tree.

Eight, nine, ten, eleven a.m. and still no movement from her mother's room. Mary peeked in every hour, but her mother lay motionless in the bed. Mary called Dockendorff's office and spoke to a nurse. Dockendorff was with a patient. The nurse said, "If it's a real emergency call 911, otherwise Dr. Dockendorff will call back later."

Mary hung up confused and almost in a panic. She did not want to call 911. Her mother would be furious. She wanted to be left alone. What if this was the end? Mary pondered. Her mind spun in different directions.

Shortly before noon, Dockendorff called. Speaking to Mary, he asked, "What's your mother's condition?" He recommended calling home health to evaluate her, even though they were not scheduled for another day.

Mary told him, "They were here yesterday and only come every two days."

Dockendorff said, "I'll make a few calls, and expect home health to arrive in the next couple of hours."

Mary thanked him and hung up the phone. A nurse from Dockendorff's office called at 1:45 p.m. to reassure Mary that home health would be visiting.

Home health knocked on the door and Mary let them in. Taking a chair close to Mrs. McDougal's bedside, the nurse took her pulse and listened to her heart with a stethoscope. After taking her vitals, she wrote down the information and reviewed her chart again. Mrs. McDougal was semi-conscious through the examination. Mary watched, arms crossed, biting her lower lip nervously.

The nurse motioned for them to go back outside to the living room. Together they sat in the living room to discuss her mother's condition. The nurse laid the file across the table. "This is not easy," she started. "We see this all the time. A patient can go from lively to lethargic at this point in their disease. Will she go to the emergency room?"

Mary said, "No."

She asked, "Have your plans changed or is what was in the file accurate?" Mary confirmed that they were still on the same plan. "At this point in your mother's care, being that she won't go to the hospital or be admitted, I have to recommend that home hospice may be your best choice." She looked at Mary for a response. Mary had a blank stare. "I know this is very difficult for you, but I really think it's your best choice at this point."

Mary came out of her daze. "What's the procedure for that?" she asked.

The nurse thought and said, "What if we start hospice on Monday? Home health will come tomorrow and Sunday to help your mother through this. Do you think this will be okay?" she asked and looked at Mary for a response. Mary nodded her head yes. "Right now all we can do is make her comfortable. I'm going to give her some morphine for her pain and start an IV to hydrate her."

The nurse opened a portal that was in her mother's chest, retrieved a drip bag and readied an IV. Reading the label of the bag, she pierced it open, straightened the line, and connected it to the line in the portal and hung the bag from the IV tree on the side of the bed. She hit the line with her fingers and the bag began to drip.

Mary watched, feeling helpless at the situation. The nurse reviewed everything once more with Mary. She thanked her and the nurse departed. Mary spent the day checking on her mother and worried.

Early in the afternoon, Mrs. Hanley dropped by with some cookies. Mary made her some tea and they discussed her mother's health. She was like family, very comforting, and asked, "Is there was anything I can do?"

At first Mary said, "Nothing, but thank you." A few minutes passed and she asked, "Can I take you up on your offer?"

"Anything," she replied.

"I've got to run a couple of errands. It will take a couple of hours, but I don't want to leave Mother alone."

Mrs. Hanley said, "Don't you worry, take your time. I'll stay right here."

Mary thanked her, got ready, and left.

The doorman, Carlos, hailed a cab. She proceeded to the South Bronx, Sedgwick Avenue, in the taxi looking over the old neighborhood. When her mother lived there while she was very young, it was an immigrant, working-class neighborhood. Through the years, it had deteriorated gradually. There was a revitalization project going on to improve the community, but it was still rough.

The taxi pulled up in front of St. Nicholas of Tollentine's parish office. Mary looked out. There were even wrought iron bars on the lower windows of the church. You shouldn't have to jail a church, she thought.

Paying the cabbie and saying, "Keep the change," she jumped out and entered the parish office and asked to see a priest.

The receptionist quizzed her, "What is the nature of your visit?"

Mary explained the situation and a woman disappeared around the corner. A young priest emerged and introduced himself. "Hello, I'm Father Romero." He asked Mary, "How can I be of assistance?"

Mary went into detail. "My mother attended school here from first grade and was married by Father Gallagher."

Father Romero explained, "Father Gallagher retired some ten years ago, but I'm still friends with him. In fact, Father Gallagher is due to visit tonight."

Mary explained, "My mother's a very sick woman. Her health has declined rapidly in the last twenty-four hours. I was wondering about the sacrament of last rites and the possibility of a funeral Mass upon her death."

"Your mother was very close to Father Gallagher then?" the young priest asked.

Mary replied, "Extremely," and she detailed, "He would come to dinner at their home, he was like a member of our family."

The priest listened and agreed to have her mother's funeral Mass at St. Nicholas. He then sat quietly thinking for a few seconds and asked Mary, "If I can arrange it, what if Father Gallagher and I make a trip to visit your mother and perform the last rites?"

Mary was stunned. She paused and answered, "My mother would love that."

"Let's plan on two p.m. tomorrow. Will that work for you and your mother?" he asked.

Mary said, "Yes," and he asked how she had gotten there. Mary told him she took a cab. He had the receptionist call Mary another taxi and said his farewell to her. He took down her phone number and address and said, "I'll see you tomorrow then."

Mary had never expected this. Her mother would be so happy to have the sacrament performed, especially with Father Gallagher in attendance.

Mrs. Hanley had dozed off on the couch as Mary walked in quietly and tapped her on the shoulder. Mrs. Hanley apologized, "I must have just fallen asleep. Your mother has not wakened since you left."

Looking at her watch, Mary grew concerned, as it was just before five p.m. Mary informed Mrs. Hanley about the upcoming visit from Father Romero and Father Gallagher. "Oh, she'll like that," she said.

Mary thanked her and walked her downstairs. "I'll let you know if anything happens," Mary told her. With that, Mrs. Hanley was off. Mary went upstairs and nibbled on one of Mrs. Hanley's cookies. She opened the refrigerator to search for something for dinner. There was nothing much of anything. She fidgeted around the apartment making a little extra noise hoping her mother would wake. By 7:45 p.m., she was unchanged.

Checking on her mother once more, she realized it was the side effect of the drugs. The morphine had done a job on her.

Mary succumbed to the leftover frozen pizza. She tossed it in the microwave and then in the oven to give it a crisp texture. It had lost most of its flavor being in the freezer for a month. It didn't matter; after a couple of tasteless bites, her appetite left her. She put on the television and aimlessly channel surfed.

Her mother emerged from her bedroom around 9:15 p.m. Mary got up and assisted her by the arm and elbow to the couch. Her mother hated to use the walker and often almost fell over. She looked as if her balance was off a bit. Mrs. McDougal asked, "Fetch me some water, would ya, Mary?"

When she returned with a glass, her mother complained, "That television's too loud." Mary complied and swiftly turned off the television and got her mother a blanket. "I didn't say you had to turn it off," she snarled.

Mary could tell the medicine was affecting her mood. Her mother was usually polite and even-tempered for the most part. Mary commented, "Mrs. Hanley dropped by."

Her mother then asked, "Why didn't you wake me then?"

Mary explained, "I tried." Her mother seemed to get more irate. She sat and brooded. "She did bring you these cookies, though." Mary got up and brought over the cookie tin.

Mrs. McDougal opened the tin and smiled, commenting, "She knows I love these."

Mary looked at her mother and asked her, "How you feeling?"

Her mother replied, "Tired."

Mary inquired, "Are your pain pills working?"

She replied, "I hate taking all that medicine, it just makes me tired and fuzzy about things."

Mary suggested, "Maybe you should just take it at bedtime, so that you can sleep?"

Her mother shrugged and a second later said, "How about you make some tea and then we can get busy on these cookies?"

Mary laughed and was glad to see her mother in a better mood. She returned to the kitchen and they talked until the kettle whistled. Mary poured the tea and the McDougal girls got busy on the cookies. In fact, they finished the last crumb in the tin. One after another, they shoved cookie after cookie into their mouths until there were none. They both sat back, legs extended on the coffee table, and picked the crumbs off their nightshirts. "I can't believe we ate the entire batch," Mary stated.

Her mother answered, "Those poor cookies never had a chance." Both of them burst out laughing.

Rubbing their stomachs, they sat on the couch to let their cookies settle. Mrs. McDougal inquired, "Did Terry mention how Mr. Wiggles is doing?"

Mary replied, "She did. She did. He's doing quite well. She said Mr. Hanley has even taken a liking to him, though he won't admit it."

They continued lying on the couch after their cookie feast, much like lions after a kill. Mary broke the silence, getting up the nerve to say, "I have something to speak to you about." Her mother waited for Mary to go on. Mary paused and asked, "Mom, have you considered the last rites?"

Her mother looked off, avoiding eye contact. There was an uneasy silence in the room. Mrs. McDougal finally answered, "Yes, I guess it's getting that time. I'll make the call this week."

"What if I made a call for you already, Mom?" Mary quietly asked.

Mary's mother asked, "What do you mean?"

She told her, "I visited Tollentine earlier this afternoon and met the new priest, Father Romero. Father Gallagher is visiting the parish this weekend and the two of them will perform the sacrament on you." She looked to her mother for her reaction.

Mrs. McDougal reached out and put her arms around Mary and said, "Thank you."

Their evening ended shortly after, as they both got ready for bed. Mary watched from down the hallway, the glow from her mother's door breaking the hallway darkness, making sure her mother made it to bed before she put in for the night.

Mrs. McDougal slept late again. Home health came at ten a.m. and went into her room to perform their usual checks. Mrs. McDougal seemed to have a weight issue. She sat up in the bed to let them examine her. They took their readings and left some supplies for Mary and Mrs. McDougal. The nurses looked over her medications and asked, "Do you need anything else?" The nurse walked out of the room and confirmed with Mary, "Home hospice is scheduled to take over on Monday, right?"

Mary showed her out and checked back with her mother. She reminded her, "Father Gallagher and Father Romero are coming over in a couple of hours."

This seemed to bring her back from her oblivious state. She got up and went to the shower, professing, "I need to get ready." As she entered the bathroom, she seemed to lose her balance, steadying herself at the vanity. Mary rushed to her side and assisted her, sitting her on the closed toilet. She claimed, "I'm okay," but Mary could tell otherwise.

She told her mother, "Stay put." Retrieving a shower seat from the closet and placing it in the shower, she assisted her mother with removing her sleeping attire. Mary turned on the shower and checked the temperature, so as not to scald her mother with hot water. Mary had installed a hand spray so that her mother could still shower while being seated in the shower.

Her mother said, "You just think of everything, don't you?"

Mary smiled and helped her into the shower. She waited there for her mother to finish showering and helped her out of the enclosure, handing her a towel to dry off, then a robe to keep warm. Mary walked her to her bedroom and sat her on the bed.

"I feel so weak. I'm just a burden to you now, I know. I'm sorry," she muttered in utter frustration.

Mary told her, "Stop saying such things, I know you'd do the same for me."

Mrs. McDougal countered, "Parents should never be a burden to their children."

Mary insisted that she stop such rants and quietly left her to get changed herself. Mrs. McDougal put on a dress, but did not feel strong enough to leave the bedroom. Instead she picked up her feet and legs and rested them on top of the bedspread. "I'm just gonna rest a bit until they get here," she said. A half-hour passed and she had fallen asleep and Mary walked in and covered her with a blanket.

At two p.m. sharp the priests arrived. Mary showed them in and explained her mother's health. Father Gallagher held her hands and said, "I remember the day I baptized you. It seems like yesterday to me." The three spoke a bit and then proceeded to Mrs. McDougal's bedroom.

Mary gently pulled the door opened. She put her hand on her mother's shoulder. "Mom, they're here."

Her eyes slowly opened and struggled to focus. Father Gallagher, in a soft voice, said, "Maggie McDougal, why it's been a long time."

Mrs. McDougal tried to sit up, but her strength was poor. They urged her to stay put. "I'm Father Romero" the younger priest said, introducing himself, and explained, "Father Gallagher and I are here to perform the sacrament of Anointing of the Sick."

Mrs. McDougal asked, "Is that the same as the last rites?"

Father Gallagher reached out and touched her arm. "It's the same thing, just that the new school has changed the name, Maggie." Father Gallagher asked her, "How have you been over the years?" as the two priests prepared for the ritual. Father Gallagher was in his mid-eighties and walked with a black cane that had a brass duck on the end. His eyes looked to be far back in his head and he smelled of some aftershave, Old Spice.

Father Romero looked to Father Gallagher, then to Mary, then to Mrs. McDougal, and reminded them of their baptismal promise, "Be with Christ so that we might rise to new life with Him." He asked them, "Are we ready to proceed?" and they all nodded yes. He went on to quote a reading from Scripture, "Amen, I say to you, whoever does not accept the Kingdom of God, like a child, will not enter it (Luke 18: 17)." He continued by telling the three of Jesus' healing and his appointed two…"They anointed with oil many who were sick and cured them (Mark 6: 7-13)."

Father Gallagher took over at this stage of the sacrament and imposed his trembling hands on the head of Mary's mother. He prayed over the oil and anointed her head and hands. Lastly, he asked all, "Please join in the Lord's Prayer."

Father Romero took out the chalice and issued Holy Communion to all, and Father Gallagher finished the sacrament by blessing all of them.

Mary looked at her mother. She was at peace and rejoicing in the sacrament. The priests concluded the ritual and started packing up, cleaning the chalice and placing it back in a leather bag. Father Gallagher handed Maggie a small Bible and held her hand, blessing her one more time. "It was really nice seeing you after all these years, " he said.

Mrs. McDougal said, "Thank you."

Mary walked them to the door. Mrs. McDougal struggled trying to get out of bed to see them out also, grabbing her walker, but she was too weak. She waved and thanked them once more, lying back on the bed.

The priests offered, "If we can be of any help, please call."

Mary opened the door and they left.

After closing the door, she leaned her back up against it. She was not a practicing Catholic and went to church sporadically, only when she would visit her mother for the weekend, but something about the day's events moved her. She felt a spiritual revival rebound throughout her body. A divine presence was there that she had never felt before. Walking slowly back to the bedroom, she peeked in to see her mother reading from the Bible Father Gallagher had just given her. Mary walked in and sat at her mother's bedside. She watched as her mother read and reflected about her own faith. She breathed deeply, feeling relaxed and joyous, an emotion that had escaped her before this.

28

BATTLE OF THE ARDENNES

Jimmy and Timmy's U.K. visit did not last long. Upon landing, they were told to grab all the gear. Transport trucks were outside the plane. Quickly they would deplane and go to the mess hall for chow with their gear left on the trucks. After their meal, the troops were gathered and informed that they would move at 0500 hours. When any of the soldiers inquired where they were going, they were met with ambiguous answers.

After being shuffled through Europe, they finally found out where their orders would take them. General Bradley had ordered First Army to Belgium to protect allied advances. The American forces had passed the Siegfried Line in late September and their advance had taken most of Allied Command by surprise. Command had anticipated heavy German resistance on this natural defensive line. The allies were stretched thin and support had been promised, but was lacking. Supplies ran low and the weather was turning frigid.

Minutes after arriving, the men jumped off their trucks and were ordered to advanced positions. To avoid enemy fire, they serpentined through the forest, taking cover behind trees. Their captain gave orders to the lieutenant for the men to stay put until sunset. Sporadic enemy fire was heard throughout the night. At this point, they dug foxholes to give them cover. It began to snow and the temperature fell to ten degrees as the wind howled, as the snow pelted their faces.

Sporadic rifle fire and machine gun bursts lasted throughout the day and into the night. Bullets whizzed by, hitting trees near their position. Training was over. This was baptism by fire. A corporal named Murphy was the first casualty in their platoon. He was hit right in the stomach. His hands covered the wound and deep red blood poured through his fingers as he tried to stop the bleeding. He cried aloud for a medic, but the bullets rained around him, preventing any member to get to his aid. The corporal began crying and asking for his mother as he lay wounded in a state of shock.

The men became frantic to get to his aid. Members of the platoon began yelling at one another to assist him. "Help him! Help him!" they yelled over and over.

Two of the men could take the screams no longer and ran to his side. Each grabbed him by an arm and leg and lifted him up. A torrent of machine gun fire erupted as bark flew off the surrounding trees and the three men were cut to pieces, almost in half. The three lay motionless, dead on the frozen tundra. Body parts lay across the snow as blood ran from the freshly cut flesh.

Screaming, the lieutenant ordered, "Stay in your damn foxholes, goddamn it!" The shock stupefied the men as they sat frozen, staring at their dead comrades from their freshly dug foxholes.

A machine gunner and his partner occupied their lead foxhole. The Fighting Irish and the Fallettis were at ten o'clock and two o'clock behind their position, about forty yards from one another. Timmy yelled to the Fallettis to make sure to identify themselves and they would do likewise, as they did not want to wind up shooting one another in the middle of the night if they got out of their foxhole or got caught in crossfire. The Fallettis agreed and told the Irish to stay low. "We will if you will stay down," they answered.

The men slept next to one another for body heat, wrapped in blankets, seated in their foxholes. Blankets did little to protect them from the cold and their teeth chattered from the temperature.

Meanwhile the Germans prepared for their Ardennes offensive. Their plan was to split the British and the American allied line in half. From there, they would encircle the four allied forces and negotiate a peace treaty in the Axis powers' favor. The Germans employed almost zero radio transmissions. The few intercepted messages suggested a German attack, but allied command was confident of their own pending plans.

Aerial reconnaissance was a week old for the allies, and the weather did not cooperate with their surveillance teams. Low cloud coverage from the weather had prevented allied planes from taking any new aerial reconnaissance. On the other side of the line, the Germans had amassed five hundred thousand men, seven armored divisions, and five hundred tanks. The allies would eventually outnumber them, but were out manned, outgunned, and surprised at this point.

At sunrise, the German assault commenced. Artillery pounded the allied lines for two straight hours. Trees shattered and splintered, smoke rose from holes, and the air stank of death. The concussions mercilessly exploded all around them. Men screamed in pain. Others sat frozen, shell-shocked in their bunkers, hands holding their helmets, crying for the madness to stop. As swift as it started, it stopped. Low groans from wounded men could be heard. "Medic" would be yelled as the corpsman would run to the wounded.

Then the utterance of German orders could be heard, screamed to their subordinates. They were advancing on the allied positions. Through a break in the trees, German troops advanced on them. The Germans ran across the field and the allies took aim and cut them down. The men shot and reloaded as fast as they could so as not to be overrun by the Germans.

The assault was the first of six that day. Artillery rounds that pelted the allies precipitated each assault, and the field was littered with German corpses, their bodies surrounded by blood-soaked snow. Each German advance gained more ground. And the front lines were now only a couple hundred yards apart.

The platoon was given orders not to break or retreat. They would have to hold on for reinforcements. The men held off the Germans for the second day.

The boys had become men, old men, and fought with all their strength. They had been showered with artillery fire and bullets for forty-eight hours now. No sleep or nourishment to reinvigorate them, only coffee to stay awake and warm them. The stubble from their beards was jagged and their hands shook as they put their tin cups to their mouths. Their platoon had taken many casualties and the dead were stacked in the rear of their position. The lieutenant collected the dead's dog tags to keep count.

As the sun set, the men gathered close for warmth again. The platoon was on edge. Every sound from the forest would result in a hair-trigger volley. The lieutenant assured them reinforcements were in route. He also said, "Air support will be here once the weather front has lifted. Hold on."

Timmy and Jimmy tried to keep their spirits up. They recalled all of their childhood exploits, their families, and the old neighborhood. "Remember the fresh doughnuts at Fleischmann's, Jimmy? I sure could go for some of them now."

"I can smell and taste 'em," Jimmy replied.

A break in their conversation as a member of their platoon announced, "Coming up from your six (o'clock)." He brought a fresh pot of coffee and some more ammunition and said, "The LT thinks they'll hit hard again first light. Be ready." He yelled to the Fallettis, "Coming up on your three (o'clock)," and was off.

Jimmy poured them both some coffee. They were freezing. Frostbite had taken hold of their feet. It took both hands to bring their tin cup to their lips from their shaking hands.

Jimmy looked at Timmy and caught him eye to eye. He was serious in tone and told Timmy, "You're the best friend a guy could have. If we don't get out of here together, I just wanted to tell you that."

Timmy looked at him and assured him the feeling was mutual. Jimmy apologized, "I'm sorry I ever got us into this stinkin' army."

Timmy cut him off and said, "We were in it together from the beginning. Don't worry, we're gonna be fine. Cold, but fine."

Jimmy lowered his blanket and opened his jacket. Inside the jacket, in the inner pocket, was a letter. He showed it to Timmy and told him, "If anything happens to me, throw the letter in the mail to make sure that Maggie gets it. OK?"

Timmy told him, "Don't worry, it won't be necessary because we're getting out of here alive."

"I hope you're right," Jimmy responded.

Sporadic gunfire and artillery landed throughout the night. None really came that close to their position, but they could not get any rest. After seventy-two hours without sleep, their bodies ached for rest and nourishment; debility had taken hold of them. Reasoning was a stretch.

The shelling stopped shortly before dawn. Birds began to chirp, returning to the forest with the stoppage. The sun came out briefly and reflected off of the snow. It hurt their eyes to look out from the glare. The silence was blessed and the men got a chance to actually eat a small amount of food. Their hands vigorously shook, trembling to open the cans of food.

Their brief reprise was over. German officers began yelling out orders again. Minutes later, artillery pounded the 106th. Trees fell over or shattered. Shells erupted everywhere around them and the lieutenant hollered, "Take cover, stay down, don't leave your foxhole." They covered their ears with their gloved hands to muffle the landing artillery shells concussions.

PFC Weisberg had been at the rear using the latrine during the break in hostilities. He was returning to his foxhole when the shelling commenced. He was hit in the legs and shoulder and could not move. He cried in pain and the LT told his men to stay put. The Germans kept aim at his position, lying in wait for some of his troops to assist him. Weisberg continued to cry out in anguish.

Seeing their friend writhing in pain, the Irish could take it no longer. Timmy cried to the Falettis, "Give us cover," and Jimmy and Timmy ran to his aid. Together, running, they dove behind a large fallen tree for cover as bullets splintered the log in front of them.

Their LT screamed, "Stay put! You're doing nobody any favors gettin' shot!"

Ignoring his commands, they sprinted from the log and dragged Weisberg into their foxhole amid a barrage of machine gun fire. Timmy was grazed on the right forearm and a bullet ricocheted off Jimmy's helmet. They had saved their friend's life for the moment.

An hour later it was over, and silence once again took the forest. The silence before the storm, the men thought as they readied themselves for the pending

German assault. They set their munitions out and took aim. The only thing between the Irish and the Fallettis and the German front line was their machine gunner and his partner.

"You keep killing dem Krauts," the younger Falletti yelled out to the machine gunner's foxhole.

The Germans advanced, hundreds of them. Racing for ten to twenty yards, they threw themselves to the ground, lying, waiting for suppressing fire. The Americans fought back with a vengeance, but still they advanced. The machine gun glowed from the heat of the bullets. Jimmy, Timmy, and the Fallettis gave supporting fire from behind.

The Germans pitched forward and the fight lasted the entire morning. Men lay dead everywhere from both sides. A few of the Germans rushed forward, having broken the allies' line, taking refuge behind the trees. The Germans took potshots at the American machine gun position from behind. Timmy quickly assessed the situation. He realized that his machine gunners were in crossfire. They had trained on how to remedy this attack, and Timmy jumped out of the foxhole and flanked the German intruders. Crawling on his belly from behind them, he shot them both and retreated back to his foxhole.

Excited, he jumped in the foxhole and frantically told Jimmy, "I got 'em. I shot them both." He took position, readying himself to continue the fight, and took aim. He realized that Jimmy had not acknowledged him. No answer. Feeling something was wrong, he said, "Did you hear me? I got 'em." He turned to see Jimmy's reaction. Jimmy's back was to him facing the other direction. Leaning over, he tugged on Jimmy's shoulder to talk to him.

As he put his hand on Jimmy shoulder, his lifeless body fell to the bottom of the foxhole, slumped over. His eyes were frozen in time, pale blue, no life to them, and blood dripped from his open mouth, a bullet hole through his forehead. Timmy fell to his knees at his friend's side. Panicking, he grabbed hold of Jimmy's shoulders, yelling at him. Letting go, he sat back, his rump on the bottom of the foxhole on the frozen dirt. He tried to scream in anguish, but nothing came out.

Saliva dripped from Timmy's mouth as a rage overtook him. Taking the knife from Jimmy's belt, he hurled himself from the foxhole. The Fallettis and the machine gunner were celebrating. "We held them. We held them again," they hollered from their foxholes.

Timmy became crazed, like a madman. He was on a mission and sought out the two Germans he had flanked and shot. The two German soldiers lay severely wounded on the ground. One had propped himself up against a tree. Unable to fight, they moaned and pleaded for help. Timmy advanced on them. His bayonet held tightly, clenched in his hand, he held a death grip upon the handle. Kicking over the German lying against the tree to the ground, he took another kick to the wounded soldier's head, and the German's helmet came flying off his head and blood spurted from his face as he tumbled to the ground. Timmy grasped his hair, pulling his head back. Pulling up the bayonet, he severed the soldier's throat. The man tried to scream, but blood filled his throat and poured from his neck from the gash. Gurgling from the blood, he quickly died.

The other German, having witnessed Timmy's massacre, tried desperately to get away, crawling on his belly and elbows. Timmy methodically walked over to the second German and jumped on his back, putting his bayonet deep into it. He began stabbing the man over and over as blood and flesh flew everywhere. The soldier was dead, but Timmy kept stabbing away; guts and blood covered Timmy from head to toe from his slaughter.

The Falletti brothers had exited their foxhole and stood aghast watching Timmy's lunatic rage. They tried to talk to him, but he was in a trance-like state. Walking past them as if they were not even there to his foxhole, he stared at his friend as tears began to flow down the side of his face. Screaming, his voice echoed through the forest. He slid his arms underneath Jimmy's frozen corpse, cradling him, and picked him up.

He carried his friend to the rear position, where some of the other men in the platoon tried to assist him, but he shook his head no, motioning them away with his head. He lay Jimmy down by the other corpses. The captain watched as Timmy lowered the body. Kneeling in front of his friend, picking up Jimmy's hands, he laid them across his body. Taking off his blood-soaked glove from his right hand, he shut Jimmy's eyes. Wiping away tears and saliva from his face with his jacket sleeve, he took a blanket and covered his dear friend, taking a long last look at his face.

Walking over to the captain, he handed over the letter he had removed from Jimmy's pocket and asked, "Will you make sure this gets delivered to his wife?"

"I will," he answered.

Timmy walked back to his foxhole.

The fighting took a brief reprieve. An hour later it started again, and the Germans unleashed a barrage of artillery and followed with a storm of infantry on the 106th's position. Fighting with a vengeance, Timmy and the Fallettis both held their ground. The Germans retreated and lobbed artillery and suppressing fire to protect their retreating soldiers. Simultaneously, artillery rounds found Timmy and the Fallettis' bunkers, killing the three instantly.

The entire platoon almost wiped out, the 106th suffered most of the casualties in the battle that the allies had called the Battle of the Ardennes. The American press dubbed it the Battle of the Bulge.

29

SPECIAL DELIVERY

Major Spellman had had a long couple of days. Spending the weekend watching the March Madness Men's Basketball Tournament and drinking beer, he was worn out. Hung over, he drove into work, forgetting to charge the battery on his cell phone. He limped into work, dragging tail from his weekend escapades, forty-five minutes late.

His corporal awaited him at the door. Stumbling down the stairs to Spellman's Jeep, the corporal half saluted as he ran. "Don't you have your cell phone on, sir?" he said squeamishly.

"No, I don't have it on. I mean, I have it, just forgot to charge it. What's the problem?"

The corporal said, "I received several phone calls from HQ and there are two officers waiting for you in your office."

Spellman looked confused. He labored to get out of his Jeep. Tucking his shirt in, he hurried up the stairs and into his office. A two-man special envoy sat waiting. They stood up and exchanged salutes, handed him their orders, and asked, "Do you have the package?"

Spellman read the orders and apologized. "If I had just known, I'd have had it all ready for you. Wait here," he instructed them.

Spellman left for the next room and tried the combination to the safe. Kneeling down, he tried the combination again, putting out his left arm to brace himself up against the wall, getting dizzy as the dehydration from his weekend exploits set in. Trying the safe a third time, he could not open it. His mind was not clear, and he tried several more times. Frustrated, he yelled, "Corporal, come here." He whispered, "Open the safe," having forgotten the combination himself.

Getting on his knees next to Spellman, the corporal entered the combination and swung the safe door open. Spellman pushed him aside, reached in, and grabbed the package with the letter in it. Trying to get to his feet, he braced himself up against a chair. He felt lightheaded and waited to gain his balance. Walking back to his office, he sat at his desk. "There it is," he said as he reached over and gave it to the envoy.

Taking the package from the major, he looked over to see if the coded numbers on the package matched his orders. After verifying the numbers, he signed a receipt and handed a copy of it to Spellman.

"If that's all," Spellman said. He escorted them out and proceeded back to his office to sleep it off.

The envoy team sped away with the package. Inside lay the letter from Jimmy, which Timmy had given to the captain before his death fifty years earlier at the Battle of the Bulge. Special orders had been drawn up from HQ. The letter was never to be out of human hands. A series of handoffs later, the next special envoy team arrived at the USPS Lost Letter Department. The postmaster had notified the Army HQ that it had located Maggie McDougal. It had taken much longer than anticipated because the army had listed Mrs. McDougal under Agnes, not Margaret, her middle name. All Mrs. McDougal's leases and phones had been under Agnes McDougal, her legal name.

The envoy reached the USPS postmaster's office late that morning. Here they met with the postmaster and his Lost Letter Department manager. It was decided that the envoy would escort the manager's courier to the McDougal residence for the delivery.

After a brief meeting, the three left in the envoy's car. At mid-afternoon, they rang the bell at Mrs. McDougal's apartment. No one answered. They rang again and proceeded to knock loudly, hoping someone would come to the door.

Mrs. Hanley heard the commotion outside her door and looked through her peephole to see who was in the hallway. She could make out the army personnel in their special blue uniforms and unlocked her deadbolt and opened her door, leaning her head to speak out to them, the security chain still attached. "Can I help you?"

The man introduced himself and explained their reason for being there. Mrs. Hanley seemed a bit confused and unlatched the chain on her door to talk to them. "You mean you're here to deliver a letter from Jimmy, fifty years later?" she questioned.

They confirmed her inquisition and asked, "When will Mrs. McDougal be back?" explaining that the package must be hand delivered.

She paused for a second before answering, "Never."

"What do you mean never?" asked the envoy.

Mrs. Hanley explained that terminal cancer had befallen her friend. They offered their condolences, but asked for Mrs. McDougal's address and phone number where she was being cared for. Mrs. Hanley complied with Mary's home information, and the men were off. They would not be able to try for a second delivery until Monday. Disappointed that they could not make their delivery, they formed a plan for an early morning delivery on Monday.

Mrs. McDougal had drifted off reading her new Bible. Mary left and was cleaning up around the house. An hour later she thought she heard some awful sounds and walked toward the bedroom. Her mother was moaning in pain, holding her side. Mary ran to her mother's bed and asked her, "Where does it hurt?" She wanted to call the doctor or an ambulance, but Mrs. McDougal replied with a stern, "No."

Mary got out some of the morphine and gave it to her mother to take. She took two of the pills and drank some water to wash them down. Mary stayed with her as she lay back trying to suppress her pain. The morphine kicked in and took affect a half-hour later. The dosage was a little high for an elderly woman of a mere hundred pounds, but Dockendorff insisted she would need it with the pain that she would be in.

She drifted off and Mary sat there wondering what else she could do, feeling helpless to assist her mother. It was torture for her, not being able to comfort her further. The medicine was very powerful and sedating. Mrs. McDougal slept the rest of the day and night, and Mary tried to keep quiet by putting the phone off the hook, so no one would wake her mother. She went about cleaning the apartment, trying to occupy her mind and not dwell on her mother's pain and suffering. The anxiety was becoming unbearable for Mary.

Around seven a.m. the next morning, Mary lay in bed sleeping. She awoke to a strange succession of sounds. Lying there, she tried to make out what they were and where they were coming from. It was a screechy, rolling sound, silence, and then a thud. It repeated itself a dozen times. She lay there wondering if they were doing some repairs in the apartment building, but then surmised it was too early for workers to be there. Perplexed, she put on her bathrobe and walked down the hallway, hearing the sound louder in the living room, repeating itself.

Looking around the corner, she saw her mother using a walker for her first time. The wheels screeched until she stopped, moved forward, then stopped and lowered the metal legs, resulting in the thud. "Everything all right, Mom?" she asked.

Turning around, her mother said, "Oh, you're up. I want to go down to the church, Tollentine, and see the tree, if that's okay with you? Remember we talked about it?"

Mary rubbed her eyes and stretched them open. "You want to do what?" she said.

"I don't like repeating myself, Mary. If you want to go, get yourself ready. Otherwise, I'll take a cab," her mother sniped back.

Mary knew her mother was headstrong and feared that she would try to go by herself if she did not join her. Mary reassured her that she wanted to go and said, "I'll get ready." But Mary made it clear that she would go on one condition. "You will have to use the wheelchair I rented if you want me to go."

At first she argued, but eventually complied with Mary's wishes. Her mother knew she could not make it alone and really wanted Mary to join her. She made a little fuss, but sat in the wheelchair and awaited Mary. Taking a taxi down to the church, they attended nine a.m. Mass. Mary had made her mother dress warmly. The temperature was unseasonably warm, but she didn't want her mother getting a chill. Mary packed a blanket in case the weather turned.

"Is all this really necessary?" Mrs. McDougal complained. Mary just smiled and ignored her.

Father Romero celebrated Mass and mentioned Mrs. McDougal during prayers. He asked the congregation, "Please pray for her health and recovery." After Mass he greeted the McDougals, "Good morning, ladies," on the steps of the church.

"It's great to see you again, Father." They spoke for a while, and several older members of the church came over and spoke with Mary and her mother.

Mrs. McDougal did not tell them the extent of her illness and assured them she was doing better the last couple of days. "I'm just feeling a little down as of late. I'll be fine."

Mary just smiled as some of the parishioners asked how her mother was feeling. She told them, "Just ask her," and looked toward her mother for an answer. Mrs. McDougal kept the same charade up as she met with some of the other parishioners from the old neighborhood.

A little while later, Mary pushed the wheelchair toward the Fleischmann's Bakery. You could smell it from a block away. She pushed at a slow pace, so her mother could take in the whole neighborhood. A young boy held the front door open and they entered the bakery. "Why, thank you."

The aroma was intoxicating. Mary took a number and they waited to be called. She ordered a dozen doughnuts, assorted. "Three Bavarians, three jelly, three chocolate, and three glazed. One coffee, black, and one tea, two sugars, to go." As she ordered, Mrs. McDougal reached from her wheelchair for some napkins. Mary placed the doughnuts and beverage tray on her mother's lap and they exited the bakery. The streets were still quiet.

Mary could hear church bells ringing for the eleven o'clock service as they strode down the sidewalk, surrounded by her mother's humble beginnings and 2251 Sedgwick Avenue. Her mother looked each building up and down, inspecting them. "That's new.

That wasn't here. I remember this," as she recalled earlier years. Mary smiled. It made her happy to see her mother excited, remembering the days of yesteryear.

They pulled up on the sidewalk across from 2251 Sedgwick. Mary grabbed another doughnut and sip from her coffee. Mrs. McDougal just kept looking up and down and side to side. "It's changed so much," she said in an indifferent voice.

"That's because it has, Mom. They tore it down and constructed a new building on the same property," Mary said.

Her mother did not reply and seemed disappointed by the new structure. There was a long, pregnant pause before Mary finally said, "Now what about that tree, Mom?"

Mrs. McDougal was having trouble letting go of the moment. She hesitated and eventually answered, "I hope it's still there."

Mary took them to a narrow path that led to the river and walkway. A few couples, some joggers, and a man walking his dog passed them. Her mother commented, "I don't recognize any of them."

Mary wondered what she was talking about, but did not argue. After all, she had been gone for nearly fifty years. Some ducks landed in the water on the other side of the river and a boy and his father played with a motorized boat. Slowly Mary kept pushing the wheelchair down the path. "How much further?" Mary asked.

"A little bit further," her mother answered.

The conversation repeated itself a few times. Finally Mary asked, "Are you sure you know where it is, Mom?"

"A little more," she responded. Her mother looked confused and disturbed that they could not find the bench or tree, at least how she remembered it. They doubled back and tried again. Coming up on a bench, Mrs. McDougal became excited, "I think this is it."

Mary pushed the wheelchair up to it, but there was no tree, just the bench, with a rusting wire trash basket chained to it. "Why is that wastebasket chained to the bench?" her mother asked.

"So people don't steal it," Mary answered. "People are crazy these days."

"This isn't it. I think it's a little further," her mother stated.

Mary was becoming tired of pushing the wheelchair, but placated her mother. Mrs. McDougal protruded her neck over the front of the wheelchair. "There, up there," she said and pointed. Mary pushed farther. The grass and weeds were overgrown at this part of the path. A cement slab, yellowed over time, sat with moss growing over it and four rusted posts stood up from it. Her mother insisted, "This is where the old bench was."

About fifteen yards behind it stood the old sycamore tree that she had spoken of. They had not seen it on their first pass because of all the new bushes and overgrowth over the years.

Mary's heart began to beat faster. This was her parents' special place that her mother had spoken of her entire life. She began looking for a clearing, to get closer to the tree. The vegetation was thick and the ground slippery. She looked down the walk a little bit. About twenty-five yards north there was an opening. She wheeled her mother to the opening and told her, "Stay here." Mary stomped down a few of the branches and proceeded toward the tree. There was a little dark path that led up to its trunk. Like discovering hidden treasure, her eyes were wide open and she put her arm and hand out to touch it.

"Mary," her mother yelled.

She walked back down the path to find her mother out of her chair, cane in hand, proceeding up the path. "There, help me up there," she cried.

Mary didn't even try to stop her. She put her arm underneath her mother's elbow and guided her up the path. Mary had to slow her down so she would not fall on the roots and undergrowth. Mrs. McDougal was breathing hard as she reached the base of the tree. Mary looked all over the trunk, trying to make out any etchings in its trunk. Out of the corner of her eye, she deciphered some markings and called to her mother. Her arm was outstretched, touching the back of the tree. It was the Holy Grail.

Excitedly her mother made her way around the tree. "This is it, Mary. This is it." Mary circled behind the tree to find what her mother was looking at. About five feet high, deep in the trunk, one could barely make out a heart about ten inches in length. Mary lifted her hands and peeled back some moss that had grown on the bark. It was thick, black, and green. Pulling it off, she revealed more of the etching. Time had not robbed her mother of her dying wish.

Mary took out her keys and removed more of the growth. Like two archaeologists, they carefully worked on the tree's surface. When they were complete, hollowed into the chest of the tree, black from time, they could see "Maggie and Jimmy, forever." A heart with an arrow ran through it, and circled with a heart stood the carving.

"I didn't think I'd ever get to see this again. God, I miss him," her mother said, choking up. Mary reached out and held her tight. They both cried joyously at their find. They gazed at the tree, lost in thought.

Mary and her mother took a long last look at the old sycamore. They each took a deep breath as their emotions and memories had come to life. Mary removed a camera from her purse and took a snapshot of her mother by the tree and then one of the tree alone. They slowly walked back down the path to the river and Mrs. McDougal got back in the wheelchair as they made their way back up to Sedgwick Avenue. Mary hailed a taxi, and they left for home.

It was late afternoon before they returned home. Mrs. McDougal doubled over in pain once in the door. Mary gave her some morphine and she went to bed. Home health had put a note on the door that they had visited, but no one was home. Mary began to call them to apologize, but there was no dial tone. She had forgotten to put the phone back on the hook from the day before. As she waited for the phone to re-set, it rang.

On the other line was Mrs. Hanley, speaking in a frantic voice, "Mary. I've been trying to call you since yesterday. Is everything all right? Your line's been busy. These men were here for your mother. They have this letter for her."

Mary tried to calm Mrs. Hanley down and slow her up so that she could understand her. She was making no sense. This went on for five minutes and Mary still did not understand the situation completely. She thought that maybe Mrs. Hanley had been drinking. Mary told her to hold on and she would be right over.

She called Rosarita, the secretary from MOD. Rosarita agreed to come over and stay with her mother until Mary got back. Mary took a taxi over and went up to see Mrs. Hanley. They sat at her kitchen table, and Mrs. Hanley got out the man's business card. "A letter from my father," Mary said. "That's crazy."

Mrs. Hanley was very deliberate in her facts now that she had calmed down. Mary began to entertain the notion that she may be right, but was still skeptical. She thanked Mrs. Hanley, and Mr. Wiggles jumped into her lap. Mary stopped for a moment and told Mrs. Hanley, "I have an idea." Mary explained her idea to Mrs. Hanley, who agreed wholeheartedly. Together they packed up Mr. Wiggles into his cat carrier to bring him to Mary's to surprise her mother. The only hiccup in the plan was Carlos, the doorman. Pets were strictly prohibited in the building. She told Mrs. Hanley, "Don't worry," and gave her a big hug. Mary would contact the army man and straighten out the whole thing the next morning.

The taxi pulled up to the building and Carlos reached out to open the door for Mary. He opened the door and said, "Good evening, ma'am."

Mary jumped out of the cab and put her finger over his lips, signaling for him to be quiet. Carlos immediately saw the cat. He looked over both his shoulders before helping her with the cat carrier and a large shopping bag. Together they briskly walked to the side of the building used for deliveries.

"Are you trying to get me fired, Mary?"

She rushed by him onto the freight elevator with Mr. Wiggles. Carlos sat the shopping bag at her feet. She took a hundred dollar bill and put it in Carlos's front pocket of his blazer as the elevator door closed.

"You didn't see anything," she said as the elevator door closed.

Mary got into the apartment and freed Mr. Wiggles from his cage. Rosarita picked him up and pet him. Mary asked her, "Will you stay and have a glass of wine?"

Rosarita said, "That sounds great. How's your mother's health?"

Mary responded, "I don't think that she has much time left," and changed the subject. "Now what about you and everything at MOD?" Mary asked.

Rosarita went on to tell her about all the office gossip. For Mary, it felt good to socialize with someone, relax, and let loose a little bit. Polishing off their first bottle, Mary uncorked a second bottle as they engaged in conversation.

Rosarita left a little before ten p.m. Mary thanked her. "Thank you so much for coming over." Cleaning up the mess, she grew tired from the stress and indulgence of the evening. They'd finished all the wine and polished off the doughnuts that Mary and her mother had purchased that morning. Mary giggled to herself thinking of her new dinner, doughnuts and wine.

She opened the door to her mother's room and woke her to take some more morphine so that she would sleep through the night. Groggily her mother took her pills. At that moment Mr. Wiggles jumped on the bed at her side. Her mother could not keep her eyes opened and whispered, "Thank you," as she fell asleep, her hand wrapped around the cat.

Mary turned away and switched off the light. She began to prepare for bed herself. While looking in the mirror, she began laughing, noticing all the powder from the last doughnut around her mouth.

The next day Mary awoke with a slight headache from the night before. Her mouth dry from the overindulgence, she drank orange juice straight from the carton. Changing into her sweats, she took a couple of aspirin. She needed to go downstairs and smooth things out with Carlos. He was outside helping some tenants get into a car. Mary looked out from the lobby waiting area. A van pulled up in front of the building. It was pale blue, the rear quarter panel dented from an accident. Written on the side, Mary could read its company and logo: Manhattan Home Hospice, Death with Dignity.

A sinking feeling overtook her. She had forgotten. They were starting their service today. The word hospice just reeked with finality. The van's rear doors were covered with wire to prevent break-ins, a cross and a Star of David on each rear window. The doors swung open and a nurse hopped out and grabbed a couple of wheeled carriers.

Mary wanted to leave and just meet her upstairs. Instead she waited, helped her inside the door, and introduced herself. "I'm Mary McDougal."

The hospice nurse introduced herself. "I'm Jenny from home health. Glad to meet you." She was very professional and explained, "I know this is a very emotional time for the family."

Mary stopped Jenny and explained to her, "I'm the only family, besides, that is, Mr. Wiggles."

Jenny asked, "I didn't read in the file that this was a co-inhabitant domicile. Who is Mr. Wiggles?"

"That's my mother's tabby cat."

Jenny smiled and said, "Pets can be very soothing to all patients."

They rode up the elevator together and Jenny explained, "I will first review home health's files, then make my own evaluation of your mother."

They entered the apartment and Mary said to Jenny, "Please sit down at the dining room table."

Jenny thanked her and began to evaluate the files. A half-hour later, Jenny asked, "Can I see your mother now?"

Mary took her to the bedroom and quietly entered. Jenny looked over the equipment and the medicines and wrote down some of the information on the prescriptions. Jenny motioned to Mary for them to exit the room. They went back out to the dining room and sat down. Jenny jotted down some more information and then asked, "When was the last time your mother used the bathroom, shower, how long has she slept, have there been any falls, when was the last time she took her medicine? Is there anything else that you would like to add that I need to know?"

Mary was very impressed. Jenny seemed concerned, but not overbearing. Jenny opened by saying, "I don't believe in waking a sick patient to check their vitals. I prefer for them to wake on their own at this stage of their care. If it gets too late, we might have to wake her. How's her appetite?"

Mary winced and said, "Very poor."

"That's not unusual," Jenny answered. She began to unpack some of her items from the bags. Jenny said, "I need to get some more things out of the van."

Mary offered her assistance. "Would you like some help?" They proceeded downstairs. They hadn't left a minute when the phone rang. It was the envoy and the postal courier. They did not want to go to midtown if no one was home. Leaving a message on the answering machine with their office and cell phone numbers, they eagerly waited to get in touch with the McDougals.

Mary and Jenny returned upstairs. Mary began to tell Jenny of the adventure she and her mother had the prior day. "I bet she's exhausted," Jenny said.

"It took every ounce of energy she had to get up to that tree. Nothing was going to stop her. We got home and she's been in bed ever since," Mary confided.

"Let's give her until noon. If she doesn't wake by then, we'll check on her," Jenny stated.

Shortly before noon, they open the bedroom door and woke her mother. They had her sit on the edge of the bed and Jenny took her vitals. Mrs. McDougal didn't speak much. She was barely awake, a skeleton at ninety-eight pounds, legs unable to touch the floor.

Mary and Jenny put a bathrobe on her and walked her to the living room. They asked her if she was hungry, but she just shook her head no. Jenny poured her a supplement drink and asked her, "Are you in any pain?"

Mrs. McDougal grimaced and opened the newspaper. "Mary, can you get my eyeglasses," she asked in a soft voice.

Jenny got up and met Mary in the bedroom. "I'm going to wash and change the sheets," Jenny said. The nurse had observed blood on the sheets. Jenny surmised that Mrs. McDougal was bleeding internally now. She would confide in Mary later, when her mother returned to her bed.

Mary got the eyeglasses and her mother ate a half-eaten doughnut from the prior day from the kitchen. She put it on a plate in front of her mother, hoping she might finish it off. Mrs. McDougal took a nibble out of it, just enough to get some of the jelly, but food had lost its taste for her and she left the rest.

A couple of hours later, Mrs. McDougal began to have more acute pain. She took some of the morphine Jenny handed her but had a violent reaction and vomited all over the couch. The vomit had traces of the supplement, but was mostly deep red in blood. She did not have much longer, with all the internal bleeding.

Mary ran for towels as Jenny cleaned up. They assisted her to the bathroom where Jenny washed her down and assisted her onto the shower seat. Mrs. McDougal began to shiver, her body hypersensitive to the change in temperature and dehydration. Jenny put a bathrobe and some slippers on her, while Mary quickly threw an additional blanket on the bed. They put the dirty clothing in the laundry and cleaned up the living room couch. Mary apologized, "I'm sorry about…" but Jenny stopped her. "This is what home hospice is all about. The patient is around their loved ones and home surroundings. Please don't worry. I am here to help."

Mary sat down to drink a soda and saw the answering machine blinking. She played the message. Mary had forgotten all about the package. She scribbled down the numbers and called immediately. The envoy answered. He informed Mary, "I have the package and would like to deliver it ASAP."

Mary informed him, "The sooner the better. We will be home."

He hung up and immediately and called the postal courier. They agreed on where to meet and proceed to the McDougals'. Shortly before five p.m., Carlos let the envoy and courier into the building and they proceeded upstairs and rang Mary's doorbell.

30

THE LETTER

Mary answered the door and showed them in. They were all dressed smartly, and one of the envoys carried a leather briefcase. Mary asked them, "Please have a seat," and they proceeded into the living room.

The senior envoy, Captain Avery, took the lead and explained how they had come to obtain the letter. During the last downsizing in the armed forces and the legislation enacted for the base closings, the army became aware of the existence of several parcels while removing a mail sorter at a European base. He added, "It has been in the army's possession for over a month now, but we could not find a Margaret McDougal."

Mary laughed and explained, "My mother never liked her real name, Agnes, and went by her middle name, Margaret."

The three men looked at one another, nodding in concurrence, thus understanding the mix-up. The envoy added that the army sought assistance from the USPS, which had a special department dedicated to lost mail. He introduced his companion. "This is Mr. Clemens from the USPS."

Mary thanked them. "Thanks for your due diligence and tracking efforts."

The envoy lifted the brown leather briefcase from between his shiny boots and rested it on the lap of his crisply pressed trousers. He put the combination in and flipped the tabs to open it. Pulling out a yellow padded envelope, he looked around and gave all of them a nod and a slight smile. Stamped on the outside, was "Hand Delivery Only," "Identification Required," "Signature Required."

"I am only supposed to release this to your mother, but due to the circumstances surrounding her health, I'm releasing it to you. I will be needing some form of identification," he stated.

Mary took a drivers license from her purse. The envoy copied down the needed information and handed it to Mr. Clemens. In turn he copied down the information for his records.

"I just need your signature on this," the envoy continued. Mary signed the documents and handed the forms back. He put the paperwork in his briefcase and handed Mary the package. "The army apologizes for the untimely delay, ma'am," he said while handing her the package. "I believe that concludes our business, ma'am. Thank you." And what that they were off.

Mary sat down and picked up the package. She sat alone thinking. In her hands, inside the package, was a letter from her father, written fifty years ago. She hoped her mother would wake so she could see it. Words would not be able to describe her happiness. With the hands of a surgeon, Mary opened the padded envelope. Carefully she tore back the tab to open it. The red string cut into the yellow envelope, and inside was a letter from PFC James McDougal. The envelope was marked with the stampings, U.S. Army, Special Services.

Mary gently reached in and took out the plastic bag that encased the original letter. On the plastic was printed, USPS, lost or damaged item. Mary could see the letter, plain as day. It was as though a voice from the past was calling her. How she wanted to open it. It mesmerized her. She read the address over and over. Mary picked up her mother's shoebox containing all of her other letters and compared the writing. Identical.

Jenny had been doing laundry but had spent the last couple of hours bedside, tending to Mrs. McDougal. Mary picked up the letter, put it back in the army's package, and put it in her bedroom until her mother woke up.

Jenny came out of the bedroom and gave Mary an update. She stated that her mother was in the end of an obtunded state. Mary inquired, "What does obtunded mean?"

Jenny explained, "It means your mother is unresponsive to any stimuli. It's sort of a coma or semi-coma-like state."

Mary was dumbfounded and distressed. Jenny spoke very calmly and tried to settle her down. "There are no rules, no guidelines, no timetables, Mary. I think she'll come out of it by morning, but there are no promises."

Mary was numb. Her body had no feeling, and she could sense that her mother had little time left. She settled down and tried to hold back her emotions.

"Everything is going to be okay, she's not in pain," Jenny said.

"I didn't get to tell her I love her or goodbye," Mary sadly said through her sobs, breaking down. Jenny tried to calm her down.

The doorbell rang and Jenny answered it. The hospice night nurse came in. Jenny introduced her to Mary, "This is Kay," and explained the situation. Together Jenny and Kay would split a twenty-four-hour shift. Jenny said goodnight and stated she would be back at eight a.m.

Kay reviewed Mrs. McDougal's chart and looked in on her. She came back out of the bedroom and gave a glass of water to Mary. She told her, "I'm going to be bedside with your mother all night and don't worry."

Mary told her, "I will be on the other side of the bed."

She nodded her head and said emphatically, "That's where I'd be too, if it was my mother."

Mary and Kay had some tea and a piece of pound cake and settled in for the long haul. They each held a book and read by Mrs. McDougal's side. Mary fell asleep just before four-thirty a.m. as Kay continued reading and monitoring her mother.

The next morning sunlight shone through the blinds and hit Mary square in the face. Her neck was throbbing, stiff from sleeping upright in the chair. It was 7:15 a.m. Kay told her, "Your mother's condition has not changed since last night." She leaned over and took Mrs. McDougal's pulse. Next Kay logged all the results from her vitals into the chart.

Mary excused herself, got up, and took a shower. She turned on the water, waiting for the hot water to kick in. She walked back out to her bedroom and took the letter out of the envelope to examine it once more. She still couldn't believe her eyes. Hoping for a miracle, she prayed aloud, "God, let my mother wake one more time to read it. Please."

After showering she dressed. The doorbell rang and Jenny arrived to relieve Kay. They spoke for a couple minutes, and Jenny got updated to Mrs. McDougal's condition. "I'll see you tonight," she whispered as Kay left. Jenny read the logs and asked Mary, "How are you holding up?"

Mary answered, "As good as I can, I guess."

The day lingered on. Now and then Jenny would come out and update Mary. Mary would spend an hour or two bedside, but was too nervous to stay still. She paced the apartment. Every fifteen minutes Mary would look in on her mother. The IVs dripped and her mother lay motionless in the bed, Mr. Wiggles curled up at her feet. Jenny would look back up from her book, and they would make eye contact. Mrs. McDougal stayed in her coma of the rest of the day.

Kay took over nightshift and encouraged Mary, "Get some rest."

She was a nervous wreck and her eyes had large bags under them from lack of sleep. At first Mary took offense to Kay's suggestion, but realized she meant bedside. Mary's reasoning and temper were slightly off due to her lack of sleep. She retrieved a pillow from her bedroom and propped it up against the wall to support her neck.

The night did not show any change. When Jenny returned to relieve Kay, the situation remained the status quo.

Mary became distraught and asked, "Can I see you in the living room?" She paced frantically back and forth as she questioned Jenny aloud," She's been in a coma for forty-eight hours. If we could stop the morphine, all but temporarily, would my mother regain consciousness?"

Jenny thought a bit and hesitantly agreed, "I'll stop the drug, but with a contingency. If I notice any signs of severe pain, I'll have to relieve it and administer the medication again."

It was agonizing for Mary as the morning turned to afternoon with no change. In her mind, she cast blame on the army for not delivering the letter sooner. Then she blamed herself for mistakenly having the phone off the hook and for not seeing the answering machine earlier. The "what ifs" played out in her mind.

Shortly before five p.m., Jenny noticed some movement in her patient. Mrs. McDougal's left arm and fingers had moved. At first Jenny thought it just to be an involuntary reflex. But minutes later her pulse increased and her head moved back and forth. Jenny got up and left the bedroom. She found Mary on the terrace looking out, lost in thought. "Your mother may be coming to."

They both sprinted from the terrace, through the apartment to the bedroom. Mary spoke to her mother, trying to touch her inner consciousness. "Mom, it's me. Can you hear me?" as she rubbed her hands vigorously.

She held her hand and spoke of a letter from her father, trying to awaken her.

This continued on for twenty-five minutes as Mrs. McDougal fell in and out of a semi-conscious state. At her bedside, Mary continued to beg her mother to wake. She frantically rambled on about the letter and how she must come to in order to read it. "Mom, wake up. I have a letter from Jimmy. Dad. Mom, wake up."

Jenny listened to her heart and took her pulse. They had both increased in rate. "Keep talking, Mary, I think she's coming out of it," Jenny encouraged. "If she does come out of it, make sure you say what you need to, because I can't guarantee how long it will last," she added.

Jenny got a cold towel and placed it on Mrs. McDougal's forehead. A minute later her head began to thrash back and forth and her grip on Mary's hand tightened. Finally her eyes twitched; gradually she blinked and then opened them.

Mary repeated, "Mom, Mom, Mom," in quick succession.

Her mother turned to her and slightly smiled as she tried to regain focus. She turned her head back the other direction to look at Jenny, gradually gaining awareness of her surroundings. Mrs. McDougal cleared her throat and asked, "Can I have something to drink?" because her throat was raspy and she was thirsty. Jenny got some crushed ice and gently put it between her lips into her mouth, telling her to suck on it. Mary ran to her bedroom to get the package. Jenny took Mrs. McDougal's pulse and listened to her heart again. The nurse informed her, "You've been out for over two days." She looked at Mrs. McDougal closely to see if she was processing what she had told her. There seemed to be a slight delay in her understanding, but she did have limited comprehension skills.

Mary rushed into the room and propped another pillow behind her mother, to boost her up a bit. She looked at her mother and placed her hand over her mother's hand that held the rosary beads intertwined through her fingers. Mary told her, "love you" and her mother put her other hand over Mary's and said, "I love you too, dear."

Mary leaned forward in her chair and told her mother, "I have something very important to tell you."

Mrs. McDougal turned her head slowly to look at Mary and said, "What's that?"

Mary began to tell her, "I have a letter from my father, Jimmy, written fifty years ago. It's now here, after all this time."

Her mother squinted and seemed to be struggling to comprehend Mary's story. "A letter from my Jimmy. Who was it addressed to?"

"You, Mom, Maggie McDougal," Mary said emphatically.

"You mean he wrote this when he was in the army and it's here now, unopened? I have all his letters in the shoebox. How can that be?" she muttered.

Mary spoke slower and showed her the letter. She explained, "It's been lost, unopened, and you haven't read this one yet."

At this moment, it seemed to set in. Her mother began to breathe faster, and her eyes blinked rapidly in succession and opened widely. Mary took the letter from the package and Jenny helped Mrs. McDougal with her eyeglasses. Mary handed the letter to her mother.

She put the letter close to her face, approximately six inches from her eyes, and whispered, "Jimmy." Her hands trembled as she tried to open it. Mary took the bedside pen, taking the letter back momentarily. Her mother's eyes were fixed on it as Mary slid the pen underneath the flap and gently opened it. Mrs. McDougal reached back to the letter and unfolded it. Her lips twitched as she began scanning the letter. It read:

December 19, 1944

My Dearest Maggie,
If you are reading this, I know
that I have fallen to the enemy
in this dreaded war. Note that
I fought my hardest and I am

sorry not to have made it back to your loving arms. I have thought of you endlessly during this campaign and missed every fiber of your being. During my loneliest times here, I know I am a poorer man never to have felt our baby's touch or seen her smile. But I have always known that I was the world's richest man, having known your love almost my entire life. I am sorry to have never met our child that you bear in your womb. Let her know how much I loved her. Bring her up to be a smart and beautiful girl like her mother. I hope you forgive me for not making it back to fulfill our life plans. Know that if there is a whisper in the dark and you see no one, it is I speaking to you and looking over you. Live your life to the fullest, Maggie, as if every day was your last. I've seen

things here I hope you never do.
Life passes us so quickly. Please
live it, love it, every moment,
every second. I will wait for
you in eternity. May God find
you well and shed his blessings
upon you and our baby. Forever
yours.

Love,
Jimmy

She read the letter over a few more times. Tears rolled over her cheeks, and she was all choked up. Jenny helped clean her glasses and gave her some tissue.

Mary wanted to know the contents of the letter, but waited for her mother to share it with her. Her mother reached in the envelope and pulled out a black and white picture. In it, Jimmy was dressed in his uniform, smiling. On the back it was dated, January 2, 1944. Jimmy had written on the back a quick note. It read, "Ready for battle, your soldier boy. Love, Jimmy."

She looked at it as memories from the past filled her mind. "Your father, your father. He was just wonderful. I miss him so." She rested the letter on her chest and pursed her lips, trying to hold back her sobs. "I'm ready to see him," she cried.

"Soon, Mom, soon," Mary answered.

Mrs. McDougal read the letter to Mary, who in turn sobbed also. Her mother began to tell Mary, "Before I was informed of his death, I had a bad feeling. He always wrote three to four times a week. I hadn't heard from him and began to get worried. It just wasn't like him not to write. When those men from the army came up the stairs, everyone in the building knew why they were there. I opened the door and I knew. Those army men tore my heart out that day. I was lost until the day you were born. I saw your face, and when you opened your eyes, I saw your father in them." She paused for a while, trying to gain her breath. Then she brought up her legs and doubled over into a fetal position, squinting her eyes and contorting her face from the severity of the pain in her belly.

Mary called, "Jenny!" who had left the room for their privacy. She immediately saw the excruciating pain that Mrs. McDougal was in and administered morphine through the IV. It entered her bloodline quickly and she lost consciousness.

Kay arrived soon after and completed her nightshift. Mary held a vigil by her mother throughout the night. Her thoughts were deep-rooted, and she thought about the letter in her mother's words to her. She was a fighter, but she was no match for the cancer.

The disease had taken a riveting toll on her body. Mrs. McDougal lay comatose again, a mere ninety-two pounds of frail humanity. It had taken its physical toll, but her heart and soul were pure.

The next morning Jenny came to release Kay and exchanged notes on the patient. Mary overheard the conversation and saw Kay shaking her head sideways, indicating where her mother's condition was at. Later that morning Jenny took Mrs. McDougal's vitals. After the tests she picked up her logbook, made some entries, and walked over to Mary. She sat like a zombie in the bedside chair.

Jenny knelt on one knee in front of Mary while putting her hand on Mary's and said, "I'm going to leave you alone with your mother now. I think it's her time. I'll be in the next room, if you need me."

Mary blinked her eyes repeatedly, trying to come out of her shock. "Okay, thank you," she said nervously. Mary looked at her mother. She lay there asleep, her breathing becoming a little erratic. Mary sat on her bed holding her mother's hands. Several minutes later, her mother's back arched up and she gasped for air.

Mary held her hands tightly as her mother lowered her back and briefly came out of her coma. Her words were garbled and she struggled trying to communicate.

In a faint voice she whispered, "Mary, Mary, are you here?"

Mary quickly answered, "I'm here, Mom, right here."

Her mother was unable to open her eyes as she squeezed Mary's hands. "I see him. He's waiting for me."

A paralyzed look came over Mary. "Who's waiting?" She was pleading for an answer.

"Jimmy, your father. He's sitting on the bench by the tree at the river. He sees me," her mother answered. Maggie McDougal's grip loosened from her daughter and she passed into eternity with her betrothed. Her head fell slightly to the side as life slipped away from her.

At first Mary's body was ready to burst into hysteria, but as she looked at her mother's face, she saw that peace had found her and a slight smile had befallen her lifeless body.

The End

About the Author

Neil Mulligan resides in New Mexico with his beautiful wife Sandra. He has a 15-year-old daughter, Casey. He plans to start work on his second novel in the near future.

Made in the USA